Praise for the novels by Jamie Brenner

"A captivating tale of family secrets and strong women."
—*People*

"Whether savored slowly or devoured in a single sitting, this heartwarming, unpredictable and witty tale of the convergence of three sisters' high-profile weddings on a single day will continue to delight and amuse readers long after the final bite."
—Pam Jenoff, *New York Times* bestselling author of *Last Twilight in Paris*

"Rich, satisfying and surprising . . . A glorious read."
—Adriana Trigiani, bestselling author of *The View From Lake Como*

"Jamie Brenner's *Blush* is a delicious, big-hearted book about love, secrets, and pleasure—a novel that's easy to devour, but made to be savored. I adored every last drop."
—Emily Henry, *New York Times* bestselling author of *Funny Story*

"Jamie Brenner has outdone herself . . . I'm recommending it to everyone I know!"
—Kristy Woodson Harvey, *New York Times* bestselling author of *Beach House Rules*

ALSO BY JAMIE BRENNER

The Wedding Sisters
The Forever Summer
The Husband Hour
Drawing Home
Summer Longing
Blush
Gilt
A Novel Summer

The Weekend Crashers

Jamie Brenner

PARK ROW BOOKS

PARK ROW BOOKS™

Recycling programs for this product may not exist in your area.

ISBN-13: 978-0-7783-1085-3
ISBN-13: 978-0-7783-0565-1 (Hardcover)

THE WEEKEND CRASHERS

Copyright © 2025 by Jamie Brenner

All rights reserved. No part of this book may be used or reproduced in any manner whatsoever without written permission.

Without limiting the author's and publisher's exclusive rights, any unauthorized use of this publication to train generative artificial intelligence (AI) technologies is expressly prohibited.

This is a work of fiction. Names, characters, places, and incidents are either the product of the author's imagination or are used fictitiously. Any resemblance to actual persons, living or dead, businesses, companies, events or locales is entirely coincidental.

TM is a trademark of Harlequin Enterprises ULC.

Park Row Books
22 Adelaide St. West, 41st Floor
Toronto, Ontario M5H 4E3, Canada
ParkRowBooks.com

Printed in U.S.A.

For my mother.

Prologue

THE NEW HOPE INN IS one of those old buildings that still has hidden doorways dating back to the days of Prohibition. It's rumored the place helped shelter soldiers during the Revolutionary War. A lot of other historical things probably happened there. Belinda, the current innkeeper, simply knows that for the past twenty-five years, her knitting retreats have made it a tourist destination.

Belinda Yarrow and her husband, Max, own the inn together. But retreat weekends are her domain. She blocks out rooms for her knitters and manages every last detail to create a cozy cocoon for her special guests. To make it feel like *their* place. And her husband should know this by now. So why is he hanging a banner over the inn's entrance that reads "Welcome Bushcraft Bachelor Party"? She marches over to him, crunching through a pile of orange and gold leaves.

"What are you doing?" she calls out. "It's my knitting retreat weekend."

She can tell by the sheepish look on his face that he forgot. And then when he recovers, once's he's processed that he messed up, he says, "There's room for both."

He doesn't understand, even after she's explained it countless times.

"It's not about the space, it's about the atmosphere," she says. Belinda likes to cultivate a certain vibe. But talking "vibes" to Max is like talking to a wall.

"I'm sorry, Belinda. But I don't think your knitters will care one whit. It's going to be fine," he says.

"I don't want this weekend to be 'fine,'" she says. "I need it to be perfect. *This* weekend of all weekends." Maybe that, at the very least, he can understand: This weekend matters.

Chapter One
Monday

THE DIRECTIONS AT THE ARRIVALS gate are confusing, and Maggie takes this personally, as if LaGuardia Airport is trying to thwart her. She hasn't seen her daughter in weeks and has no patience for circling for the right place to pull over. The curbside is a sensory overload of honking horns, rolling luggage wheels and traffic marshals wearing neon vests shouting at drivers to keep things moving. It's too much to handle on only one cup of coffee.

To her right, a stream of yellow cabs jostle for position alongside a logjam of sedans and black SUVs. A police officer raps on her driver's-side window. She lowers it and a rush of crisp autumn air fills the car. "This is a no-standing zone," the policeman says. He's handsome, and it irritates Maggie that she notices.

She can't leave this spot. Piper will be out any second. But from the look on the officer's face, she's about to get a ticket.

Really, Maggie has no one to blame for this 7:00 a.m. stress bomb but herself: Piper had insisted she could just get an Uber, but Maggie wouldn't hear of it. There are few things left to do that make her feel useful. And they have so little time together anymore. But Maggie has an idea to fix that: a three-day weekend at a rustic knitting retreat. If Piper will say yes.

Maggie's eyes sweep the curb, and she spots Piper's familiar long-legged stride heading toward her. "She's here!" Maggie jumps out of the car and waves her arms wildly. She doesn't care if she gets a ticket. Piper is home!

"Mom," Piper says, running into her arms. The embrace feels like a giant exhale.

The officer barks something at her, and Maggie ushers Piper into the car. She avoids a ticket—probably because of Piper. Grown men lose all reason around her stunning daughter. Piper is nearly six feet tall with white-blonde hair and remarkably big blue eyes.

"Thanks for picking me up," Piper says. "But honestly, next time Ethan will do it. He always offers."

Maggie ignores the comment as she steers into the queue to exit the airport. Ethan is Piper's boyfriend of the past three years. Maggie has nothing against Ethan, but she does think her daughter is too young—and has too much going for her—to be tied down in a serious relationship. Maggie learned the hard way that nothing could derail a career like the distraction of a romance.

"It's my pleasure," Maggie says. "Now tell me all about the trip."

Piper's been in Milan the past two weeks modeling. Her return to Manhattan is for walking in a runway show tomorrow night for the designer Betsy Toledo. Her career is so glamorous; Maggie can't imagine living Piper's life. At her age, Maggie struggled to make ends meet in a studio apartment alone with a two-year-old. Piper's twenties are the opposite: Freedom. Money. The world is her oyster.

"I've told you pretty much everything," Piper says. Then, with a little smile, "Except last week, Ethan flew out and surprised me," she adds.

"He was with you in Italy?"

"For a few days, yeah."

Maggie feels a flash of annoyance. It was a work trip. Modeling is a brutally competitive business, and it's difficult enough for Piper to fight her way to the top. She really needs to set some boundaries.

"Don't you think it's a little inappropriate that he showed up?"

"I invited him to come. It was my idea."

Maggie has to dial back her negativity. It doesn't matter what she thinks. She doesn't want to sound like her own mother. She shudders at the thought. So she keeps her mouth shut while Piper spends the remainder of the hour drive to the Upper West Side talking about all the romantic things she and Ethan did in Europe. Barely a mention of work, something Maggie is more curious about. But it's her job to listen, and she does, and then before she knows it, they've reached Ethan's apartment building on West 82nd Street.

Only when Piper opens the passenger door to step out does Maggie realize she forgot to ask her about the knitting retreat.

EARLY-MORNING CLOUDS HAVE rolled in by the time Maggie gets to her job at an Upper East Side clothing store called Denim. The boutique is on a quiet block just east of Lexington Avenue in the sixties. It used to only sell high-end denim (hence the name) but over the past thirty years has expanded its inventory to include expensive cashmere in muted colors, cult designer jewelry and the occasional handbag.

Since the neighborhood clientele have proven themselves skittish in the rain, Maggie unpacks some knitting from her bag to pass the time.

"Good morning, Maggie," her boss says, breezing in fifteen minutes later. "I have some news!"

Elaine Berger is more like family than an employer. Maggie's known her for so many years, Piper calls her "Aunt Elaine." She fills a void left by the absence of Maggie's own mother.

Elaine pats down her damp hair, a silver bob never a centimeter longer than her jawline. Her dark, heavy-lidded eyes are always behind the thick wall of her glasses, of which she always keeps an extra pair on a chain around her neck. Her nose is prominent, balanced out by strong bone structure. The word *handsome* comes to mind. Handsome, and chic: The only jewelry she wears is a Tiffany triplet ring and a Cartier watch on a leather band.

Maggie is forever grateful that she walked into that particular store on that particular day in the summer of 2000. Up to that point, not a single employer had been willing to overlook the fact that Maggie was seven months pregnant. Elaine offered minimum wage plus commission, and she'd jumped at the opportunity. It would be a temporary job until she figured out something permanent. Twenty-three years later, she's still here.

"What's the news?" Maggie asks, unable to imagine what it could be.

"I've gotten you a ticket to the Betsy Toledo show tomorrow night."

Scoring a ticket to a New York City fashion show is a near impossible feat. In fact, Piper's been modeling for two years now and it's never happened. But Elaine, who made a fortune as a banker in the 1990s (the clothing shop is mostly a hobby) sits on a lot of prestigious boards throughout the city. One of them happens to be for the venue hosting tonight's show. Elaine knows how much it would mean to Maggie to get to see her daughter walk.

"Elaine! I don't know what to say . . . except I hope you're coming with me."

Elaine shakes her head no. "I could only get one ticket. But I'll be waiting eagerly to hear all about it."

Maggie gives her a hug, thanking her, telling her she can watch the show on a livestream.

"I'll do that," Elaine says. "It's a big night for our girl."

Maggie smiles. The biggest.

Chapter Two
Tuesday

*B*EHIND THE SCENES, A FASHION show is barely controlled chaos. That's the thing that had surprised Piper Hodges the most when she started working: If beauty is, as they say, suffering, then style is anarchy. Piper isn't a huge fan of anarchy.

The thing is, she'd grown up watching runway shows online with her mother, and the models always seemed like they were walking in a flawless dream. Now she realizes it's more like a rock concert sharing the stage with a ballet: wild creative energy funneled into torturous precision.

"Let me fix this, Piper H." A stylist adjusts the silk-lined trench coat on her shoulders. The coat feels sumptuous, and at three grand it's a privilege to wear it even for the minute it takes to walk the runway. But lately, her heart has been racing and she breaks out into a cold sweat moments before it's her turn to walk. Tonight, a feeling of absolute dread washes over her. But she shakes it off, reminding herself that it's the most important show of her career so far.

"Excuse me, people! Has anyone seen Piper's other boot?" A member of the designer's team waves a Polaroid of Piper's footwear, a mid-calf boot with a six-inch heel and three-inch platform. Piper stands barefoot while one of the makeup artists touches up her eyebrows. Her missing boot appears thanks to an assistant, and Piper quickly pulls it on.

She peeks out from behind a curtain to a dark room with only a single spotlight. It's hard to believe that somewhere in that darkness, her mother is watching. And Piper knows exactly how much this means to her mother—not because of anything Maggie ever said to her, but because of a conversation with her grandmother, Birdie. Piper was in fifth grade when she mentioned, with that unbridled certainty of a ten-year-old, that she wanted to be a veterinarian when she grew up. Her grandmother looked at her and said, "Well, then you'd better not get pregnant and drop out of college like your mother."

Piper never mentioned the conversation to Maggie. But it forever changed Piper's understanding of their life together. The sacrifice she'd made to have her. She was determined to make her mother proud.

The show choreographer appears by her side. She wears a headset and carries two iPhones at all times. "Piper, you're up: Countdown to five, four, three, two . . ."

Piper advances from the shadows of the staging area toward the bright lights of the runway.

A strange sensation overcomes her, something like nausea but not quite. The light appears to blur and the music, so loud a second ago, sounds like its coming from underwater. She feels herself pitch forward, but rights herself.

Headset girl snaps her fingers at her.

"And Piper . . . now . . . go!"

She steps out onto the runway. And everything goes dark.

THE BETSY TOLEDO show is held in a cavernous room that buzzes with the energy of a crowd that is certain they are, in that very moment, the center of the universe. Maggie can hardly believe she is one of them.

The space holds the chill of the autumn evening, but she's happy for the excuse to keep her coat on. It's wool, chocolate brown with oversized lapels and a belt that cinches at the waist. She'd found the treasure at a resale shop in the village years ago, never imagining one day her own daughter would be walking on the designer's runway.

Maggie settles into her seat, taking it all in and savoring the moment. Fashion journalists, photographers and fabulous people buzz all around, but quiet when the lights dim. Loud music fills the room: Rihanna's sultry ballad "Love on the Brain." And the first model saunters out, followed by another. They strut and sashay in crushed velvet dresses and quilted coats and cargo pants in sumptuous material.

And then there's Piper. Her baby!

The moment is so overwhelming, Maggie's eyes play a trick on her. Piper, wearing towering platform boots, seems on the verge of toppling over. An illusion, of course. But gasps in the audience tell her that this is real—this is happening.

Piper collapsed on the runway.

Chapter Three

THE WEILL CORNELL HOSPITAL WAITING area is chaotic. Maggie is just thankful Piper's location is still trackable on her phone or she wouldn't have known where the ambulance took her. The thought makes her shudder.

Maggie hunkers down in an uncomfortable plastic seat waiting for an update on Piper's condition from the medical staff. She wishes she had something to do with her hands, but she left her knitting bag at work. Usually she has it with her, but she didn't want to schlep it to the fashion show.

It's been at least a half hour since Piper was taken by ambulance to the emergency room. Even though she's already texting Maggie, telling her she's "fine," Maggie won't exhale until she gets to see for herself, to talk to her face-to-face.

"Mrs. Hodges?" A nurse in blue scrubs appears. "You may go back and see her now."

Maggie is not a Mrs., but it's an irritating assumption she's been dealing with for twenty-three years now. No matter. The important thing is that she's finally getting to see Piper.

A different member of the nursing staff shows her through two wide doors that require an electronic pass. Inside is a large pen buzzing with voices and the beeping of machines and curtained-off partitions. Behind one of these, she finds

Piper sitting on a cot wearing a pale blue hospital gown. Her golden-blond hair is slicked back, her blue eyes rimmed with a shimmer of black shadow. The pronounced cleft in her chin and small bump in her nose give her face just enough character to go from blandly pretty to striking. She looks just like her father, a man Maggie hasn't seen since the night Piper was conceived.

It's a strange thing, having a beautiful daughter. Especially now, when the nurse looks at her skeptically when she declares she is, in fact, this young woman's mother. Part of the reason it seems unlikely is how close they are in age. (Many of Maggie's peers have children in elementary school.) But also, Maggie doesn't look like Piper. She's only medium height, with light brown hair (still no gray) she wears straight to her shoulders, passably slim though not without increasing effort. Still, she always felt attractive enough. She wants to believe all that stuff about beauty coming from the inside, and having a positive attitude, and eating right so her skin has a glow. But when she walks down the street next to her daughter, she knows it's all nonsense. Some people are just born beautiful.

Maggie swoops in to hug Piper. She smells like antiseptic. "Are you okay?"

"I'm fine," Piper says, pulling back. "Just totally humiliated."

"Piper?" a male voice calls from outside the curtain.

Maggie closes her eyes. She knows that voice. It's Ethan Brandt, Piper's boyfriend.

"In here!" Piper calls out. "Mom, can you get him?"

Maggie steps outside the curtain and waves him over. Ethan is tall, taller than Piper, and he bends down to give her a hug as she rises awkwardly to meet his embrace.

"Thanks for holding down the fort," he says, turning to Maggie. "I got here as soon as I could. I thought an Uber would be faster than the subway but the traffic . . ."

He frowns, his brows furrowed, his big brown eyes concerned. Ethan has glossy brown hair and cheekbones Maggie herself would kill for. He's adorable. She can't blame her daughter for falling for him. After all, she'd fallen for a gorgeous guy once. Once, and never again. *Fool me once, shame on you. Fool me twice, shame on me.*

"You didn't have to rush down here," she says, fighting her annoyance. She likes Ethan, but at the same time she thinks her daughter is too young—and has too much going for her—to be tied down in a serious relationship. Maggie learned the hard way that nothing could derail a career like the distraction of a romance. And she'd been younger than Piper when she learned it.

"Of course I rushed down here." His face is pinched with worry. "So what happened? Are you sure you just fainted?"

That was more information than Piper had given Maggie, and this hurts her feelings. It's irrational, she knows that. But it's difficult to be the parent of a grown child. It's cruelly ironic that for the first eighteen years of Piper's life she was the most important person in it: She was the authority, the point person. Now, suddenly she's an afterthought. Extraneous. And it's a painful adjustment.

"We're still waiting to hear what the doctor has to say," Maggie says.

An older man in a white coat steps into the little area.

"Piper, you're just fine," he tells her. Maggie has questions and doesn't hesitate to jump in. She's aware that Ethan is waiting to say something, but she doesn't bother including him in the conversation. He's crowding her.

"People faint," the doctor says. "The room might have been overheated, her clothing might have restricted her breathing. Maybe she was light-headed from not eating all day?"

"My daughter eats! She's naturally thin."

"Mom," Piper says. "I'm *fine*."

"I know you're concerned, Mrs. Hodges," the doctor says. She resists the urge to correct him: Mrs. Hodges is her mother, the last person she wants to think about at that moment. "The best thing you can do is take your daughter home, make sure she keeps that ankle elevated tonight. If she experiences nausea or a headache, call us."

Piper stands up and starts looking around for the hospital-issued plastic bag holding her clothes—the Betsy Toledo trench, now all balled up. The doctor issues the discharge paperwork, and Ethan helps Piper with the bundle of clothes. Maggie starts to say something about the logistics of finding a cab, but Piper's not listening. Ethan's hugging her and they kiss and now Maggie feels like an interloper.

"Let's get you home," he says, then turns to Maggie. "I've got it from here."

PIPER LEANS AGAINST Ethan in the back seat of the cab, where she is sandwiched between him and her mother. Despite the professional humiliation of the evening, Piper feels physically fine—a few bumps and bruises, but no real damage. Except to her pride.

Still, Maggie insisted on seeing her back to Ethan's apartment, and Piper figures if it makes her mother feel better, why not just indulge her? After all, she can imagine how much she's disappointed her tonight. But Maggie is doing a good job of pretending everything's fine.

"It's actually very fitting that you fainted at a collection dedicated to Vivienne Westwood," Maggie says with forced cheer. She reminds Piper that one of the most famous runway falls of all time was when Naomi Campbell stumbled and fell at the Vivienne Westwood show in 1993. Her mother is a walking encyclopedia of fashion history. But this little bit of trivia doesn't make her feel any better.

What on earth happened back there? She doesn't remember stumbling or falling. She felt hot and dizzy and the next thing she knew she was looking up at the ceiling with people hovered around her. Now all she can imagine is her mother watching her live from the audience. It must have been horrifying.

Her phone buzzes with a call from her manager, and she lets it go to voicemail.

"Is that Gretchen?" her mother says.

Piper nods. "I'm too tired. I'll call her in the morning."

She's not looking forward to the conversation. This is bad. Her career was at a crossroads *before* tonight's epic fail. She can't admit this to her mother, but in Milan, at every go-see, she was surrounded by models who were taller, prettier, with bigger Instagram followings. It's ironic that she's never felt more unattractive than since she's become a professional model. And she's had the limited bookings to show for it. But then, the Betsy Toledo show—it was supposed to change everything.

Beside her, she can feel her mother watching her, looking for signs that she's upset or not feeling well. Piper regrets letting her join them in the cab. She needs some space.

It's a relief when they finally reach Ethan's building. Piper shares his third-floor apartment in a brownstone between Amsterdam and Columbus on 82nd Street. On their first date, they discovered they'd grown up directly across Central Park from each other. The realization seemed like something out of a romantic comedy. It felt like a sign.

They've been living together for a year, but she still can't get used to using her own key. The apartment still seems like his place, and she wonders if that will change once they're engaged. *If* they're ever engaged.

For months now, she's felt certain Ethan was on the verge of proposing. It's embarrassing how much she thinks about this, how weighted every little suggestion to go to dinner or away for the weekend has become. But in her defense, he brought it up first by asking what type of rings she liked. And ever since that conversation, she can't put it out of her mind. (And even if she could forget about it, her phone keeps bombarding her with ads for engagement rings.)

And then, over Labor Day Weekend, she accidentally found It: An antique diamond in a white gold filigree setting. It was in a small box underneath the bedroom dresser, where a ball of yarn had rolled after falling from her lap.

She did what any sensible person would do under the circumstances: She shoved it right back under the piece of furniture. And she didn't tell anyone—not her closest friends, not even her mother. Now, she's thankful she kept it quiet.

So much time has passed, she's starting to think he's changed his mind.

Chapter Four
Thursday

MAGGIE PUSHES OPEN THE DOOR to the shop, relieved to see Elaine already behind the front counter. She's eager for the company. It's hard to be patient waiting for Piper to wake up and let her know how she's doing.

"You look terrible," Elaine says, adjusting her glasses as if her eyes might be failing her.

"Sugarcoat it, why don't you," Maggie says, walking around to the back of the counter to make sure that's where she left her knitting bag. "I didn't get much sleep."

"I understand that. I just thought you'd dress up a little for tonight."

Tonight? What's tonight? Oh no. She forgot: Elaine set her up on a date. This had been in the works for a few weeks, before Maggie knew Piper would be returning home. She didn't have any interest in going in the first place, but Elaine wouldn't take no for an answer. The way she saw it, Maggie was single, an empty-nester, and still arguably young. Too young to give up on men.

"I can't go," Maggie says. "You *know* what happened last night." Elaine, watching the show's livestream as promised, texted her when Piper fell.

"You told me she's fine," Elaine counters.

"*Physically*, yes. But I'm sure she's upset and needs moral support." Seeing Elaine's skeptical expression, she adds, "Come on. My daughter's very public humiliation merits a rain check."

"Canceling a date won't cheer her up."

"Well, it will cheer me up," she grumbles.

"Did you ever register for that knitting retreat?"

"No!" In all the excitement, she'd forgotten to ask Piper about this weekend. Elaine was the one who'd told her about it in the first place. She discovered it online, following her hometown's Instagram account. Elaine, though the epitome of a Manhattanite, isn't actually a native New Yorker. She's from a small Pennsylvania town called New Hope where, apparently, a quaint riverside inn hosts knitting retreats. Elaine had grown up going to the inn for Sunday tea, and described the place as timeless. "I'm going to register today. Thanks for the reminder."

"I wish I could go with you. I miss New Hope," Elaine says.

The front door opens with a screech of the metal hinges, heralding the arrival of one of their regulars, a personal shopper. Maggie likes the woman, who, like herself, is a single mother. They got to talking one day when Maggie was knitting, and the shopper shared her own knitting addiction. "It's expensive, but so is a bottle of wine a night. And this is healthier."

Today, the woman has a cobalt-blue sweater draped over her arm.

"This isn't a shopping visit," the woman says. "It's a knitting emergency; I made this for one of my clients' birthdays, I'm giving it to her tonight and . . . look. I just noticed this now that I'm finished."

Maggie leans closer and sees a slight change of color where two separate balls of yarn, both technically the same shade of blue, are joined together.

"They're the same brand, the same shade—I bought them together on the same day."

"Well, they're probably from two different dye lots. Or one of the yarns could have faded. I don't know. But to avoid this in the future, before you start a project, take the end of one ball of yarn and twist it with the beginning of the other ball. If you have a striping effect, you know the yarns don't match."

The woman looks crestfallen.

"So there's nothing I can do about it now? I know that sounds ridiculous. The colors are the colors."

Maggie thinks. She remembers—

"There is a way to camouflage the color discrepancy. You do a duplicate stitch." She takes the piece in her hands and moves her forefinger to trace the demarcation spot. "Work across this row using yarn from the other dye lot to cover over other stitch. Do this on both sides."

"You think that will work?"

Maggie nods, and the shopper hugs her. "You're a lifesaver."

After she's gone, Maggie turns to Elaine and jokes, "You heard it: I just saved her life. I should be allowed to cancel my date."

Elaine folds her arms across her chest. "Maggie, I say this from a place of caring: Maybe you should stop being a lifesaver for everyone else, and start paying attention to your own."

PIPER WAKES UP to a phone full of voicemail, the most humiliating of which is from Betsy Toledo's people asking where a messenger can retrieve "their *property*." The way they emphasized the word, it's as if to remind her that they'd be more than happy to take legal action should she fail to return the thousands of dollars of clothing she was wearing when she was carted away by ambulance.

The second message is from her manager, Gretchen Lundgren. She wants Piper to meet her at the management company office—a bad sign. Typically, they go out for coffee or drinks. She hasn't been to the actual office since the day she signed her contract.

Piper takes the subway to Midtown, trying not to look at her phone. The video of her fainting—teetering for a moment on her high heels like a skyscraper in an earthquake—has gone viral. There are versions set to music, versions with people talking over it, versions edited with footage of other runway mishaps.

People just have a lot of time on their hands, she tells herself, walking through the revolving door to the office building. An elevator whisks her to the twenty-fifth floor, where it would be clear to even the most casual observer that this is a company built around fashion and style. Every aesthetic detail is optimized, from the lighting to the chic employees to the sleek modern furniture to the framed photos of clients featured in editorial layouts and runway shows.

An assistant who towers over Piper shows her to Gretchen's office. Everyone is tall, with the exception of Gretchen herself, who is maybe five foot two. When Piper walks in, she stands and comes around the desk to give her a hug.

"Oh, you poor little doll. Are you okay?"

"I'm fine," Piper says, feeling a fresh wave of humiliation.

Gretchen returns to the seat behind her desk. She's wearing a plaid ankle-length wrap skirt, Prada combat boots and a cropped denim jacket. Her black hair is, always, parted in the center and stick-straight to her shoulders. Piper's not sure how old she is. Maybe early forties.

"I'm really sorry," Piper says, sitting in the leather chair closest to Gretchen's desk. "I'm still not entirely sure what happened. I've never fainted before in my life."

"It's fine," Gretchen says.

That's a relief. If Gretchen says it's okay, then it's okay.

Gretchen Lundgren discovered Piper when she was a sophomore in college. At the time, Piper was working at an animal shelter in Union Square. She always took her break at Joe Coffee, right across from the park. She was waiting in line when a woman walked up to her and said, "I'm sure you get this all the time, but you could model. If you're interested, I have my own management company." She gave Piper her card. Piper didn't take it seriously. But when she mentioned it offhandedly to her mother, Maggie immediately checked out the manager's social media.

"Piper, this woman is the real deal," she said.

Piper didn't have time or the interest. She had school, she had the animal shelter and she'd recently started dating Ethan.

"You should give this serious consideration," Maggie had said.

Piper knew that she should. Models can make a lot of money. Since finances were always an issue—maybe not an issue, but certainly a concern—she couldn't dismiss the opportunity without at least a conversation. It would be disrespectful to her mother, who had raised her as a single parent in New York City on a retail sales salary. Her mother comes from a very wealthy family, but since they shamed her so much over her single motherhood, Maggie always refused to accept financial help from them.

And so Piper took a leave of absence from school to pursue it. The plan was to save up for her tuition and expenses and then finish her degree debt-free. It was a solid idea. It was just taking a little longer than expected to bank serious cash.

She looks closely at Gretchen. If everything is "fine," then why is she sitting there in the office?

"I sense a 'but,'" Piper says nervously.

Gretchen sighs. "Unfortunately, yes. Now, this has nothing to do with last night, but since your contract is almost up for renewal, I feel it's time to have an honest conversation." She clasps her hands in front of her and leans back in her chair. "I simply don't have a vision for how to get your career to the next level."

Piper takes a sharp intake of breath. "You're dropping me as a client?" Her first thought, her primary concern, is *My mother is going to be so disappointed.*

And then she realizes that's a strange reaction.

Chapter Five

MAGGIE IS LOCKING UP THE shop. Outside, she finds that it's raining—a light, irritating drizzle. But there will be no rain check: She's going through with the date.

She's regretting this fact with every fiber of her being when she spots, of all people, Ethan just a few feet away. She's never run into Piper's boyfriend in this neighborhood, and it takes her a few seconds to process that this isn't a coincidence.

"Maggie, hi. Do you have a minute?" he asks, instantly putting her on high alert.

"Is Piper okay?"

"Yeah . . . yeah. She's napping. Didn't get much sleep last night."

The drizzle really is no more than a mist at this point. She checks the time on her phone and decides she's going to walk to the restaurant instead of taking the subway.

"I'm meeting someone for dinner. Can you talk while we walk?"

It's just after five but the street is blanketed in the fall's early darkness. They turn right on Lexington. Some storefronts already have seasonal twinkling lights, and with the last glimpse of daylight on the horizon, the moment makes her feel wistful and oddly alone.

"I assume you're here because of Piper's fall last night," Maggie says. "And I appreciate that you're that concerned. She needs both of our support so she can dust herself off and get back to work."

"I'm actually not here about last night," he says, and stops walking. "I've been trying to get ahold of you for a few weeks now."

Yes. The texts. A voicemail. Maggie is embarrassed she never got back to him. If pressed, even now, she can't explain why, exactly, she's been avoiding him.

"I apologize," she says. "Things have been busy."

He nods in understanding. "I thought about talking to you last night when we were waiting for the discharge paperwork, but figured it wasn't the right time."

Maggie feels the hair rise on the back of her neck, her motherly intuition tingling like a sixth sense.

"The right time for what?"

Ethan smiles sheepishly. "I want to ask Piper to marry me."

Maggie's stomach drops. Piper is twenty-three years old. Ethan is a decent guy, and if this were five years later she'd be thrilled for the two of them. But what's the rush?

"Look, Ethan. Please don't take this personally. But I think Piper should be focused on her career and just being a carefree young woman right now. There's plenty of time for marriage down the line."

Ethan looks incredulous. "With all due respect, Maggie, we've been together for three years and taking the next step feels right."

"But she's trying to get her career off the ground."

"And I'm proud of her."

"I know you are. I'm just concerned that getting married right now would derail that."

"Why would it?" he says.

"Because I know my daughter, and she loves with her whole heart. She'll be torn between you and work, and you will always come first. There's certainly a time for that. But that time is not now." She pauses, looking into his big brown eyes to see if any of this is sinking in. It's tough to tell. So she keeps going. "Clearly, something has her stressed out. Look what happened last night. She's never fainted before in her life! So if you want what's best for her, you'll give her some space to be selfish for a little while. Let her make her own money, and have a career she can look back on when she's older and say, *Yeah—I did that*. And then, when you do get married, she won't have any regrets."

Ethan looks stricken. "Okay. Well, you've given me something to think about."

Maggie smiles at him, resisting the urge to pat him on the shoulder. He looks very young himself in the moment. She knows she's given good advice. That's all she can do.

Maggie walks the rest of the way to the restaurant alone.

HER DATE TAKES her to an expensive French restaurant. Allan is ten years older, a lawyer with a tan that suggests he has a second home somewhere warm. He reminds her of one of her mother's favorite old movie stars, George Hamilton.

She doesn't want to think of her mother, Birdie Hodges, who is relentlessly vocal in her disapproval of Maggie's single status. According to Birdie, Maggie is willfully making life unnecessarily difficult by failing to find a man to take care of her. This is Maggie's second unforgivable mistake in life. The first, of course, was getting pregnant at age twenty.

Maggie met Piper's father backstage at a fashion show. It was her second year at Parsons and she had an internship with a major designer. Maggie's job was to assist the assistants. One night, in the flurry of backstage activity, she ended up working with a male model from Iceland. Kris was sweet and self-deprecating and she went home with him that night. It was six weeks before she realized she was pregnant. And, that being the dark ages before iPhones and social media, she had no way to get in touch with him. And even if she did, it would be pointless. He was in his early twenties, based in Europe, traveling the world as a model. She was on her own.

But a decade later, after some online sleuthing, she did find him: He owned a furniture design company in his hometown of Höfn. They messaged briefly on an app. He was married, with no kids, and no interest in Piper.

Her last serious relationship ended when Piper was twelve. Daniel was an architect she'd met at a friend's birthday dinner. They dated happily for a few years, but when she kept declining his invitations to move into his apartment, they reached an impasse. She said she'd consider it once Piper was off to college, but he said he couldn't "put his life on hold." And that was the end of her romantic life, essentially. She didn't do the whole online dating thing. The construct was so flawed. How could a true love match ever come from it? So she'd accepted that she'd missed the boat on romance. Her own mother had told her as much: "You always overreach and then you wonder why nothing works out." She liked to add, "If you don't watch out, you'll spend the rest of your life alone."

Maggie didn't bother explaining that she'd never be alone as long as she had Piper. Birdie would never understand how fulfilling a mother-daughter relationship could be because they themselves didn't have one. Once she got over the initial shock and logistical worries of being pregnant at twenty, Maggie stopped viewing it as a mistake. It was a second chance at a good mother-daughter relationship, just reversed. The day she gave birth to Piper was the day she stopped aching for her own mother's love.

Maggie listens to Allan the lawyer talk about his home in Palm Beach (She knew it!) while she sips her glass of wine.

"I feel like I'm doing all the talking," he says after a while. "What about you? Where are you from?"

"Outside of Philadelphia," she says.

"The Main Line?"

She nods. The wealthy suburb was made famous by the Katharine Hepburn film *The Philadelphia Story*.

"You don't look like a Main Line girl," he says.

She resists the urge to say, *Well, because I'm not a girl, I'm a woman.* Instead, she tells him, "I moved to New York for college."

"Me too. Columbia, class of 1993."

She smiles politely and offers, "I was at Parsons." She omits the part about dropping out before getting her degree. She's not ashamed of it; she just doesn't see the point in expending the energy to explain it. She already knows she won't be seeing this man again.

The bottom line is that she doesn't have any interest in sharing her life with a man. She's tried, it hasn't worked, and she's moved on. She has everything she needs: A good job. Friends. Knitting. And most importantly, she has her daughter.

Before they've ordered food, Piper texts, Ru around?

Maggie excuses herself for the ladies' room. She takes the wide staircase leading to the bathrooms on the second floor. Upstairs, she stands outside the bathroom and texts back, I'm around. What's up?

She doesn't mention she's on a date. Piper would be horrified to know she'd interrupted.

Can you meet at the diner? Need to talk.

Maggie doesn't have to ask what diner. She and Piper have a shorthand for everything. See u in 15, Maggie writes.

She has until she reaches the bottom of the staircase to think of an excuse to tell her date.

GRACIE MEWS DINER has occupied the corner of East 81st Street and First Avenue for decades. The portions are huge and the prices are outrageous, but it's the dining equivalent of a warm cozy blanket. The place has had the same staff for as long as she can remember, and when she asks for her usual, LEO (lox, eggs, onion) omelet—her server comments:

"Breakfast for dinner."

Maggie exchanges a look with Piper. Dimitris, their server, says this same thing every time, in the same deadpan expression, as if he's never made the comment before. And she plays along, not sure if it's a reprimand, a question or a suggesting for framing her order.

"He never disappoints," Piper says. Maggie and Piper are seated in a booth next to windows overlooking 81st Street. It's dark outside, and all she sees are car headlights. Piper moves French fries around her plate, but doesn't take even one bite. Across the aisle, Maggie spots a familiar old woman sitting alone at a table for two. She has dyed red hair and overly rouged cheeks and cartoonish blue eyeshadow. She's been eating at the same table every night for all the years Maggie's lived in the neighborhood.

"You're finally quiet enough to appease the Dragon Lady," Maggie jokes. Piper dubbed the old woman Dragon Lady back when she was in fourth grade because the woman used to scold her for talking too loudly.

"She still fucking terrifies me."

Maggie steals a glance at the woman. It seems she hasn't

aged, but that's probably because she's the type of person who looked eighty when they were sixty.

It's sad, really. Maggie wonders, with a shudder, if that will be her fate. Sitting alone at a table in Gracie Mews eating overpriced breakfast food for dinner and snapping at small children. But no, she will never be alone. She has Piper.

Maggie reaches across the table and pats her arm.

"I know you're embarrassed about last night. But trust me, no one else is thinking about it anymore. The important thing is to get right back on the horse." *Right back on the horse?* Oh god. She was turning into Birdie. "You know what I mean," she adds.

Piper exhales. "Yeah, well, it's not that simple. That's why I wanted to have dinner—to talk to you in person. But I don't want you to get upset."

Maggie's stomach tightens into a knot. "Now I'm already upset. What happened?"

Piper reaches for a lock of her hair, twisting it around her forefinger.

"Gretchen dropped me."

"Dropped you meaning...what?" Maggie knows, but she can't believe it.

"Meaning, she no longer represents me."

She understands that Piper's manager would be upset, concerned even. But to drop her?

"That doesn't make sense," Maggie says. Piper starts talking about her contract being up, that she doesn't have enough momentum—but that she's fine with it. Clearly, she's determined to put up a brave front. But Maggie knows deep down she must be heartbroken. Maggie feels helpless. Motherhood was so much easier when almost anything could be fixed with a trip to the ice cream shop or toy store. She wonders, what's the adult equivalent?

She remembers the knitting retreat.

"Piper, let's get away this weekend."

Piper shakes her head. "Mom, you don't have to fix this for me. I'm fine."

"I know you're fine," Maggie says. "But Elaine told me about this amazing knitting retreat. It's just two hours away. I think it would be good for both of us."

She shows Piper her phone, where's she pulled up the retreat website.

Welcome to New Hope: Indulge your passion for all things yarn in the heart of a charming historic town nestled on the Delaware River. Our exclusive knitting and crochet retreat offers a sanctuary for creativity and relaxation . . .

"A sanctuary for creativity," Piper says.

"Are you making fun?" Maggie says, swiping the phone away.

"No! Come on—show me again."

Maggie hands the phone back, and Piper reads aloud: "Craft in comfort. Your accommodations will be the cozy New Hope Inn, blending old-world charm with modern amenities, providing the perfect backdrop for your crafting endeavors." She looks up. "I like old-world charm."

"As do I," Maggie says, and they share a smile. She has the rest of the post memorized:

Something for Everyone: Whether you're an experienced crafter looking to refine your skills or a novice eager to learn the basics, our knitting and crochet retreat promises an enriching experience for all.

"What do you think?" Maggie says.

Piper nods. "I mean, it sounds great. But it starts tomorrow. I'm sure it's sold out."

Maggie's thinking the same thing, and that's why she's not going to bother trying to register online. "Let's see about that."

She dials the number for the inn, and a man answers.

"New Hope Inn."

"Oh, hello," she says, glancing at Piper. "I'm calling about the knitting retreat? Are there any spots left?"

"Hold on," he says. "That's my wife's domain."

Maggie hears the thunk of a landline receiver hitting a hard surface. Across the aisle, The Dragon Lady gets up and grabs hold of her walker.

"Hello, Belinda speaking."

The woman's voice is warm and mellifluous.

"Oh, Belinda, hi, my name is Maggie Hodges. I'm calling to see if you have any spots left for your retreat this weekend."

The woman asks how many people are in her "party."

"Two. Just me and my daughter."

"I have space in my workshops," the woman says. "The only issue is . . . I'm looking at my occupancy now . . . you'd have to share a room. We have a deluxe twin available."

Sharing a room is even better. It will be just like the old days when Piper lived at home and they ate popcorn on the couch and watched *Gilmore Girls*.

"We'll take it." She looks at Piper and gives her the thumbs-up.

They're going to have the perfect mother-daughter weekend.

Friday

New Hope Knitting Retreat: Day 1

Noon: Welcome Tea & Yarn Market

Course Offerings: Intro to Crochet; Intro to Knitting; Know Your Yarn; Color Theory and Stranded Knitting; Lacework; Reversible Knit-purl Color Combinations; Classic and Cozy: Shetland Hap Shawl

Evening Activity: Group dinner at Bucks Tavern

Chapter Six

PIPER KISSES ETHAN GOODBYE. HE'S on his way to work, and she's waiting with her packed bag on Columbus Avenue for her mother. New Hope, here they come.

Ethan agrees the getaway is a good idea. He knows she's upset about the fashion show, but he has no idea she's also wondering if Ethan's changed his mind about getting married.

Last night, while Ethan was in the shower and she was packing for the trip, she checked under the dresser for the ring box. It was gone.

So she's happy for the excuse to get away for a few days. She needs to process this, figure out what it means. And she's annoyed with herself for feeling this way, because she never thought of herself as the kind of woman who would freak out trying to read the tea leaves of a relationship. But the minute they started talking about a future together, something changed.

Maggie arrives at the pickup spot in front of the apartment, and Piper opens the trunk to stash her suitcase. It's already full. Piper manages to cram her bag inside.

"How much did you pack?" Piper says, climbing into the passenger seat. "I thought you said it's only three nights?"

"It is. But I have one suitcase for the clothes I'm wearing, and one suitcase full of clothes I knit. It says in the info that sharing your work is part of the retreat. Oh, that looks adorable on you!" she says when Piper shrugs off her coat.

She's wearing a sweater that Maggie knit for her last winter. It's cobalt blue, with a fitted bodice that flares out at the waist. She'd been deliberate in packing it, hoping her mother hadn't noticed how rarely she wears it. It's cute but feels like something she would have worn in middle school. But she put it on today to make Maggie happy.

Sometimes, she wonders if she thinks more about her mother's happiness than her own.

MAGGIE OPENS HER window and breathes in the unmistakable scent of wood smoke and the earthiness of freshly raked soil. Two hours outside of Manhattan and they're driving underneath a canopy of fire-colored leaves. Crossing over the small bridge between Lambertville, New Jersey, and Pennsylvania, it's like driving through an oil painting come to life. The roads are lined with the red, yellow and orange leaves of the maple and birch trees. They pass a farm with miniature ponies grazing near a fence, and beyond it, endless rolling hills. The light is particularly crisp, and when she catches sight of herself in the rearview mirror, the glow of sunshine makes her look twenty years old again. Almost.

Beside her, Piper scrolls through her phone. Personally, she's happy to ignore her own phone for a few days. The most recent text was from Allan, her Thursday-night date, saying he was sorry their evening was cut short and that they should try to meet up again soon. She wrote back that it was lovely to meet him, but she was really focused on work and her daughter at the moment.

And it's true. She can't stop thinking about Piper losing her manager over the unfortunate episode this week. Everyone has a bad night—how could Gretchen be so unforgiving? Is the industry that callous? Or is something else going on that Maggie doesn't know about?

"Piper, was everything okay with work before the show the other night? Between you and Gretchen, I mean?"

"I don't want to talk about that this weekend, okay?"

Maggie won't push. Maybe it's too soon. Still, it feels strange to walk on eggshells conversationally. Maggie and Piper could talk about anything. At least, they used to be able to. But come to think of it, the first time she felt a little shut out by Piper also had to do with Gretchen.

Maggie only learned about the manager scouting Piper by accident. Piper had tossed Gretchen's GMI Model Management business card in the garbage, where Maggie found it one morning covered in used coffee grinds. That was back when Piper was still living at home—before she got serious with Ethan. When Maggie asked Piper about it, she was maddeningly nonchalant: "Oh yeah. She came up to me at the coffee place I always go to."

"Piper, that's incredible. You're going to follow up with her, right?" Maggie had said, barely able to contain her excitement. But Piper just shrugged and Maggie realized if she didn't give her a little push, she might actually miss the opportunity of a lifetime. Ultimately, Piper came around. But her ambivalence was surprising.

Now, just like that morning when she fished the soggy business card out of the trash, she feels a disconnect between them.

"Whatcha thinking about over there?" she says, glancing over at the passenger side.

"I'm thinking about deleting all my social media accounts," Piper says.

Maggie is horrified. Quitting social media would basically be quitting her career. And Maggie will not let one little bump in the road derail her entirely.

"Hon, don't make a major decision like that when you're upset. Why not just stay off your phone for a few days, and see how you feel next week?"

She's thankful for the timing of the knitting retreat. This weekend away will be the perfect reset.

In New Hope, the streets become winding and narrow. Hilltops are dotted with Victorian homes. And then, on the bank of the Delaware River, looms a grand colonial revival building with a classic redbrick facade, white trim and intricate cornices. The New Hope Inn. Even Piper seems to perk up at the sight. Right next door to the inn is the historic theater Bucks County Playhouse. Maggie read in the retreat info that it's one of America's oldest and most famous summer theaters.

"Isn't it beautiful here?" Maggie says. "Look at that little bridge. It's probably been standing there since the Revolutionary War."

"This place looks like a movie set," Piper says, snapping photos.

A gravel drive leads to a small parking lot on the far side of the inn, where Maggie gets a view of a promenade stretching along the river.

"How beautiful. We should take a long walk after we get settled in," Maggie says, pulling the bags from the trunk. She feels a flutter of anticipation. She imagines a lobby filled with knitters sprawled out on couches and armchairs, a crackling fireplace. And hopefully, coffee.

They walk with their luggage to the front entrance, where a giant banner hangs suspended from second-story rafters. Maggie stops short.

The banner reads, *Welcome, Bushcraft Bachelor Party!*

No mention of a knitting retreat.

"Is this the right place?" Piper says.

Of course it's the right place. How many New Hope Inns could there be?

A Jeep pulls up and deposits three burly men. They're laughing and one stops just short of the front doors, cups his hands around his mouth and hoots, "Scott!" A second-story window opens, and a young man sticks his head out and tosses out a can of . . . beer? The guy on the ground misses the catch, and the can crashing to the ground erupts into a fizz of liquid.

"Party foul!" the guy calls from the window, as the others brush past them, up wide stone steps to the inn's front porch.

"I can't believe this," Maggie says, bending down to retrieve her luggage handle. "This is not what I signed up for."

"What's the big deal?" Piper says and walks toward the steps.

Maggie has no choice but to follow. The porch is grand but welcoming, with white balustrades and railings. Wrought-iron lanterns flank the front door, which is a bold red. On the far end, she spots a porch swing. Two wicker chairs and an end table are stationed nearer to the door. At the top of the steps she finds decorative gourds and pumpkins.

"The big deal," she says, hoisting her suitcase, "is that this is a girls' trip. A knitting retreat. I thought we'd have the place to ourselves. A bunch of . . . lumberjacks completely ruins the mood."

"Mom, men knit."

"You think those guys are here to knit?"

Piper shakes her head. "I'm sure they're even less interested in us than you are in them."

That's entirely not the point.

Chapter Seven

SOMETIMES, BELINDA YARROW WONDERS HOW she's made it through thirty-five years of marriage. Clearly, it's not due to great communication. She still can't understand how Max could have booked a bachelor party during her knitting retreat weekend. She brought it up again last night.

"Belinda, everyone can fit. We have plenty of room," he said.

"Barely."

"And besides, with everything that's going on, I couldn't turn down the chance to have full occupancy."

She can't be too cross with Max. Things are, as he said, "going on": A businessman from Philadelphia recently approached them about buying the inn. They hadn't been thinking about selling, but the big numbers being tossed around were slowly changing their minds. Max's mind, especially.

"Bee, the bachelor party isn't just anyone—it's the Cavanaughs," Max said. "You know Barclay Cavanaugh. His son-in-law owns Danby Markets."

Of course she knows the Cavanaughs. It seems everyone knows everybody in Bucks County. She likes the Cavanaughs. That isn't the issue.

"My retreats are supposed to be a mood board come to life.

A half dozen rowdy bachelor party attendees is not part of that mood."

"These are outdoorsmen. They will barely be around the inn except for meals—if that. Your retreat ladies will have the run of the place every day."

That was what he told her last night. Now it's the morning, and the lobby is jammed with both groups checking in at once. And all she can do is damage control.

"Can you at least put up a banner for the knitters, too? Maybe inside over the desk?"

A few years ago, Max's friend in the printing business started selling canvas banners customized for local businesses. Sometimes Max hung banners that read, "Go Eagles!" or "Happy Holidays!" The one today welcomes the bachelor party.

The front desk is one of the first things guests see when they walk in: a heavy wood piece they saved from the previous owner, with the nicks and scars to signal it's a sentinel of bygone eras. They keep an antique copper bell on the front ledge, along with a leather-bound guestbook.

The lobby is wide and accommodating. To the right of the check-in are two chocolate-brown leather couches facing each other with an antique chest serving as a coffee table between them. Beside that, a stone hearth and fireplace. When they bought and renovated the inn they preserved as much of the lobby interior as possible. The charm of the place is in its imperfections: the patina on the banister, a slight unevenness of the walls, and well-worn tapestries. The high tin ceiling typically absorbs noise in a way that keeps the lobby pleasantly muted. But it seems the entire bachelor party arrived at once, a group that has so much energy they seem to take up all the space in the room.

Looking around to make sure her knitters are navigating the logjam, she spots a woman in a lavender cable-knit cardigan busily tapping away at her phone. She has thick brown hair pulled into a low ponytail. The sweater is intricate and constructed with obvious skill from good yarn. Beside her sits a striking young woman, tall and willowy with long blond hair. Belinda approaches them.

"Welcome to the New Hope Knitting Retreat," she says, extending her hand. "I'm Belinda."

The brunette stands. "Yes, I'm Maggie Hodges. We spoke last night. I didn't realize there'd be so many . . ." She looks pointedly around the lobby.

"I assure you, once check-in is finished, you won't even know anyone else is here aside from our group."

Two of the men are busy tossing a football back and forth. The catcher misses, and the ball hits the tower of paper coffee cups at the coffee station, sending them toppling to the floor.

"Dude, you suck!" the thrower says, running over to fix the mess.

This is embarrassing. This is not what walking into a knitting retreat should feel like.

"Stay right here—I'll get you checked in," Belinda says quickly.

She walks behind the desk, where Max is busy handling the bachelor party. They still use physical keys on brass key rings engraved with the room numbers. She pulls the keys for room 226 and delivers them to Maggie Hodges.

"You're in the Margaret Meade Room. One of my absolute favorites."

When Belinda and Max left Center City Philadelphia for the Bucks County countryside thirty years ago, they felt defensive explaining the move to their city friends. Max got into a habit of reciting the names of all the brilliant people who spent time in the Pennsylvania countryside: Gertrude Stein. Margaret Meade. Pearl S. Buck. And those were just the women! So when they undertook renovations of the inn, in homage to their newly adoptive town, they'd name each room after one of Pennsylvania's long list of luminaries. (In 2018, when they learned Taylor Swift was from nearby Berks County, Ben Franklin got bumped.)

Maggie takes the key, but seems to be eyeing the front door.

"Our welcome tea begins in an hour," Belinda says. "And our on-site restaurant is right down that corridor, and they have a full-service bar. Please order some refreshments on the house."

The young blonde woman reaches for the keys. "Thank you. I'm Piper, by the way. Maggie's daughter."

Belinda wouldn't have assumed that. They don't look alike. Or maybe she's just unskilled at noting that sort of thing. She and Max don't have any children. The inn is their baby.

Maggie follows her daughter's lead and heads to the stairs without another word to Belinda.

Not a great start to the weekend.

Chapter Eight

PIPER OPENS THE DOOR TO the guest room, Maggie just one step behind her. The walls are a muted sage color with off-white crown moldings. It has polished wood floors and two full-sized beds with crisp white linens and patchwork quilts. Ornate frames containing sepia-toned prints of historical New Hope decorate the walls. A sideboard table features an antique porcelain teapot and a copper clock.

Piper doesn't understand why the bachelor party triggered her mother so badly. Personally, she thinks the guys add to the festive atmosphere. She couldn't help but notice one is about her age and looks like the actor Austin Butler. The world is full of attractive men.

"Well, this is more what I'd expected," Maggie says, and Piper is relieved. Back on track for a good weekend. Maggie walks into the bathroom and calls out, "Oh, Piper. Come in here—there's a clawfoot tub!"

"In a sec," she says, flopping onto one of the beds. She didn't sleep enough last night.

She woke up at two in the morning thinking about Gretchen, about what happened at the Betsy Toledo show. And about Ethan and the disappearing engagement ring.

The irony is that she has this whole weekend with her

mother, someone she usually talks to about everything, and she can't talk to her about this. If she admits to Maggie that she's fretting about an engagement ring, she knows what her mother will say: *You're too young, you should be focused on your career, now's the time . . . live it up.* The subtext of all of this being, *Don't make the mistakes I made.*

"Have you had time to look at the workshop itinerary?" Maggie asks, sitting on her bed with a hank of burgundy yarn that she starts winding around her knees. Her mother always insists on hand-winding instead of investing in a yarn spinner. She told Piper that the act of winding it before knitting a project creates a sense of intimacy with the yarn that she finds integral to the whole process.

"Not yet."

"We have a welcome tea in an hour and then an all-day yarn market. I signed us up for Know Your Yarn, a lacework class, and Beginner's Brioche. I texted you a link. They have the instructors' bios listed, too."

Piper picks up her phone, sends Ethan a check-in text telling him they made it and that the inn is "super cute" and that she'll talk to him later.

"Hey, why does this name sound familiar?" Maggie says, squinting at her phone screen.

"What name?"

"This instructor. Hannah Elise."

"Wait," Piper says, pulling up the retreat on her own phone and scrolling through it. "Hannah Elise is teaching here?"

"That's what it says. Do we know her?"

Hannah Elise is a crochet designer whose edgy knitwear made her famous on TikTok. Her pieces are intricate and bold, with cutouts placed strategically to accentuate curves and bright color-blocking that made even the simplest pieces stand out.

"From TikTok," Piper says. "@HaloHannahKnits. I've sent you her videos."

"Oh, right. I like her stuff."

"I can't believe she's here," Piper says. She never imagined she'd have to go to New Hope, Pennsylvania, to meet Hannah Elise from Brooklyn. She follows the link to the classes she's teaching. It appears she's mostly doing crochet workshops, not knitting.

"Let's learn crochet," Piper says.

Maggie looks up from her winding. "We only have a few days here. I think we should focus on the advanced knitting workshops."

Their first disagreement of the weekend. Piper is eager to meet Hannah Elise, but she'll try to do things Maggie's way for the next few days. Judging from her overreaction to the bachelor party, her mother needs some R & R. And really, this whole weekend is a gift. Piper shouldn't be a brat about it.

"Sounds good," she says. "Wanna go check out the yarn market?"

AIDAN DANBY LOOKS around the lobby of the New Hope Inn, a place he'd been visiting his entire life. Back in the late eighties, he'd go with his grandparents and parents for dinner and special occasions. Today, all these years later and with new ownership, it feels almost exactly the same.

It's strange to be standing there with his son and his father-in-law on a Friday morning. Aidan doesn't typically do long weekends. In the twenty-five years since he'd opened his first grocery store, Danby's Market, the idea that he needed a break never crossed his mind. But it's his nephew's bachelor party, and family is one thing Aidan always makes time for.

Now that his son, Cole, is grown up, there are fewer occasions to see his in-laws; the Cavanaughs are his late wife's family. And Nancy has been gone twelve years.

"Good morning, Aidan. Welcome," Max Yarrow says from behind the front desk.

He hands over his credit card. Beside him, Cole flips through a printed itinerary.

"Seriously, Dad," he says, holding up the sheet of paper. "What's all this stuff we're scheduled to do?"

"Wilderness training," his father says. "I told you the theme's bushcraft."

"When you said theme, I thought you meant for drinking games. Or commemorative T-shirts."

"It will be fun."

Cole looks dubious.

"I'm twenty-four years old. I've made it this far without knowing how to build my own firepit."

"Where's your sense of adventure?" a voice booms behind them. It's Barclay, his father-in-law. Barclay Cavanaugh has a deep voice, ragged from years of nicotine and yelling from the sidelines of football games, and it gives every statement he utters a certain gravitas. In his seventies, Barclay still has a thick head of salt-and-pepper hair and, today, a mustache. Nancy once told him that all her friends in high school had crushes on him.

"Hi, Grandpa. No offense," Cole says.

Back when Cole was a child, Aidan was praised for making so much effort to keep Cole close to the family on his mother's side. But now, friends seem to raise an eyebrow at his continued determination to be a part of the Cavanaugh clan. "What do you call your former father-in-law?" one of his buddies asked last week when he mentioned the bachelor party weekend. Aidan told him, "He'll *still* my father-in-law. I call him Dad." The thought of the conversation still irks him.

"These are things boys used to learn just in the regular course of growing up. We didn't have a fancy name for it," Barclay says, holding up his bushcraft itinerary.

He walks over to Aidan and gives him a half hug, half backslap. "We're doing beer and bratwurst in the restaurant in an hour. I was there during Oktoberfest, and trust me, you don't want to miss it."

Cole consults his phone.

"Do we have time for beer and bratwurst? This itinerary says we have to get to fort building."

"I think we can fit in a few beers first," Barclay says. "It's a bachelor party, not basic training. Am I right?" He shadow-boxes Cole's arm.

"You got it, Grandpa," Cole says.

Across the room, a group of women sit on couches chatting, a few of them furiously working knitting needles. Barclay lets out a low whistle. "Who invited the ladies? I told your grandmother this is strictly a boys' weekend." He gives Cole a wink, but Cole seems not to hear a word of it. He's staring at the group of knitters like he's seen a ghost.

"Everything okay?" Aidan says.

"I need to make a phone call," says Cole. And then he rushes back outside.

SHOPPING FOR YARN has the same effect on Maggie as browsing fresh fruit at the Yorkville farmer's market. She wants to devour everything in sight.

Belinda's pop-up yarn market is held in a large first-floor space. Floor-to-ceiling windows overlook the river. The windows are dressed with sheer linen drapes to let in all the natural light. The furniture is a mix of rustic and contemporary: polished wood tables and upholstered armchairs, velvet sofas, and a grand stone fireplace complete with an antique iron grate. And everywhere, tables are piled high with yarn.

There's yarn in bins, skeins clipped to metal frames and pre-wound balls of yarn in lined baskets. Small, delicate bundles of cashmere are nestled side by side on a table along with a display of fluffy mohair. Beside it is a basket of hand-dyed merino wool.

"Mom, look," Piper says, pointing out a pile of Quince & Co. yarns, a brand Maggie finds particularly elegant. She picks up a few skeins in a deep charcoal color, Finch, and places them in one of the lined wicker shopping baskets.

"Maggie, hello," Belinda says, walking over. "I hope you both are settling in."

Belinda is slender and tiny, no more than five foot three. Her white hair trails down her back in a single braid. She wears large round tortoiseshell glasses and coral lipstick. Her button-down denim shirt is paired with wide-legged, rust-colored corduroys with embroidered pockets.

"Yes, the room is great," Maggie says. "And so is this one. It's a beautiful place you have here, Belinda."

Belinda compliments the sweater Maggie's wearing, asking her about the buttons she chose for it, the brand of yarn. All the while, she looks Maggie directly in the eyes, making her feel like she's the only person in the room.

Belinda's attention warms her like sunshine. Older women have that effect on her, and it's not a mystery why: Her own mother never had time for her. Even before Maggie got pregnant and dropped out of school and refused to return home, Birdie Hodges seemed alternately bewildered by and resentful of her. Birdie didn't do "fun." She'd never heard the expression "quality time." And so Maggie formed a habit early in life looking for mother figures. She knows, on some level, that's what made her dynamic with Elaine Berger work so well.

Maggie was basically motherless, and Elaine only had sons, no daughters. Maggie wonders if Belinda has children.

Now she feels bad for making an issue out of the bachelor party. She wants to apologize, but before she can say anything two young women walk over.

Belinda makes introductions. The women are Laurel Hayes and Kalliope Dimitriou, best friends from elementary school on their annual girls' weekend. They're physical opposites; Laurel is slight and fair with a heart-shaped face framed by stick-straight, wheat-colored hair just skimming her shoulders. Kalli is tall, with long dark curls and eyes so brown they appear black.

"The selection of yarns here is amazing," Laurel says. She has hazel-gray eyes with nearly invisible lashes.

"Thank you." Belinda smiles. "We used to have a yarn shop in town, and I'd take all my knitters on a field trip the first day of every retreat. But it closed a few years ago, and so I started this little tradition instead."

Maggie comments that she especially likes the brushed yarn selection.

"You know, I used to favor mohair in this category," Belinda says. "But lately, I've been impressed by the softness of alpaca and alpaca blends."

A woman comes barreling toward them, waving her hands. "Belinda, I forgot to register for Know Your Yarn," she says.

She's a whirlwind of energy, mid-fifties, curvaceous and busty with dyed red hair and dressed in a flowy caftan and a chunky beaded necklace.

"Sheila, you know that won't be a problem," Maggie says. "Sheila, meet Maggie, Kalli, and Laurel. Ladies, Sheila Bevins is a retreat regular."

"I've been coming since the very first one," Sheila says. "Summer of 1999. That's right. Never missed a retreat, never will." Sheila beams at Belinda, then turns to Maggie and Kalli. "Belinda's classes are the best, and I'll tell you why: One, she always has a clear agenda, and two, she doesn't waste time. Oh, and three, she teaches *technique*. Not everyone does. You'd be surprised."

"That's lovely of you to say, Sheila," Belinda says, before she excuses herself to help one of the other retreat attendees, who wants to pay for a bundle of cashmere.

When she's gone, Sheila says to them, "I'm hosting a yarn swap in my room later. It's a retreat tradition. I'm in Edgar Allan Poe."

"Oh, thank you. I'll check with my daughter."

Maggie looks around the room. Where did Piper go?

PIPER SPOTS HANNAH ELISE, aka @HaloHannahKnits, across the room talking to two other twentysomething women. Hannah Elise is easy to spot, with distinctive strawberry-blond corkscrew curls that fall halfway down her back and hooded, pale blue eyes. She has fair, faintly freckled skin. Her nose is pierced with a tiny gold hoop. She's dressed in a crochet tank with a divine matching ankle-length jacket paired with faded wide-leg jeans.

It feels strange to just walk up and introduce herself. And before Piper can decide how to approach her, Hannah Elise notices her and waves her over.

"You look so familiar," she says with a smile. "I'm Hannah Elise—one of the instructors this weekend." It's strange to hear her voice in person instead of through a video on her phone. Here, her Brooklyn accent is more pronounced.

"I know you from TikTok," Piper says. Now that she thinks about it, she hasn't seen Hannah Elise's posts for a while. Her feed is now overly crowded with fashion accounts she follows for networking. She makes a mental note to unfollow some of them so she can see more posts that actually bring her joy—especially considering what happened this week. The last thing she wants to think about now is the fashion industry.

Hannah Elise introduces the two women standing with her, Lexi Takahashi and Dove Sullivan. They're both artists from Philadelphia. "This weekend is our honeymoon," Dove announces, then gazes lovingly at Lexi. Dove is medium height, sinewy, with fair skin and short brown hair marked with a premature streak of gray.

Piper feels Hannah Elise looking at her intently.

"Now I know why I recognize you," she says.

Piper can tell, just from the tone of her voice, that Hannah Elise has seen the video of her falling on the runway. But she doesn't elaborate, and Piper is grateful. Dove and Lexi seem to have missed the comment entirely.

"You know I hate that term, honeymoon," Lexi says. Lexi is shorter and broader than Dove, with delicate facial features and black hair feathered like Joan Jett's circa the 1980s. "So patriarchal."

"Congratulations," Piper says. "When did you get married?"

"Monday," they say in unison. Then Lexi adds, "We went to City Hall. Kept things simple."

"But we're going to have a real ceremony at some point," Dove says.

"That *was* a real ceremony," Lexi corrects gently.

"You know what I mean."

Dove reaches for Lexi's hand, and Piper notices their matching platinum bands. She wills herself not to think about rings.

She's not about to let the fact that her boyfriend might be having second thoughts about their future ruin her weekend.

Chapter Nine

MAGGIE LOOKS AROUND THE ROOM for Piper. She's already bought a bunch of yarn, most of it for Piper, and wants to show her.

She finds her talking to a small group standing in front of a wall covered with framed photos. Maggie recognizes one of the women from Instagram: Hannah Elise. She always posts some impossibly gorgeous sweater or elaborate throw and insists the patterns are easy.

"Sorry to interrupt," Maggie says, coming up behind Piper and touching her shoulder. "But I picked up a few things for you and don't want you to double-buy," Maggie says.

Piper picks through the basket. "A few things? Mom. I think you got enough for the whole retreat."

Her basket *is* a bit stuffed. She snagged a deep, dusky brown baby alpaca, soft and plush with a subtle sheen. And blue Malabrigo lace, hand-dyed and exceptionally soft, made from 100 percent baby merino wool. She found a bulky yarn in a heathered, rustic tweed that seems made for the autumn weekend. Everything she sets her eyes on looks special, each holding the promise of happy hours to come.

"Nice stash," Hannah Elise says, introducing herself and a couple who are apparently on their honeymoon. Maggie thinks, *If I met someone willing to go on a knitting retreat as a honeymoon, I'd get married, too.*

A loud burst of male laughter, followed by some shouting, comes through the wall from the restaurant next door. Maggie had almost forgotten about the bachelor party.

Belinda calls out, asking for everyone's attention for a moment, and the buzz of conversation quiets down.

"Welcome, everyone. For those of you who are new to my retreats, a special welcome. We are standing in what I think of as the sort of home base of the retreat, the Pearl S. Buck Room—named after the author of *The Good Earth* among many other titles. But since the room has become knitting retreat central, we have come to call it affectionately the Purl." She spells it out to clarify and is met with appreciative laughter.

"I'm delighted to see everyone chattering away and getting to know one another already. And I can tell you from many years of experience: By the time you leave here, you'll have made at least one new forever friend. As a memento, I'll take a group photo before the end of the weekend. It's a retreat tradition, as you can see from the frames covering that entire wall over there."

So that explains all the photos behind her.

Piper leans over and whispers, "Mom, I'll catch up with you later."

Later? "Where are you going?"

Piper says something to elaborate, but Maggie can't hear because her voice is swallowed up by noise coming from the restaurant next door.

"What?" she whispers back.

"I *said*, Hannah Elise is going to show me some things from her latest drop."

"Wait—you're leaving? What about yarn shopping?"

Piper glances pointedly at Maggie's full basket. "I think

you've got that covered." She leans over and hugs her. "I won't be long. Have fun!"

Maggie knows it's irrational, but she feels a little rejected. She and Piper should be experiencing the opening event together. And worse, she can't even hear the tail end of Belinda's remarks because of the men making so much noise next door. What if it's like this during the entire retreat? How is she supposed to lose herself in the pleasure of creation if it sounds like they're at Madison Square Garden?

She looks around, but no one else seems to notice, while she simmers with a building rage. Rage at the bachelor party for being loud, rage at Gretchen for firing Piper as a client, and yes, maybe rage at Piper herself for leaving her in favor of a knitting influencer.

There's another roar from the restaurant and it sends her over the edge.

AIDAN AND HIS father-in-law, Barclay, sit at opposite ends of the group table at the inn's restaurant, Bucks Tavern. Everyone is hooting and hollering, and Scott, the groom-to-be, is doing a shot of bourbon. They're going around the table toasting Scott. Aidan didn't, as a rule, drink during the day, but now everyone at the table is looking at him expectantly. It's his turn to speak.

"You're up, buddy," Ritchie says. Sometimes, Aidan almost forgets that Ritchie and Nancy were brother and sister. They didn't look alike and never acted alike. Aidan had always felt more of a connection with Barclay.

Aidan stands and raises his glass, surveying the group. In addition to Ritchie and Barclay, and Scott, there are four of Scott's Penn State fraternity brothers.

"Scott, it's incredible this day is already here." He remembers the day Scott was born. He and Nancy rushed to Doylestown Hospital at four in the morning. Cole would be born eight months later, but at the time, Nancy hadn't even known she was pregnant yet. "And I know if your Aunt Nancy were here with us, she'd want me to tell you how proud she is of you, and how much we both wish you both every happiness in your lives together."

He hadn't planned on evoking his wife, but the occasion made it impossible not to think of her, to want to acknowledge her in some way. Now, after so much time has passed, he'd gotten over the constant feeling that he was being robbed of her presence.

They met as lifeguards down the shore. It was the summer after college, and his father told him to take the summer to do outdoor work as a sort of last hurrah before adulthood began and he was stuck working in an office all day. So he went to the beach and there was Nancy, with her white-blond hair down her back and the freckles across the bridge of her nose. And those long, tan legs. He'd be the first to admit he'd noticed the legs first. In fact, he did admit it to her, on their third date—when he already knew they'd be together long enough to someday laugh about it.

She'd been gone now longer than they'd been together.

"To you, Scott." He takes his seat and downs a shot of whiskey, just as a woman appears at the table. She's wearing a sticker name tag that reads "Maggie."

"Excuse me," she says, hands on her hips. "You know, you're not the only guests at this inn. Can you please keep it down a little? We're at an event right next door and we can barely hear ourselves think."

"I'm sorry—I can't hear you," Scott says, clearly messing with her.

"I *said*, we're right in the next room and can barely hear ourselves think!"

"Well, this is a bachelor *party*," Scott says, emphasizing the word *party*.

"You're being very rude," the woman says. She has wavy dark hair to her shoulders, bright blue eyes, and would probably be very attractive if she didn't have such a sour expression on her face. Scott starts to snicker.

"You don't have to be a dick about it," Cole says to Scott.

Okay, this is enough. Aidan stands up again. "Sorry we disturbed you. We'll try to keep it down."

The woman starts to say something, stops, and turns and walks out. Beside him, Cole is bickering with Scott. What's gotten into those two?

"Boys, come on now," Barclay says. "I thought you'd agreed to play nice this weekend."

Aidan doesn't know what that means, but from the look on Cole's face, he does.

"Am I missing something?" Aidan says.

"Apparently, everyone at this table is missing something: I'm twenty-four. I'm a grown man. I think you and Grandpa and Uncle Ritchie forget that sometimes."

Cole gets up and leaves.

Ritchie? What does his brother-in-law have to do with anything? He looks over at Ritchie, who just shrugs and takes a swig of his beer. Aidan doesn't like feeling clueless, especially not when it comes to Cole. He prides himself on being a hands-on father. It was shocking to find himself a single parent when he first lost his wife. But he gained his footing. He learned to juggle running the business and being both Mom and Dad. Still, he always envied friends who were able to provide their children with a two-parent home. They took turns playing bad cop; no matter what issue or crisis they were dealing with, one of them always had the bandwidth to be the good guy. To be a friend and not just a parent. Aidan never found that balance.

Once, when Cole was a freshman in high school, he discovered Cole trying to make a bong out of a cored apple. It was funny, really. He was so far from getting it to work. But there was no margin for error, for laughing, when he needed to be stern and set an example. And there was no one to talk to about it behind the closed bedroom door after Cole went to sleep. Aidan always felt like there was a third dimension to parenting he couldn't experience.

But now, it's time to relax. Time for the victory lap; he'd done his job. Cole was a decent, responsible young man. But clearly, something is going on. Fortunately, he has an entire weekend to figure out what that something is.

In the meantime, he'll make sure to avoid the angry brunette.

Chapter Ten

PIPER FOLLOWS HANNAH ELISE TO a small room on the second floor that appears to be serving as a makeshift knitwear studio. It's filled with bins of yarn, boxes of needles, an automated yarn spinner, a sewing table and clothing racks on wheels filled with handknits on velvet-cushioned hangers.

"This rack is all my designs," Hannah Elise says, separating a few of the hangers. "Feel free to try anything on."

"Really?" Piper is thrilled. She truly is a fan of her work. "These are extraordinary," Piper says, pulling out a pair of patchwork pants with a drawstring waist and flared bottoms. "Is this the pair you made from all the different leftover yarns?" They were spectacular. Weeks ago, Hannah Elise posted a video showing a pile of half-used balls of yarn in every color and shared her obsession with "scrap wear."

"Yes, and they'd look amazing on you. Can I take a few photos? I haven't had a decent chance to post them yet," Hannah asks.

Piper wants to say yes, and at any other time would have. But she can't put herself out there after what happened at Betsy Toledo.

"I've sworn off social media for the weekend," Piper says.

She means for it to come off as light and half joking but it sounds like she'd just announced she's in rehab.

"Hmm," Hannah Elise says.

"What? Don't tell me you wouldn't feel the same if it were you."

Hannah picks up a pink metal crochet needle and works it casually through bulky butter-colored yarn. "Maybe at one point I would have. But now I know better."

Piper is skeptical. "I find it hard to believe you ever had a bad moment on social media."

"No, but I once did an internship at a crisis PR firm."

"Really? That's interesting. Do you work there now?"

"No. I have the most heinous bureaucratic job in the world."

"Doing what?"

"I literally don't want it entering my mind long enough to tell you."

"That bad?"

"Soul-crushing," she says. "I'm just biding my time until this knitting influencer gig starts bringing in real money. But that's a whole other story. My point is this: At the PR firm, one thing I learned is that when something negative about you is out there, you have to reframe the narrative."

"Meaning what?"

"Meaning—if there's a viral video of you falling on your ass, you better put out a video of yourself doing something more interesting."

"Like what? Modeling your clothes?" She raises her eyebrows. "I don't think so."

"No! Knitting. Show yourself *creating* something instead of wearing something. Do it now. Right here. I'll record it. Use something of mine. Here . . ." She leans over, fishing through a wide-open canvas bag, and passes her knitting sample. "The part of the pattern I'm at now is simple stockinette for a few rows, so you can pick that right up here."

"Are you sure?" Piper arranges the piece on her lap and takes hold of the needles. "I don't want to mess it up."

"It's just a swatch for one of my classes. You won't mess it up, and if you do I can fix it."

Well, okay then. It's worth a try.

She picks up the first stitch and Hannah Elise starts recording.

MAGGIE DOESN'T KNOW what came over her back there in the restaurant. But as soon as the man at the table stood and apologized, it was like a spell broke and she saw herself from the outside, shrieking at people simply enjoying themselves at a restaurant.

She's becoming the Dragon Lady. And she needs to reset, immediately.

With Piper otherwise occupied, Maggie takes Sheila Bevins up on her invite to stop by the room for the yarn swap. Ever since her favorite knit shop closed, yarn swaps have been one of her favorite ways to build her stash without breaking the bank. Especially as she's completely adopted the philosophy that there's no such thing as having too much yarn.

The Edgar Allan Poe Room is on the top floor. She knocks, and Sheila's low, raspy voice calls out, "Come in!"

Maggie opens the door and finds Sheila sitting on the edge of the mahogany canopy bed, surrounded by balls of yarn, needles in her hands. One half of the honeymoon duo— Alexis? Lexi—is sorting through piles of yarn on a wood side table. The room has blue-and-white toile wallpaper and wainscotting—just magnificent. It's much larger than her twin room, and she assumes after so many years at the retreats Sheila knows exactly what to book for her stay.

"Welcome, welcome. You just missed the rush—and you get to peruse all the goodies left behind. Help yourself."

Maggie holds up her offerings: some worsted-weight yarn with a plush smooth texture in a shade called Lettuce, then a felted tweed in an orange-brown color called Cinnamon. Sheila gestures for her to leave them both on the table. "If they don't have labels, use the Post-it pad to note the fiber and yardage if you know offhand."

"I like this green," Lexi says, picking up the Malabrigo.

"Isn't it great? I used it for a fantastic little shawl and miscalculated how much of that color I'd need," Maggie says.

"Where's your daughter?" Sheila says.

"I think she's doing something with the crochet instructor. They know each other from social media."

"KnitTok," Lexi says.

"I guess." In the swap pile, Maggie spots a deep, dark blue she needs for a quilt she started and never finished.

"What do you think of the retreat so far?" Sheila asks, not looking up from her clacking needles.

Maggie is about to offer the expected *It's great!* But she's still feeling a bit hungover from the encounter at the restaurant. So she says, "I guess I just imagined it to be a more intimate, knitters-only vibe here."

Lexi, having claimed the Malabrigo Rios for herself, starts winding the yarn on her knees.

"Oh, you mean the dudes? They're harmless. Weekend warriors," Lexi says.

Maggie had been tempted to confide in the two women about somewhat losing it and reprimanding the bachelor party. But she reconsiders.

"I think it's nice to have some male energy," Sheila says. "You young gals take it for granted. But at my age—I'm happy for even sideline viewing."

Maggie can't help but smile. "I'm not that young. But I appreciate your point." Now she feels even more foolish for losing her temper. She needs a weekend reset. "So, anything I should do while I'm here aside from the workshops? This is my first trip to New Hope."

Sheila looks up from her knitting. "Oh, honey. Then you must take the walking tour."

Maggie isn't really a guided tour person. She's more of a "wander around and stumble upon things" tourist. But Sheila is emphatic, and says, "I'll even go with you. This town is such a treasure. Always something new to learn." She waves her phone. "I'm signing us up now. And wrangle your daughter. She won't want to miss it."

BELINDA HAS A short break between the yarn market and her first workshop of the afternoon, and she steals a few alone moments on the back deck. Max comes out to join her, and she pulls her chair closer to his, brushing the dried fallen leaves off the seat cushion. He hands her a mug of their local hot chocolate that tastes like liquid molten lava cake.

It's brisk when the wind picks up, but the heat lamps do their job. They're a relatively new addition. Belinda and Max bought them during Covid, looking for any creative way to create space for guests. Turned out, people really loved sitting outside into the late fall and even the winter.

Like a good marriage, the inn is constantly evolving. When they assumed ownership in 1996, the building—dating back to 1871—needed a lot of work. Originally constructed as three separate buildings, two were combined in 1902 to form a hotel. The third building was added as an expansion after Prohibition, when the property had been used as a speakeasy. Somewhere in storage on the property is the preserved, original speakeasy side door with sliding peephole.

When they bought the place, it hadn't been in service as a hotel for almost a decade. Belinda and Max were in complete agreement about the interior renovations, as they were about most things in life. They decided the common areas and guest rooms should be a mix of antique and reproduction furniture, including four-poster beds, wingback chairs, settees and plaid tapestry. They maintained as much of the original hardwood flooring as possible, covering any problem areas with patterned rugs in deep, warm colors. The lighting was also warm and soft, with antique-style chandeliers and wall sconces. They added new brass fixtures with wrought-iron detailing and glass shades. They filled empty wall space with large ornate mirrors with gilded frames. In the lobby, shelves were decorated with hardcover books and framed black-and-white photos of New Hope dating back to the early 1900s.

A year after they assumed ownership, Belinda had the idea to host knitting retreats, and this inspired another set of renovations. She initiated a project to combine three ground-floor rooms into a private event space with doors opening to a back deck. She knocked down an interior wall to combine two rooms into one, then expanded the footprint by a thousand square feet. That extension has floor-to-ceiling windows, a river view and a sliding glass door leading to the back deck. The Purl was born.

"How's it going so far?" Max asks.

"Good." She nodded. "It's a nice group."

"I'm sorry about the double-booking. I just have to be practical right now."

She looks at him. "It's fine. It's really not a big deal."

"Okay, good. Because—"

"Max!" Barclay Cavanaugh, standing in front of the patio

on the river promenade, waves to get their attention. "I've been looking for you. I need a minute."

He walks briskly around the wooden-beamed barrier between the public space and the deck to get closer to them. "Sorry to interrupt, Belinda."

"You're not interrupting," she says, wondering what Max had been about to say before Barclay interrupted.

"The boys and I were having lunch in the tavern, minding our own business, having a good time—and one of the knitting ladies marched in and let us have it! Said we're making too much noise. Is there some sort of new protocol around here I don't know about?"

Belinda looks at Max as if to say, *See. I told you.* But he's focused on Barclay.

"We apologize for the disruption," Max says.

"I suspect one of my retreat attendees might just be having a bad day," Belinda says. "Did you happen to catch her name?"

Barclay crosses his arms. "Her name's Karen, I'd guess."

Max laughs and she shoots him a look.

"Can you describe her?"

"Medium height. Brown hair. Wearing some sorta fluffy purple sweater."

Maggie Hodges.

"She'd be damn attractive if it weren't for the bad attitude," Barclay says. "But that just ruins the whole picture, you know what I mean?"

"Absolutely," says Max.

Absolutely? To that sexist remark? She shoots him a look, but he doesn't notice.

"Well, I'm going to excuse myself," she says. She'll leave them to their juvenile conversation.

She's got a retreat to run.

Chapter Eleven

THE WALKING TOUR OF NEW Hope starts across the street from the inn. Maggie hopes the outing will include some shopping. That's always been a reliable bonding activity for her and Piper. And, to her relief, Piper is enthusiastic about the tour.

"You picked the perfect weekend for this," Piper says, inhaling the fresh air. "We don't really get the full autumn vibe in the city. I never think about it when I'm there, but as soon as we go away it's, like, wow—nature in full force."

The weather is beautiful, and so is the town. New Hope feels frozen in time, though she isn't sure what time, exactly. The vibe is 1960s free-love bohemian meets 1990s grunge rebellion. Just two blocks away from the inn, they'd already passed an indie bookshop crammed with paperbacks, a shop selling tie-dye T-shirts and ponchos, a Wicca supply store, and a candy shop that sold treats she hadn't seen since her childhood. Lampposts are covered with band stickers and posters advertising local events, like an outdoor movie night in nearby Peddler's Village.

Their guide is from the New Hope Historical Society, a man named Edward who wears jeans, a button-down shirt and bow tie. They pause on the street in front of an old stone Georgian-style house.

"This is the Parry Mansion, now a house museum. It was built in 1784 by Benjamin Parry, known as the Father of New Hope. Benjamin Parry played a key role in the town's development. After his Hope Mill burned down in 1790, he rebuilt and christened it the *New* Hope Mill."

Beside her, Piper takes a selfie with the museum in the background. Sheila offers to take a photo of the two of them together.

"You should come back for the winter retreat in December," Sheila whispers so as not to disrupt the history lesson. "It coincides with the annual ice sculpture garden. It's five days long and all the projects are holiday themed."

It sounds lovely, but Maggie can't imagine a more perfect time of year for the retreat than autumn. The town, bathed in gold and burnt umber and deep reds, bordered by the river and threaded with creeks and canals, feels like a film set.

"Today, this home showcases a hundred years' worth of local art, and each of the rooms is decorated to represent a different time period spanning the era of 1775 to 1900." Their guide waves them along and they pass an embankment overlooking a canal. The waterway is lined with old stone houses, the Great Barn Taproom and a sign for a vintage shop.

"This body of water is Aquetong Creek, which flows all year long and is fed primarily by a natural spring located two miles west of here. It was one of the main draws for people settling in this town. The strong currents supplied the energy for waterwheels that powered the many mills that made New Hope one of the foremost industrial towns of that time."

The group murmurs their appreciation and they all make a turn onto a side street called Mechanic. Their guide points out a time-worn stone building marked with a big copper plaque, but Maggie's more interested in a vacant storefront next door. The wooden windowsills are painted pale yellow, and she peeks through at the interior, a space with high tin ceilings and clean hardwood floors. The front door is also a soft buttery yellow, and a Realtor's sign hangs from the brass knob.

Maggie looks around the block for nearby cafés or stores. Across the street, halfway down the block, Maggie spots a shop with a black taffeta dress with crinolines hanging from the closed front door. The purple-and-black painted sign above the window reads, "Velvet Revival: Vintage."

Maggie turns to Piper. "Come with me to check out that place," she says.

"You want to ditch the tour?"

"We'll catch up with them after," Maggie says.

Piper hesitates. Frankly, she expected more enthusiasm. Sometimes Maggie doesn't understand her daughter. For someone who works in fashion, she has very little curiosity about clothes or style in general. When Maggie was a teenager, *Nylon* magazine was her bible. Fashion, art, music—it was the promise of a future. It showed her the world that awaited beyond the Main Line suburbs: New York City. Paris. Seattle.

The front door of the store is half covered with a posterboard that's scrawled with the following:

> 2 People at a time! Yes, even if you're related, came as a group, or are joined at the hip. No one under 16! No dogs. If you just want to browse, everything is posted on our website.

Maggie hesitates. "Maybe we should knock?"

Piper shrugs. Maggie turns the knob.

"Hello?" she calls out, slowly opening the door. "Is it okay to—"

"Come in," someone barks from deep within the dim room. The only window is covered with band stickers. It reminds her of the clubs in the bowery during the nineties. She reaches for her phone to take a photo, then notices a "No phones! No photos!" sign on the wall.

From behind the counter, a young woman with dyed black hair and heavy eye makeup watches them with barely concealed irritation. Maggie feels like they just barged into someone's personal closet. There are piles and piles of Doc Martens. Everywhere. They're spilling off shelves, arranged in the corners, peeking out from under racks of dark clothing.

Every inch of space is filled with *stuff*: plastic dolls and CDs and Christmas lights and twentieth-century ephemera. But the shoes are clearly the thing.

"Are these Docs vintage?" Maggie asks.

"Guaranteed. I only sell Docs manufactured before the year 2000. That's when the company movied production to China. Everything I got here—made in the UK." She points to a hanging Union Jack.

They step farther into the room. It smells musty, like all good resale shops. Piper pulls a pair of blue velvet Docs from a shelf.

"Are these organized by size or is it just sort of random?" Maggie asks. The woman sighs impatiently, then says, "Sevens, eights, nines . . ." pointing to various shelves. Maggie can't follow. She gives up and just looks at whatever catches her eye. She hasn't worn a pair of Docs in thirty years. The last time had probably been when she was still in college.

Piper pulls out a pair in classic black leather.

"There's no returns, so make sure they fit," the woman says.

Piper sits on the floor and tries them on, and then something else catches her eye.

"Mom, look at this." Piper pulls a violet embroidered coat from one of the racks. She opens it to reveal silk lining. It has a faux-fur collar and cuffs. "You used to have one just like it."

She did. She'd sold it at a consignment shop years ago and regretted it ever since.

"It's like when I used to play dress-up in your closet," Piper says, before trying on a pair of hunter-green Docs. Maggie's about to say that they look great on her, that she should get them, when Piper's phone rings.

"No cell phones!" the woman says from behind the counter.

Piper heads for the door, telling Maggie, "I'll be right back."

The store proprietress rounds the counter and makes a beeline for her.

"Did she walk out of here wearing merchandise?"

She did. Maggie produces her credit card. Moments later, Piper reappears.

"I forgot to take off the—"

"They're *yours* now," the shopkeeper says.

Piper looks at Maggie, confused.

"I've got it—don't worry about it," Maggie says, waving her credit card.

"Thank you," Piper says, looking apologetic. At first, Maggie thinks her expression is about the shoes. But then she says, "Would you mind if I head back?"

"To the inn?"

Piper nods.

"What about the rest of the tour?" Maggie signs the credit card slip.

"I'm kinda tired. I'll just meet you at the first workshop in . . ." Piper checks her phone. "About an hour."

Maggie nods. "Um, okay. See you there."

Piper leaves, unsmiling. The call seems to have spooked her. Strange. Maggie wonders if there's something Piper isn't telling her. If so, she has the rest of the weekend to find out.

Chapter Twelve

AIDAN AND COLE STAND WITH the rest of the party on the outskirts of the nearby state park. Aidan, having lived his whole life in the area, knows the terrain well. It's a mix of woody forest, open fields and the riverbank. The sun is shining and it's warm for October. A perfect day to be in the great outdoors. And judging from his outburst at lunch, Cole needs the time to decompress.

Barclay, assuming the role of bushcraft guide, gathers them around and addresses them like they're a bunch of troops. He's fully committing to his leadership role, dressed in an army-green all-weather jacket, brown tactical boots and wraparound black sunglasses.

"I'm sure every one of you standing here considers yourself handy, capable, and self-reliant. But if you stop and really think about it, those beliefs are contingent on certain conditions we take for granted: Food. Shelter. Hell, having our phones. Bushcraft is about sustaining yourself using only what nature provides."

One of Scott's friends makes a crack about nature providing him with "plenty to work with" with an accompanying lewd hand gesture. But the laughter comes to a quick stop when Barclay announces he's collecting everyone's phone for the duration of the activity.

"True survival skills mean relying on your own strength—mental and physical," he says.

Aidan glances at Cole, who's staring straight ahead. His expression is unreadable, and Aidan suspects his mind is somewhere else entirely.

"We don't have technology in the wilderness, but we can have tools. Starting with something simple but possibly lifesaving: a reliable compass," Barclay says, holding up an old-fashioned copper variety. "And, again—don't let me hear you say you have an app on your phone for that. Phones run out of batteries. They can get ruined in water. Phones offer a false sense of security."

Nearby, a stream rushes with a faint burble, and Aidan remembers taking Cole to find salamanders in the very spot as a child.

"A compass is not just about general directions—you can use the sun for that. A compass's main value is helping you avoid lateral drift. Does anyone here know what lateral drift means?"

No one says anything. Without their phones to look up the phrase, Aidan suspects no one will. He's pretty sure Cole knows the answer, but he's staring off into the distance.

One of Scott's fraternity brothers finally pipes up, explaining that it's impossible to walk a straight line over a long distance without having an object in sight that you're walking toward.

"You got that, Cole?" Barclay says, pointedly calling him out.

"Got it," Cole says, expressionless. Detached.

What is going on with him? Since they work together, Aidan gets to spend more time with his adult son than most fathers. But he still has no clue what's going on.

Aidan was pleasantly surprised two years ago when Cole informed him, after graduating cum laude from Villanova University, that he wanted to join him in Danby Markets. For a while, it seemed like Cole was going to pursue a law career. And sure, Aidan would have been proud to tell everyone his son was an attorney. But he was even more proud when Cole changed his mind and joined him in the grocery business. It was something he'd hoped for, but never pushed. Aidan believes it's important to have a job you care about, one that gives you a reason to get out of bed in the morning. In the first few years after Nancy's death, work was his lifeline. Sure, he had parenthood. But work gave him a sense of control.

Maybe Cole feels touchy this weekend because Scott and all his friends have white-collar jobs. But why would that bother him? The grocery business has been lucrative, and Cole had always been proud of his work. But something's got him on edge. That's evident.

Barclay passes out analog compasses.

"What we have here is an extensive trail system, including the Towpath Trail, which runs for miles along the river."

By now, Scott's wise-cracking fraternity brothers are paying close attention, and probably regretting the fourth and fifth beers at lunch.

What an odd meal. First, Cole and Scott snapping at each other. Then, that brunette barreling over to the table. Very attractive. But clearly neurotic as hell.

Maybe that's why Cole is in a bad mood. Aidan is pretty sure Cole had a breakup a few months ago. Maybe he'd been looking forward to a guys' weekend and there they were, surrounded by a bunch of women. Or, as Barclay put it after the lunchtime confrontation, "Harping women."

Raising Cole alone, every weekend had been guys' weekend. Aidan hasn't had a significant woman in his life since his wife died. Back when Cole was in high school, at the urging of his friends, he tried to date. At one point, he actually met someone he could see himself with long-term. But at the seven-month mark, the holidays rolled around and the thought of taking her to the Cavanaughs for Christmas made him shudder. It wasn't the Cavanaughs' fault—they only wanted him to be happy. He knew that. But he also felt that as a single father, he had to put family first. And a new woman would always be a piece of the puzzle that didn't quite fit. It wouldn't be fair to her. And maybe not fair to Cole. It just didn't feel right.

"I think you're punishing yourself," said the overpriced therapist he'd reluctantly agreed to go see. That didn't last long. And no, he didn't feel guilty about Nancy's death—he had nothing to do with the rare cancer that interrupted their lives so mercilessly. And he didn't feel guilty about being alive while she was gone. It was more complicated than that.

"Grandson, is that a phone?" Barclay looks at Cole, who shoves something back into his jacket pocket.

Cole didn't hand over his phone when they were collected?

"What's going on?" Aidan whispers.

"It's still a weekday," Cole says.

Aidan wants to believe it's just a strong work ethic making Cole violate the spirit of the afternoon. But he's not so sure. He gives him a nudge, and Cole hands his phone over to Barclay.

"Our first exercise is collecting materials to build a lean-to shelter. We won't have time today to build an entire structure, but the assignment is to gather material as if we must do so with a ticking clock—sunset's in two and a half hours. So we're splitting up into two groups that we're gonna called Team Boone and Team Crockett—named of course for the two greatest outdoorsman that ever walked this fine earth. Now, fellas, choose your team partners wisely. Because to keep things interesting, we're awarding points for every activity this weekend, and the team with the most points on Sunday wins the weekend."

There are hoots and hollers. And then Barclay opens one of his backpacks and hands out T-shirts that read, "Scott's Bushcraft Bachelor Party" on the front and "Win the Weekend" on the back. Even though it's chilly, everyone sheds their coats to change into their T-shirts. Cole is the only one who doesn't, instead folding the shirt into his own knapsack.

Barclay goes on to explain the rules and points system, and Aidan's brother-in-law, Ritchie, taps him on the shoulder. "Partners?" They fist bump. This is going to be fun.

"Your assignment, should you choose to accept," Barclay says, a nod to Scott's favorite movie franchise, *Mission: Impossible*. "Collect branches and twigs for a lean-to shelter. The team with the most viable materials wins."

The group disbands as everyone heads off deeper into the woods.

"Dude, you can't go one hour without your phone?" Scott says.

"I could. If it were for a good reason. I don't think this qualifies."

"Cole, what kind of attitude is that?" Aidan says, surprised.

"Oh, so you think this is stupid?" Scott says in a way that makes Aidan wonder if maybe Scott thinks it's stupid. Maybe he and Barclay are the only ones who think the bushcraft angle was a good idea. He hopes not.

"No," Cole says in a tone Aidan knows all too well. Whatever he says next will be sarcastic. "I've been thinking recently I really need to improve my fort-building skills."

"Sure," Scott says. "Since you've already mastered the skills of sneaking around and lying."

Aidan doesn't know who hits who first, but fists start flying, and the boys drop to the ground. He jumps in to pull Cole away from his cousin, and Ritchie does the same with Scott.

"Knock it off!" Aidan yells.

"What the hell is going on with you two?"

Cole brushes the dirt and twigs off his jeans. He shakes one hand, rubbing his wrist with his thumb. And he walks off without another word. Aidan turns to Scott, and he just shrugs.

This isn't the bonding weekend he'd had in mind.

WHEN PIPER SPOTS the Bucks County Playhouse, she knows she's almost reached the inn. She feels bad for ditching her mom, but there will be plenty of time for togetherness later. Right now, she needs to deal with that phone call.

The lawn between the inn and the theater is dotted with red wooden Adirondack chairs. She sits in one facing the river and the promenade. The sun shines on her face, and she tilts her chin up, giving herself a moment to enjoy the moment before dealing with the unexpected voicemail from Gretchen. She can't imagine why she's calling Piper a day after firing her. Whatever it is, she didn't want to have the conversation in front of her mother. So she let it go to voicemail.

But now that she's alone, she decides not to bother listening to the voicemail. If there's paperwork or some exit bureaucracy, she'll deal with it when she gets back to the city. The whole point of a getaway is to actually *get away*.

In the distance, on the inn's back terrace, Kalli and Laurel are drinking from mugs, bundled in cozy cardigans they no doubt crafted themselves. They seem so relaxed and happy. She knows it's what her mother wants for the two of them this weekend. Piper wants that too.

She looks out at the water. The afternoon sunlight gives the river an amber sheen. Flower beds filled with purple asters, fountain grass, stalks of small red berries and pinecones decorate the railing that runs the length of the promenade. Across the river, an ornate spire topping a church reaches toward the blue sky. And in the water, a gaggle of ducks paddles by.

"Excuse me," someone says. She looks up. A tall guy with sandy-brown hair stands in front of her. Austin Butler from check-in. "Sorry to bother you. You're with the knitting group, right? I saw you in the lobby earlier."

"Yeah. I'm with the group. You with the bachelor party?"

He nods. "Unfortunately. I'm Cole."

"Piper," she says.

"Listen, I know this sounds weird, but can I borrow your phone for a minute? My grandfather confiscated mine for this sort of . . . outward bound situation we have going on. And I really need to make a quick call."

She's distracted by a fresh, angry-looking bruise on his right cheek.

"I think your face is bleeding," she says.

"You should see the other guy." He smiles, and she resists the impulse to tell him no, seriously, he'd better get some ice on his cheek.

"So can I use your phone?" he says.

She hesitates.

"Look," he says, "I'm not a psycho. I promise. My family is just a big pain in the ass. And I need to make a call."

Fair enough. He seems harmless. Plus, he's injured.

She hands over her phone.

"Thank you. You're amazing. I'll be right back."

He turns toward the water and walks a few yards away. She feels twitchy without her phone. The wind picks up, and she glances back at the inn. Laura is still in her spot, but Kalli has moved to the promenade. Laurel must sense her gaze, because she turns and gives her a wave. Piper waves back, feeling a stab of guilt for ditching her mother. Maybe she should head back to the walking tour after all.

She looks over at Cole, who's turned away while he talks. And talks. He said a minute, but he doesn't appear to be ending his call anytime soon. This is ridiculous. She walks over to him, but he's too wrapped up in his conversation to notice.

"I didn't plan this, but I'm here. It is what it is. So let's—"

Piper taps him on the shoulder and he stops talking.

"Sorry to interrupt, but I really need to get going," she says. He nods, tells the person on the other end, "I'll see you later," and then ends the call.

"Thanks," he says, handing over the phone.

"No problem."

They look at each other for a beat longer than necessary. She feels the frisson of unexpected chemistry.

"I have a boyfriend," she blurts out.

He nods. "And I really just needed the phone."

She feels herself flush with embarrassment.

"Right. Okay then—have a good . . . bachelor party."

"Happy knitting," he says.

She shakes her head, thinking, *What was that?* It was nothing, really. It's probably displacement—all of her relationship anxiety and missing Ethan.

She walks back to the inn.

The lobby is warm and smells like chocolate. Piper looks around for the source of the delicious aroma, but doesn't see any food. And then she forgets all about the guy Cole and the scent of cocoa and everything else, because her phone suddenly feels like a hundred-pound weight in her hand. Who is she kidding not listening to the voicemail? Of course she has to find out why Gretchen called.

Across from the fireplace she spots an inviting, velvet-cushioned wingback chair. Settling into it, she takes one more glance around to make sure she has privacy. Aside from the man minding the front desk, she's alone. Satisfied, she plays Gretchen's message, pressing the phone to her ear.

"Piper, I'm so sorry our last meeting got off track. And if I said anything to offend you, I absolutely didn't mean it. In fact, I have some fabulous news, so give me a call back ASAP . . ."

She listens to it three times to make sure she isn't missing something. The meeting "got off track"? That's quite the euphemism for firing her as a client. And as for the great news, Piper can only assume it's a potential booking. Why else would Gretchen backtrack like that?

But really, the reason doesn't matter. Piper should be thrilled—overjoyed. She should be calling Gretchen back immediately. But she isn't.

And she doesn't.

Instead, she turns the phone on Do Not Disturb and heads back to her room.

Chapter Thirteen

MAGGIE IS HAPPY TO BE reunited with Piper for the first workshop of the day, "Know Your Yarn." It's held in a second-floor room dominated by a large farmhouse table piled with balls of yarn in the center.

Belinda stands in the front of the room, but she hasn't started the official lesson yet. Everyone is chatting casually, and this gives Maggie a chance to ask Piper, "So who called earlier? When we were in the vintage shop?" she says.

"Oh, it was just Ava," Piper says, naming a friend from high school.

Maggie nods. She'd been hoping it was something work-related—something positive. She still can't believe Piper's manager dropped her. Surely, this can be fixed.

Belinda stands at the foot of the table.

"Welcome, everyone, to Know Your Yarn. It's the topic that inspired me to teach workshops in the first place. It dawned on me, a few years into owning a knitting shop, that many of my customers were tremendously skilled craftspeople but sort of flying blind when it came to what yarn to choose for their projects. I was somewhat guilty of it myself. So the year I turned thirty, I took an opportunity to spend a summer at a sheep farm in the UK."

Stories like this always make Maggie feel a little wistful. She never had the chance to leave her worries behind and just go wherever life would take her the way her friends had in their twenties.

"So many of us make decisions about our projects without some important practical considerations," Belinda says. "Do you know that cashmere is eight times warmer but twenty times lighter than wool?"

Maggie and Piper share a little smile. She starts to take notes on the pad of paper set in front of her. She exhales, finally feeling the closeness to Piper she'd been aching for all day. Longer than a day. It's actually been a while since she felt connected to Piper, and it hurts. Their relationship hasn't been the same since Piper moved in with Ethan. Maggie knows it's a normal progression, one that every parent goes through. But it's always been just the two of them.

She's thankful they have knitting to bring them together.

Maggie hadn't learned to knit until after Piper was born. It began as a source of stress relief and quickly became an integral part of her life and happiness. She was determined to expose Piper to the craft as early as possible, and as soon as she was old enough to grasp the basics, Maggie sat her down and taught her.

But Piper's intolerance for her own mistakes made knitting a source of frustration, not joy. She'd known going in that Piper had a bit of a perfectionist streak—a stubborn trait from Maggie's own mother that had apparently skipped a generation. Maggie tried and tried to cajole Piper into sticking with it, but with no luck. When she shared her frustration with Elaine, who is also a knitter, she said, "Just tell Piper there's no such thing as mistakes in knitting. With children, so much is how it's presented to them." Maggie gave it a try, but her smart little girl just rolled her eyes. But Elaine's words stuck with her. It was true: many knitting "mistakes" are actually just advanced stitches that the beginner accidentally stumbles into—like a yarnover. A yarnover is a way to create an extra loop on the needle, resulting in a deliberate hole or "eyelet" in the fabric. Beginning knitters can accidentally create a yarnover when they unintentionally wrap the yarn around the needle in a way that adds an extra stitch. So instead of telling Piper that a knitting "mistake" was often a technique she just didn't need yet, she *showed* her. And it changed everything.

"I signed us up for the brioche class after this," Maggie whispers to her.

Piper shakes her head. "Ooh, can't. I'm taking intro to crochet."

Crochet? She thought they'd already discussed this and agreed on other knitting workshops. *This is because of Hannah Elise.* Of course, it's fine that Piper made a new friend—it's great. But the weekend is supposed to be *their* bonding time.

"Mixing and matching yarns can improve the way your fibers perform," Belinda says. "For example, since mohair can be heavy and drapey, you can add wool to stabilize it. And weaving in some silk controls the fuzz."

Maggie jots down these notes, then turns to Piper.

"I thought the whole point of the weekend is to spend time together."

"Mom, of course," Piper says. "We'll just meet up after. It's not like we have to be together every minute, right?"

Maggie doesn't answer.

HER MOTHER IS really being *a lot*. Piper almost feels guilty enough to change her mind about taking the crochet class, but ultimately doesn't give in to it.

After Belinda's workshop, Piper makes her way back to the

Purl, where Hannah Elise is teaching intro to crochet. The space is arranged slightly differently than earlier, with a large round table now dominating one side of the room, an island surrounded by the colorful yarn displays. The space is bright and toasty from sunshine streaming in through the large windows.

Piper takes a seat at one of the spots set with a crochet hook and a skein of an acrylic wool blend. Kalli and Laurel join her at the table, and she detects a tension between them that she didn't notice earlier.

Or maybe she's just projecting because she herself is tense.

"Welcome, everyone," Hannah Elise says, standing in front of the room. She's dressed in head-to-toe crochet, including a cream-colored crop top with bell sleeves and intricate floral motifs in orange and teal. She's paired it with high-waisted pants with a whimsical, tasseled drawstring that matches the orange and teal of the top. "Like many of you, I came to crochet as a second love, after knitting. Crafters often message me asking which is better, and the simple answer is that it depends on the individual. But personally, as someone who's become partial to crochet, I can tell you there're a few advantages—especially for beginners."

Piper's phone buzzes with a text. It's from Ethan: the cat-with-heart-eyes emoji. She smiles. They always use that cat emoji as shorthand for *I love you* because of the way they met. She feels a little guilty for finding that guy Cole attractive. It wasn't that she was attracted to him—she just couldn't help but note the obvious. Piper had absolutely no reservations when it came to her commitment to Ethan. She hadn't been with any other guys since the day she and Ethan met, and she'd never wanted to. Maybe it was less than ideal to find her Person so early in life; she was missing out on all the drama her friends were going through, both good and bad. But people spent their entire lives looking for the sort of connection—physical, emotional, spiritual—that she has with Ethan. But maybe Ethan is having doubts because their relationship timeline is more advanced than that of their friends.

"It's easier to correct mistakes in crochet because you can usually unravel a few stitches and redo them versus unraveling entire rows in knitting," Hannah Elise says, and Piper wonders what her mother would think of that. There was never a knitting mistake that Maggie couldn't tackle. She loves finding creative ways to save an errant stitch. Piper prefers to just rip out rows quickly and get the suffering over with. That's a major difference between the two of them: Maggie doesn't mind messiness. She goes with the flow—except when it comes to Ethan.

Piper knows that her mother thinks she's too young to be in such a serious relationship. She'd only said so once, and after Piper's resounding rejection of the idea, she never brought it up again. At least, not overtly. But Piper continues to feel her disapproval. Her mother, usually so warm and bubbly and open, is just not herself around Ethan. It's frustrating sometimes, but Piper understands that Maggie's simply afraid she'll make the same mistake she made. Of course, Maggie would never put it like that. She'd always insisted that having Piper young was the best thing that ever happened to her. But Piper can tell Maggie wants something different for her.

"As you get more experienced, crochet is faster because it only involves one active loop at a time. And because I like to make things that are structured, like bags and jackets, crochet fabric tends to be denser and more stable. But again, this is about you discovering your unique relationship with crochet."

Hannah Elise talks through the instructions for what she calls a single change, and Piper follows along with her hook and yarn. She pushes down the negative thoughts about her mother, like a tough piece of meat she can barely swallow. She waits for the magic of crafting to kick in, making everything else recede.

And soon, it does.

Chapter Fourteen

MAGGIE IS IMPATIENT TO REUNITE with Piper, and while she waits she changes into black corduroy pants and a black cashmere turtleneck for the welcome dinner. Then she heads downstairs for a glass of wine.

Bucks Tavern has a warm, intimate vibe. Rustic wooden tables are set with handmade pottery. There are thick timber beams overhead and windows looking out to the river. The crowd seems to be a mix of locals and out-of-towners. There's a lot of flannel and all-weather footwear.

The horseshoe-shaped bar is dark wood with an inner bank of shelves displaying glass bottles filled with aged whiskey and gin and colorful liqueurs. Two bartenders buzz around shaking cocktail mixers.

Maggie's lucky to find an empty seat in the center facing the river. It's a lovely spot, one she should enjoy. But she hears her mother's voice in her head, saying: *A lady never drinks alone.* It makes absolutely no sense on any level, but every time Maggie sits alone at a bar or at a table for one, she feels like a failure. And considering her track record with men, that's fairly often.

But tonight, men are the last thing on her mind. She's hurt over how readily Piper keeps choosing to spend time apart this weekend. Fine, she wanted to take crochet. But the class ended an hour ago, and Piper's still hanging out with Hannah Elise; she texted her to say they were doing knitting videos for social media, that she'd meet her at dinner. Maggie knows, on a practical level, she shouldn't take it personally. But she can't help feeling rejected. And, she has to admit, also a little scared.

The conversation with Ethan yesterday has left her a bit unmoored. She doesn't know if he's going to heed her advice and wait to propose or if he's going to ignore her. These next few years are Piper's chance to establish a career that's interesting and rewarding. While Maggie's grateful for the steady paycheck Elaine's store has provided for her, she can't help but want something more for Piper. People in their twenties simply don't realize how their decisions will reverberate for decades to come.

And then there's the other fear: the fear of what her life will look like without Piper in it. Oh, sure—Piper will always be her daughter. But a marriage will change things. Maggie knew this day would come at some point. She just thought she'd have a lot more time before it did.

The bartender, a cheerful guy with a man bun, appears for her drink order, and she has a better idea than wine. With the crackling fireplace and the earthy aroma of hearty stew and something sweet and caramelized, she wants something autumnal.

"I'll have a coffee with Baileys, please," she says.

The man beside her turns to her. "I haven't heard anyone order that in a long time." And then he tries to pretend he didn't say it. Because they recognize each other.

It's the guy from the bachelor party. The one who stood up and apologized to her. He's very attractive, with dark auburn hair and eyes to match. She glances at the table where he'd been sitting just a few hours earlier. The table where she yelled at him.

"Um, I think I owe you an apology," she says. "That wasn't me at lunch. I mean, it was me, but I think I was just upset about something else and took it out on your group. So, sorry about that."

"Aidan Danby," he says, holding out his hand. "And no apologies necessary. Nothing more stressful than a relaxing vacation, right?" he says.

"I'm Maggie Hodges," she says, shaking his hand. She notices the firmness of his grip and looks up to meet his direct gaze. His eyes are remarkably the same colors as the autumn leaves, and the shared glance gives her a little shiver. Surprised by the feeling, she pulls her hand back.

"You're with the knitting ladies?" he says.

"Well, yes. But when you say it like that, it makes me sound like I should be in a rocking chair with a cat on my lap and wearing spectacles." She hates to admit that's kinda the way she envisions herself in the future. And she's just fine with that.

"Not at all. Clearly, you are a very youthful and, might I say, feisty, knitter."

"Your group seems very feisty—if I may say."

He laughs. "You just caught us at a bad moment. I'm mostly along for the ride to spend time with my son. He's not the one who mouthed off to you, by the way."

"Thanks for clarifying," she says. She reflexively glances at his left ring finger. Bare. These days, that doesn't necessarily mean anything. And really, his marital status is irrelevant. She's not looking. "Well, I hope you're having better luck spending time with your son than I am with my daughter."

Aidan looks pointedly at the empty seat next to him on the other side. "Apparently, I'm not. How old's your daughter?"

"She just turned twenty-three. How 'bout your son?"

"Twenty-four."

She has the impulse to make a little toast, to say something like, *Well, here's to getting ditched by our kids.* But she's afraid it will come off wrong, like a flirtation. So she says nothing, and neither does he, and they fall back into a silence as if they'd never started talking in the first place.

"Well," he finally says, "hopefully things will improve by the end of the night."

"Bachelor party out on the town?" she says.

"More like bachelor party in the woods."

The woods? "Oh. Right." She remembers the banner draped across the entrance. "Bushcraft. So basically you're doing overnight camp for adults."

"Overnight camp?" Aidan says. "I think you're underestimating the challenge. It's a lot harder than knitting, I can tell you that."

"Oh, really? I think you're the one underestimating the challenge." She frowns, mildly insulted.

"No offense. My point is that bushcraft is hard."

"Like what? What are you guys doing tomorrow that's so hard?"

Aidan consults his phone. "Okay, tomorrow we're trout fishing in the morning. Afternoon, we're foraging for campfire materials. Then we have an axe-throwing competition."

"None of those things are any more difficult than knitting a blanket. In fact, I'd say they're easier."

He laughs. "Every one of those things takes physical exertion and exposure to the elements. They only *sound* simple."

"You'd be a lot more 'exposed to the elements' without the *knitted* sweater you're wearing," she says.

Aidan smiles appreciatively. "Point taken. Look, there's no real debate here. It's age-old, right?"

"What do you mean?"

"Well, from the dawn of time, men are hunters and gatherers and women tend to the nest."

"Wow. That's not at all sexist," she says sarcastically.

"Am I wrong?"

"I think you are, in fact, wrong. And what does that have to do with our respective weekends?"

"It means we're both acting according to our natural strengths: Men build fire and shelter, and women darn socks."

Maggie's jaw drops. "You did *not* just say that. You know what? I bet you couldn't last through a single knitting class. I bet you can't even get the yarn on the needle."

"That's a bet I'm willing to take. If you admit you wouldn't last a day out in the wilderness. You couldn't start your own fire next to a tank of gasoline." He's grinning, and she knows he's simply teasing her. But she's a little offended because he probably also believes it to some extent.

"I'll admit no such thing. I raised my daughter in New York City alone. Self-sufficiency is my middle name."

"New York City? Hailing a cab is not a survival skill."

"I have plenty of survival skills."

"Prove it."

She shakes her head no. They fall back into silence. After a minute, Aidan turns to her.

"I've been thinking," he says. "Cole, for some reason, isn't getting along with his cousin. They got into a fight earlier—a literal fight. And I can't get through to him. At this point, I'll try anything to salvage the weekend. So maybe you and your daughter come along for one of our outings tomorrow."

"Are you trying to set her up with your son? Because she's got a serious boyfriend," Maggie says.

"No! Absolutely not. I don't meddle in my son's personal life. That's a line I cross at my own peril. But I'm thinking maybe together, we can jolt Cole out of his funk. And have a friendly competition while we're at it. What do you say?"

Is he joking? No. He seems absolutely serious.

"We're here to take knitting workshops."

"Nice excuse," he says.

She shakes her head and smiles. "It's true."

"Also true: You can't hack it out there in the wilderness."

She laughs. "Right. And you couldn't knit a simple potholder to save your life."

He seems to consider this. "Well, put your money where your mouth is: I have fifty bucks that says I'd be a better novice knitter than you'd be trying to survive an hour in the wilderness without a cup of coffee or your phone."

He holds out his hand to shake on it. Is he flirting with her? She can't tell. And she also can't tell whether or not she wants him to be.

"You're on. I'll be using your fifty dollars to buy more yarn."

"So we're doing this," he says, smiling.

"I guess we are."

He asks for her phone number. And she gives it to him.

Chapter Fifteen

PIPER FINDS THE KNITTING GROUP at a table in the back of the inn's restaurant, near a crackling fireplace. Piper's the last one to arrive, but Maggie saved her a seat. She hopes her mother isn't upset with her for being MIA the past two hours.

Hannah Elise was absolutely right: Posting the knitting content gives her a sense of control; she served the algorithm gods an offering in hopes they soon bury her viral runway fall.

"Nice of you to make an appearance," Maggie says.

Okay, so she *is* upset with her.

Bottles of wine are set along the length of the long table, and Maggie is already pouring herself another glass. A waiter hands Piper a menu of craft cocktails. Kalli, to her right, is drinking something that smells like bourbon and spiced apple. Across the table, Lexi and Dove sip amber-colored beer. Piper decides she'll stick with wine and pours herself a glass of merlot.

Laurel is on Maggie's opposite side. Piper finds it curious that the best friends aren't sitting together, but maybe she's envious of their secure attachment. *God forbid Mom and me aren't glued at the hip.* Then she feels guilty for the ungrateful thought. She turns to Maggie.

"Mom, sorry I ran off with Hannah Elise. But honestly,

it felt good to have fun and post stuff that has nothing to do with work."

She tries not to think about Gretchen's voicemail. Her mother would be upset to know she's ignoring a message from her manager. Former manager. And she doesn't need Maggie's input when she's wrestling with her own mixed feelings.

"Well, I'm glad you didn't delete your accounts after all. I'm telling you, what happened Wednesday night is going to blow over. It will be like it never happened."

Maggie probably feels the sting of Piper's failure as much as she feels it herself. That's always been the double-edged sword of their closeness. And the older Piper gets, the sharper that edge feels.

Belinda stands up from her seat to address the table.

"Welcome to our opening-night festivities, everyone. I hope you're all getting settled and that you've had some time to explore our beautiful little town. As I mentioned earlier, one of my retreat traditions is taking a group photo."

Belinda's husband appears with a digital camera. Max seems to be in his seventies, possibly a little older than Belinda. He's medium height with a slender build, thick gray hair and deep-set brown eyes.

"I hope you'll indulge me for a moment while my husband, Max, immortalizes our little ensemble. And I'd like to point out that one very special knitter has made it into every photo: Let's hear it for Sheila."

The table breaks out into applause. Piper stays seated, but half the table gets up to fit into the frame, shuffling around for position and debating who's too tall for what spot.

"Say—we love yarn," Max says once they've found a configuration that works. Maggie looks at him, her arm around Piper's shoulder, and smiles. Okay, so they're all good.

Everyone returns to their seats and the hum of conversation

resumes. Beside her, Kalli hunches over to tap away on the phone she's half hiding under the table. Then, sensing her gaze, Kalli looks up.

"Sorry," Piper says, though she's not sure why she's apologizing.

"No, I'm being antisocial," Kalli says, shoving the phone away in her bag. "So—you and your mom having fun so far?"

Piper can tell the brightness in her tone is forced.

"Yeah. It's great. How about you and Laurel?"

Kalli glances across the table at her friend.

"As far as knitting? Hands-down the best workshops. And we've been to Vogue Knits Live twice."

"And the non-knitting?" she says.

Kalli starts to say something, then stops herself. When she finally speaks, she says, "This trip was Laurel's idea. A girls' weekend, a 'get your head straight' weekend. But she's annoyed that my head isn't in the place she thinks it should be, so we're arguing."

"You mean, you're not into the knitting as much as she is?"

"I wish it was that simple. Long story short, I'm getting divorced and she wants this weekend to be the start of me moving on. I want that too. But we have different ideas of what moving on should look like."

Piper nods. Kalli doesn't look that much older than she is. And she's already getting divorced? She hopes Maggie doesn't hear the story. It will just validate her anxiety over Piper getting so serious with Ethan.

"How long have you been married?"

"Three years. But we've been together since high school. So—a long time. And it's a big deal because I'm the first in my family to get divorced."

"Really? No one in your family has ever gotten divorced?"

"I'm Greek," she says, as if that explains it.

Piper sees the waiter taking orders at the opposite end of the table and she scans the menu. The main courses are hearty and locally sourced, dishes of braised meat and roasted root vegetables.

Beside her, Maggie orders the wild mushroom risotto and goes right back to talking to Laurel. Piper hopes her mother is genuinely engaged in the conversation and not trying to make a point of ignoring her. Her mother isn't usually passive-aggressive, but something seems to be making her extra sensitive this weekend.

By the time the entrées are served, several cocktails later, Kalli shares the story of her failed marriage: Apparently, she met someone else, fell madly in love and realized she'd never experienced it before.

"And once I experienced real love and, yeah, *passion*, I couldn't go back."

"I get it," Piper says. "So now you're with the other guy? The man you actually love?" Piper says.

Kalli shakes her head. "No. I ended things with him back when I still thought I should save my marriage. And by the time I tried to get him back, he wanted nothing to do with the whole situation. I guess I can't blame him. But I've been pretty messed up over the whole thing," Kalli says, her eyes glassy. "And so . . . the knitting retreat." She raises her near-empty glass to toast Piper, and she dutifully raises her own.

"To mistakes," Kalli says. "To living and learning."

"To living and learning," Piper says.

Maybe her mother has a point. It could be a mistake to settle down too young. Ethan's second thoughts—if he is, in fact, having second thoughts—might be doing them both a favor.

Still—it hurts.

MAGGIE IS SEATED next to Laurel, and the two strike up a conversation over dinner. She learns that Laurel and Kalli are both teachers in a nearby local school district—Kalli at Lenape Middle School in Doylestown, Laurel at Central Bucks West. And that they've been friends since their days at those same schools.

"Do you want to switch seats with Piper so you can sit next to one another?" Maggie offers.

"No," Laurel says. "But thanks."

The vehemence in her voice when she says no tells Maggie that the two of them are in an argument. Maggie can relate; she herself nearly started a fight with Piper over her ditching her and then being the last one to show up for the group dinner. But she knew she was probably being overly emotional, possibly even irrational. That it was the fear again.

She turns to look at Piper, vivacious and chatting away with Kalli, and experiences a warm rush of love for her daughter. Beside her, Laurel orders another cocktail.

"I know it's none of my business," Maggie says, "but if you two are fighting over something, whatever it is, it's not worth it."

Laurel nods. "So it's that obvious?"

Maggie smiles with empathy.

One of the waiters reappears for their dinner order, and she asks for the mushroom risotto. She hears Piper order the roasted chicken.

"Can I ask you something?" Laurel says. "Have you ever had to sit back and watch someone you really care about do something colossally stupid? And there's nothing you can do about it?" Her eyes look teary.

Maggie nods. "Absolutely. But the trick is, that's when you need to stay even closer—not pull away."

Maggie can't resist mentally patting herself on the back for this bit of wisdom, because she's been following her own advice: As much as she disapproves of Piper focusing more on her boyfriend than on her career, she hasn't let that come between them. If anything, Maggie's been working even harder to spend time with her.

She turns back to Piper, to tell her how happy she is that they're away together for the weekend, but Piper is standing up with the phone pressed to her ear.

"Where are you going?" Maggie says to her back, a question Piper either doesn't hear or ignores. But before Maggie has a moment to register this latest irritation, Belinda slides into Piper's freshly vacated seat.

"Maggie, I hope you haven't had any more aggravation from the bachelor party," she says. Maggie feels sheepish, wondering if Belinda heard about her little tantrum at the lunch table.

"Oh, it's all fine. I shouldn't have made a big deal out of it. Really. I'm sorry."

Maggie finds herself looking over at the bar where she'd sat talking to Aidan Danby. It had been fun chatting in the moment, but now she regrets having given him her number. The whole bushcraft/knitting challenge is fun in theory, but she's not actually going to go through with it.

"Don't be sorry. I understand completely. My goal is always to provide a tranquil, intimate experience at the retreat. Somehow this weekend, my husband and I got our signals crossed."

"No problem. Really. I understand. I mean, I'm not married. But if I were, I'm sure I'd get my signals crossed too."

"How long have you been divorced, if you don't mind my asking?" Belinda says.

"Oh—I've never been married. It's just Piper and me."

"Well, aren't we flip sides of the same coin: I don't have children. It's just Max and me. Anyway, we typically have an agreement: On my retreat weekends, none of the other rooms are booked."

Maggie feels terrible she made an issue out of it in the first place, and hopes she didn't cause problems between Belinda and her husband.

"Really, it's fine. In fact, I was talking to one of them earlier. Seems like a decent guy."

Belinda looks happy. "Now, that's nice to hear! I always hope the retreat members end up becoming friendly, but I didn't dare hope for some cross-pollination with the bachelor party. Who'd you end up chatting with?"

Maggie tells her Aidan's name, and Belinda nods. "I've known the Danby boys—Aidan and his son, Cole—for quite some time."

"You have?"

"Well, yes," Belinda says, as if it's obvious. "He's local. This is a small town. I know Aidan's father-in-law, the cousins. Never met his late wife, though. That was before we moved here."

Late wife.

"Oh. Well, we have a little friendly competition going," Maggie says. "A bet." She explains the challenge Aidan posed to her.

"I'd pay money to see one of those men with a set of knitting needles," Belinda says with a wink. "Feel free to bring him to any workshop I'm teaching."

Maggie smiles. Maybe it's not the worst idea after all.

And maybe it will shake things up enough to keep Piper's attention. She's willing to chalk today off as a bumpy start. But tomorrow . . . let the bonding begin.

She can't wait to tell Piper.

Chapter Sixteen

AIDAN AND HIS FATHER-IN-LAW, two out of the three "old" guys at the bachelor party, break off from the rest of the group and duck out, just the two of them. It's been years since he's had one-on-one time with Barclay, and the conversation while they walk a few blocks to a bar is superficial: the Eagles' Super Bowl odds. Ballooning local real estate prices. The new duckpin bowling spot in Doylestown.

The bar is packed, a place that hasn't changed since Aidan first snuck in with a fake ID when he was a senior at Central Bucks West. He used to go because it was the one bar he could get into. Now he chooses it because it's the last of a dying breed: no flat-screen TVs, no craft beer and a bartender over the age of thirty.

Inside, the scent of decades of cigarette smoke and spilled drinks have seeped into the pores of the place. It has an old-school jukebox that still works, and tonight it's playing Bruce Springsteen's *Born to Run*. Memories of his late wife set off a fierce wave of nostalgia.

The long bar is lined with wobbly leather stools. Shoulder to shoulder with Barclay, Aidan orders a Sam Adams on tap. He probably had enough to drink at the inn but can't bring himself to order a water. Actually, he might have had too much to drink. What had gotten into him, inviting Maggie Hodges to join them tomorrow? It had seemed like a fun idea in the moment, but that's where it should have stayed: a passing moment. He was sure, in the sober light of day tomorrow, she'd feel the same. Aside from the episode at lunch, she seems pretty normal and chill. And he can relate to her frustration with her daughter. And yes, she's attractive as hell, with luminous skin and flirtatious eyes.

"To young love," Barclay says, raising his glass. Aidan is momentarily confused, as if Barclay read his mind about Maggie Hodges. Then, embarrassed, he realizes it's a nod to Scott's impending marriage.

"I'm glad we have this time together, Dad," Aidan says. It feels weird to still call him that after all these years since Nancy's been gone, but it feels weirder to revert back to calling him Barclay. Actually, he never had called him Barclay. It had gone straight from Mr. Cavanaugh to Dad.

"I am too," Barclay says. "But I gotta admit I'm a little surprised you're here."

Aidan is taken aback. "Surprised? I wouldn't miss it."

"Don't get me wrong. You're family. But even so, I'd think you had better things to do over a long weekend."

Aidan lowers his mug to the bar top. "You don't want me here?"

"Of course I do. When I say you're family, I mean it. And as family, I just want to be real with you. For your sake, and for that grandson of mine."

"Cole? He's fine. I don't know what happened between him and Scott." Aidan can only assume that's what he's talking about.

Barclay frowns. "They'll work that out. No, I'm talking

about Cole himself. I think it's been hard on him without a mother all these years. Not that you haven't done a fine job—that boy couldn't ask for a better father. But there's gotta be some reason Cole's making bad choices with women."

Aidan feels blindsided. What is Barclay talking about? He realizes now that Barclay invited him out specifically to talk about Cole. He also realizes that if there's a problem in his son's life, he himself is clueless about it.

"Barclay, I gotta admit I'm a little lost here. What 'bad choices' are you talking about?"

His father-in-law leans forward and lowers his voice. "I promised Ritchie I wouldn't get into it this weekend. So let's just leave it at this: Cole's last relationship was inappropriate. People got hurt."

Aidan feels a flash of annoyance. How does Ritchie know something about Cole that Aidan doesn't?

"I doubt Cole is confiding in Ritchie. He's a very private person."

Barclay shakes his head. "Ritchie only knows about this from Scott."

Scott? Aidan thinks of the fight between Cole and his cousin earlier. And his gut tenses.

"I'm confused. Is Cole dating one of Scott's ex-girlfriends or something?"

"No, nothing like that," Barclay says. "I don't think Scott knows the woman in question. But Ashley—Scott's fiancée—does. And from what I understand, he had some words with Cole about it a few months ago. I'm guessing there's still some hard feelings there."

Aidan starts putting some pieces together. Yes, he'd noticed Cole had become moody and distant toward the end of the summer. Then he seemed better, then regressed again.

Yesterday, during the brief drive over to the inn, Aidan casually asked how his dating life was going. Cole just shrugged, and that was the end of the conversation. Aidan didn't think much of it. Cole could be quiet sometimes.

The jukebox plays Billy Joel's "Innocent Man." Barclay finishes his beer and signals to the bartender for another round. Aidan quickly downs the rest of his before saying, "I appreciate you wanting to keep me in the loop. But Cole is a grown man, and if he's with someone Scott doesn't like, that's not something I need to know about. Not unless Cole wants to tell me himself."

"Understood. But I'm letting you know what Cole and Scott are fighting about."

The bartender sets the fresh mugs of beer in front of them. Aidan knows it's a good time to change the subject. But now he's pissed. "It's not really Scott's business. What does he care?"

Barclay raises an eyebrow. "What does he *care*? We're family."

Aidan sighs. "Are you asking me to talk to Cole? Or somehow broker the peace between him and Scott?"

"No, no, no," Barclay says, shaking his head. "Just the opposite; I know that's asking a lot, but for the sake of the boys' friendship, don't say a word. Cole got pissed at Scott for telling Ritchie. If he knows this has gone all the way up the food chain to you and me, he'll never forgive him."

Aidan feels hurt. Doesn't Cole know he can confide in him? That he can talk to him about anything? Barclay must read this on his face, because he says, "That boy thinks the world of you. He doesn't want to let you down."

That could never happen. "Everyone makes mistakes," Aidan says.

"Ritchie thought the boys had mended fences before the

weekend. But I guess he was wrong. And Aidan, I hold you partly responsible for him going down the wrong path here."

"Me?" Aidan says defensively. "What's that supposed to mean?"

"Look at the example you set. You've never brought anyone to a holiday, a dinner. Never mentioned anyone in your life. Not in fifteen years. I can't blame Cole for not knowing up from down when it comes to relationships."

Aidan can't believe it. He prides himself on having avoided the pitfall of bringing a parade of girlfriends into his son's life. Of course he'd gone out with a few people over the years. Recently, one of his vegetable purveyors, a woman named Beverly Cricket, asked him out for coffee. He gently turned her down, but maybe he should reconsider. After so many years of making Cole his priority, he'd maybe forgotten how to nurture his own life.

But Barclay, of all people, should understand all this. After all, it's the memory of his daughter that Aidan's was trying to honor. He knew she'd want him to put their son first.

"I've done the best I can, Dad."

Barclay nods. "I know you have. And I mean no disrespect. Just wanted to loop you in, as they say."

"I don't know what to do with this information," Aidan admits.

"Forget I mentioned it," Barclay says. "At least for now. It's a party weekend, right? A few drinks, good food, the great outdoors—he'll get over this bump in the road." Barclay raises his glass and Aidan mirrors him with his own.

"Okay. Well, thanks for telling me."

Really, he almost wishes he hadn't. How's he going to spend all day tomorrow with Cole and not talk about this?

Maybe having Maggie Hodges and her daughter along is a good idea after all.

PIPER LEAVES THE table to take a call from Ethan. She finds a quiet spot in the lobby, curling up on a soft armchair near the crackling fireplace.

"How's it going?" he asks as the sound of his voice warms her like a shot of whiskey. In the background, she hears cars honking and an ambulance siren, a sharp contrast to her current surroundings. For the weekend, it's a welcome change of pace. But her life with Ethan is in the city and they agree they never wanted to move, not even after they get married and have kids. (And yes, they'd discussed that far into the future—making the mystery of the vanishing ring all the more perplexing.) Even if she considered living somewhere else, the guilt over abandoning Maggie would dissuade her. She saw how upset Maggie got when Piper applied to college and suggested schools that weren't within driving distance. She had no interest in repeating that drama.

"Yeah, it's really cute here," she says.

"I saw your posts," he says. "You met some good people?"

"Yeah, everyone is so nice." She identifies everyone in her latest posts: Hannah Elise, and Lexi and Dove.

"Lexi and Dove are on their honeymoon," she says pointedly, but he clearly doesn't pick up on it.

"Piper, you know I miss you already. But I'm glad you had the chance to get away for a few days."

"Gretchen called, but I don't want to talk to her."

"I get it. And you shouldn't," he says. "You're on vacation from all that."

She appreciates the validation.

"I know. I need it. I've got to hand it to my mom: This trip was a great idea. I just wish she wasn't so sensitive. I took *one* workshop without her and I can tell she's pissed."

There's a pause, and then Ethan says, "No comment."

Piper sits up straighter in the chair. "What's that supposed to mean?"

She hears him sigh.

"Nothing."

But she can't let it go. "Clearly it's something. Why're you being negative?"

"I'm not being negative. Just . . . have fun. I'm heading into the subway, but we'll talk later."

They exchange the usual *I love you*s, but the call leaves her with a bad feeling. She puts the phone back in her handbag and stands up to go back to dinner. A few feet away, she spots Cole from the bachelor party. He sees her too and calls out, "We meet again." He's dressed in a navy blue all-weather coat and a green-and-white Philadelphia Eagles scarf.

"Don't tell me you still need to borrow my phone," she says, smiling.

He shakes his head and holds up his own cell. "Back in business."

Raucous group laughter comes from the direction of the stairs. Cole's expression shifts, his face tensing.

"Shit," he says. "This is going to sound crazy, but I'm about to pretend we're long-lost best friends, so just go with it?"

The bachelor party descends on them before she can question him.

"Where've you been hiding, bro?" one of them says.

"We were about to leave without you," says another.

"Uh, I actually just ran into an old friend of mine. This is Piper. Piper, this is my cousin Scott."

Scott has wavy brown hair cut short and fair skin with freckles. She towers over him.

"Nice to meet you," she says, feeling the eyes of the rest of the group on her.

The cousin asks how she and Cole know each other.

"The city," she says, mostly out of habit. That's usually her answer to that question.

"Philly?" one of them says.

"Yeah," Cole says quickly. "Look, you guys go on ahead. I'll catch up."

The cousin points at her. "Don't even think about tagging along. No girls allowed. It's a *bachelor* party."

"Wow. Okay. My loss." When they're out the door, she says to Cole sarcastically, "You sure you don't want to go out with them?"

Cole, checking his phone, looks up at her. "I absolutely do not."

"Well, that's not very bachelor-party-friendly of you," she says, aware she sounds flirtatious and willing herself to dial it down. She doesn't know why she's doing it. Except that she's hurt by Ethan. What was with that snide comment about Maggie just now on the phone?

"I'm really only here for my dad," Cole says. "It's important to him."

"I feel that," she says. "My mom wants a girls' weekend."

"Makes sense. Left dad at home watching football?"

"Actually, it's just me and my mom."

"Divorce?" he says.

She nods—it's easier than explaining the real story. "How about yours?"

"It's just me and my dad too. But not because of divorce. My mother died a long time ago," he says.

"Oh!" She feels stupid, though how could she have known? "I'm so sorry."

"It was a long time ago," he repeats, his tone casual. He's probably had to explain it a thousand times over the years, and she understands how that, in itself, is as much a burden as the absence. She's always hated explaining the situation with her father, although she knew the two situations weren't comparable. She'd never mourned the loss of her father. It had always just been the way it was.

It helped that Maggie was always open and honest about him, encouraging Piper to ask questions: Where did they meet? A fashion show. Were they in love? No, it was one night of passion. Did they keep in touch? No. Do you have any photos of him? No. Does he know Piper exists? Yes.

There was a brief time during middle school when she was consumed with the fantasy of tracking him down. This was when she'd gotten her first laptop, and she sat in her room at night going through his Facebook page. He was living his best single life in Iceland. And then it became normalized—her father wasn't a mythic being, but just a regular guy and probably a selfish one at that. She knew by that time that any thoughts of a reunion were one-sided. And that was enough to leave it at just that: thoughts.

Her mother had loved and cared for her enough for two parents. And she'd done it all on her own. Even Piper's grandparents hadn't been around much. They sent Piper a Hallmark card and a check every birthday until she was eighteen, and there had been times in their earlier years when they spent holidays at that big old house on the Main Line. But one day Maggie had announced that she wasn't going back—there'd been some falling-out with her mother. And then even those rare visits stopped.

Piper realizes she's been an ingrate all day long. The least she can do is put her relationship issues aside and give Maggie the mother-daughter weekend she wants. The one she deserves.

Cole's phone buzzes, triggering some furious texting. After a minute or so she wonders if he remembers she's standing there.

"Well, see you around," she says. Completely distracted, he doesn't respond.

Piper heads back to the group dinner and decides that tomorrow, she'll join her mother for whatever she suggests. It will be their day.

It's the least she can do.

Chapter Seventeen

IT'S AFTER TEN BY THE time Maggie and Piper finally slip under the covers of their respective beds. Walking up to the room from the tavern, she'd been exhausted. But the silence outside is so complete, it has the unexpected effect of making her feel highly alert. Now she thinks she might need to listen to a podcast to get to sleep.

"Are you awake?" Piper says.

"Piper, of course. We just turned out the light."

"If we were in middle school at a slumber party, this would be the time someone tells a ghost story."

"Don't remind me. I had to pick you up in the middle of the night from more than one of those things."

"No, you didn't."

"Oh yes, I did!" Maggie sits up, even more awake now. It's like the old days when they lived together. Even on school nights, sometimes they fell asleep in front of the living room television streaming *Gilmore Girls*.

She feels silly for begrudging their time apart earlier in the day. What does an hour, or a day, or even a month apart here and there matter? Those times are temporary, whereas their fundamental, blood-deep mother-daughter connection is forever.

"Okay, so no ghost stories," Piper says. "How 'bout a little harmless gossip?" She launches into what Kalli Dimitriou told her, some drama about a soon-to-be ex-husband and a former lover she can't get over. It all sounds very messy and complicated, and Maggie is thankful her own personal life is simple. Frankly, hearing Kalli's story, she can't imagine being so consumed by any man. She wonders if she's even capable of experiencing enduring romantic love. She always told herself things might have been different if she hadn't been a single mother in her twenties. But maybe she never would have met The One, regardless. Maybe for some people, that simply doesn't exist. She tells herself she's fine with that.

"I saw you talking to Belinda for a while," Piper says. "What's her deal?"

"She and Max used to live in Philadelphia," Maggie says.

"I thought they'd had this inn forever."

"No, just twenty years."

"That's what I mean."

Maggie smiles to herself. A twentysomething thinks twenty years *is* forever. But as a woman in her forties, she's already experiencing the phenomenon of life chapters. She can already identify two of her own: BP and AP—Before Piper and After Piper. She'd never really thought much beyond those two, because there's no *after* After Piper. She's always going to be a mother. Except she's starting to realize motherhood looks a little different from the other side of forty. Again, the fear creeps in, and she pushes it away.

A stripe of moonlight comes through the gap between the window curtain and the wall. Maggie gets out of bed to pull them more tightly closed. Their room overlooks the front of the inn, and she sees a few guys from the bachelor party clustered together, bundled up in jackets. She can't tell if they're coming or going, but she notes Aidan Danby isn't among them.

She still hasn't told Piper about the bet with Aidan, the little competition tomorrow, but she should. She feels her way carefully along the unfamiliar space back to her bed thinking how to explain the conversation with Aidan without it sounding ridiculous—not an easy task. But before she can bring it up, Piper says, "Mom, thanks for this weekend. I really needed something to help me clear my head."

Maggie feels a swell of happiness. "It's my pleasure. Last week was rough, but we'll tackle this temporary professional bump in the road together."

"I'm not thinking about *work*," Piper says, her tone incredulous.

Maggie is confused. "Oh. I thought when you said 'clear your head' . . . So what's bothering you?"

There's silence for what feels like a full minute, then Piper says, "I think something's going on with Ethan."

Maggie sits up. "What do you mean?"

She hears the squeak of Piper's bed as she sits up as well.

"Well, during the summer we had lots of conversations about the future—our future. But lately, we don't. So I wonder if he's changed his mind."

"About what?"

"About me. About us."

"He's hasn't," Maggie says firmly. "I'm sure of it."

But she can tell by Piper's silence that she's not convinced. Well, she's just going to have to take her word for it. She can't very well tell her that Ethan is thinking about proposing. For one thing, it would spoil the surprise. And for another: Maggie *discouraged* him.

Wait—she hadn't discouraged him from proposing. She'd *encouraged* him not to rush. To wait for a better time for Piper.

"Piper, I know he loves you," Maggie says carefully. "But maybe right now you should just enjoy what you two have together and focus on your career. That's what this stage of life is all about. When the time is right, I'm sure those conversations about the future will pick up right where they left off."

Piper lets out a sigh. Maggie's eyes have adjusted to the dark, and she can make out faintly that Piper is propped up on one elbow.

"What does that mean, when the time is right?" Piper says, her voice pinched. "Life is only going to get busier, get more complicated. People who blame timing are just making excuses. It was like, our relationship had this forward momentum, and then it stopped."

"Is it possible you're imagining that?"

"I found a ring," Piper blurts out. "A diamond ring."

Maggie's heart starts to beat faster. If she'd known this before Ethan spoke to her last week, she might have said something different. But it's too late now.

"When?" she asks, trying to sound nonchalant.

"A month ago. Thirty-two days ago, to be exact. But then when I checked before leaving last night, it was gone. And it's not like we have a trip coming up or anything where it's like oh, obviously he's waiting for that. And sure, he could have moved it somewhere else. But why would he? No, I feel there's a disconnect."

Maggie is panicked.

She and Piper do not lie to one another. They've had it pretty easy as far as mother-daughter relationships go. She'd been warned by countless articles and books about the Terrible Twos, and then it was *watch out for middle school*, and then the common knowledge that her daughter would hate her throughout high school as she established her own identity. But none of those things happened. And Maggie felt not just lucky, but a little smug. She and Piper are different.

"Piper, again, I think maybe he's waiting for the right time.

And I give him credit for that. You have other priorities right now."

Piper doesn't say anything.

Maggie, her eyes wide open, is thankful for the darkness.

There's only one way to fix this: She's going to have to tell Ethan to disregard what she said about the timing. She'll tell him she was wrong, that if he thinks this is what Piper would want, then he should act accordingly. But for now, she just wants to end the conversation.

"Piper, try to get some sleep."

"Okay. I will. Thanks for listening," Piper says. "You're the only one I can talk to about this."

Maggie swallows hard. The joy she experiences from the compliment is tempered by a fresh wave of guilt. As soon as they're back in the city, she'll talk to Ethan.

Until then, she'll make sure she and Piper have so much fun this weekend, neither one of them gives it another thought.

BELINDA HAD AN epiphany earlier that night. An unwelcome one.

It happened somewhere between the braised lamb shank and the chocolate custard with blueberry-lavender compote: She heard herself telling the story of how she and Max fell in love with this historic place—not just the inn, but also the town—and realized it was home. Until that moment, it had somehow still felt temporary, an experiment, a phase. But now that they were leaving, she realized it was the longest she'd ever lived in one place since childhood. No wonder she doesn't want to leave.

After dinner, she convinced herself the nostalgia was because of the wine. But as she settles into bed next to Max, she understands that it wasn't the wine. This was her first retreat since agreeing to explore a sale. And it's giving her second thoughts.

Their living quarters are two guest rooms combined into one suite with a full kitchen, a living area, and a bedroom. Briefly, years ago, Max had converted the living room into a second bedroom because Belinda hit perimenopause and needed the room to be so cold at night, Max couldn't sleep. Separate bedrooms seemed to be a logical solution, until Max came storming into hers one day and announced, "Do you know we spend the equivalent of twenty-five years of our lives asleep? I refuse to spend that much time apart." From that night on, they negotiated a compromised sleep climate.

Really, so much of their lives together in New Hope had been a compromise. Moving there in the first place. After spending the first decade of their marriage in center city Philadelphia, she agreed to the experiment in small-town living, certain Max would get it out of his system and they'd be back downtown in time for the next SEPTA strike.

But then he discovered the inn for sale. It wasn't something they'd planned, but it had fallen into place so easily. Like it was meant to be.

Beside her in bed, Max is reading *The Philadelphia Inquirer*. As a former reporter for the newspaper, he still insists on getting the print edition, and she also likes having physical copies around. If it wasn't for the *Inquirer*, they never would have met. Max was covering the local beat and was assigned to do a piece on South Street businesses. She'd recently opened her knitting shop, South Street Knits, and he interviewed her. When the piece published, Max hand-delivered a few copies to the shop and asked her out to dinner. The rest, as they say, is history.

"How's everyone getting along down there?" he says, turning the page absently.

"You mean my knitters and your bachelors?" she says, reaching down to the canvas bag on the floor next to the bed. She pulls out the scarf she started last night. At the end of each day, she relaxes by knitting something mindless, a habit that's resulted in endless hats, scarves and socks that she donates to Goodwill. "I have a feeling this might be an accidental stroke of scheduling genius."

She watches his mouth curve into a slow smile, one that still surprises her with its charm. But it's his eyes—those dark, steady eyes—that truly captivate her. They still catch her off guard with their intensity, like they did the first day he walked into her knitting shop.

Max reaches out and touches her, and they kiss. For now, the issue of the inn is forgotten. Her entire body stirs with desire for him, and she drops her knitting to the floor. Max unties the sash of her robe. Being with him now, physically, is about more than just passion—though the passion is still there. It's also about memory, weighted with what they've built and endured together.

Afterward, she lies in the crook of his arm, the covers pulled high to her shoulders. She feels a chill and moves closer to his body.

"Max, I'm having second thoughts."

"About what?"

"About selling."

He sighs. "Bee, we've discussed this. If we're going to have another chapter, another adventure, the time is now."

Max has always been a searcher. A dreamer. It's part of why she's his perfect counterbalance: She's practical. Methodical. Rooted. It's what gives her the patience to knit. Stitch by stitch, she creates beautiful things. Some projects take months of devotion. Errors are made, rows ripped out, progress. Max would never be capable of knitting.

But Belinda is not afraid of mistakes. There'd been a time when Max made a huge one. And they almost separated over it. Instead, they moved to New Hope.

Buying the inn had given them a good excuse to uproot themselves from the city. The inn was something they could tell their friends in art and journalism. Falling in love with a charming, small-town inn for sale was a good narrative. It was unassailable—admirable, even.

Up until the moment they signed the paperwork, she'd never fully believed Max was serious about it. She felt the bid was an exercise to show how far he'd go to save their marriage. But then to both of their surprise, they got it. From that point on, she viewed their worst relationship crisis as a happy accident that served to bring them to the place where they belonged.

"I know we discussed the offer on the inn. And I know you're already making plans. But I think it's a mistake."

"You're just getting cold feet," he says. "That's normal."

"Max," she says carefully. "We've built a life here."

He takes her hand. "Life should be fluid. It's not a stake you drive into the ground and then say, 'I'm done.' I'm *not* done."

Belinda looks around for her robe and pulls it on. "This isn't just about you. And nice to know you feel like living here with me is like a stake driven into the ground."

She leaves the room.

MAGGIE CAN'T SLEEP. Long after Piper is softly snoring, she's thinking about the conversation with Ethan. She replays it in her mind on an endless, tortuous loop. The more she thinks about it, the worse it gets, until there's a version in her mind in which she's not only telling him to wait for a more practical time to get engaged—she's telling Ethan to actually *break up* with Piper. It's like a waking nightmare.

Unable to take it anymore, she slips out of bed and dresses in sweatpants, the nearest sweater she can find in the dark and her boots. She tiptoes out into the hall, closing the door slowly behind her so it doesn't make more than a small click. Then she pads down the hall to the stairs.

The inn is quiet. At this hour, with the shadows of night and the creaking of the old bones of the building, she feels its history. She wonders how many people have roamed those halls, sleepless with their own secrets and problems and mistakes.

And then she nearly collides with someone.

"Oh!" she yelps.

It's Kalli Dimitriou, and she looks every bit as startled as Maggie feels.

"Sorry," Kalli says. "I was just heading out."

"Out?" Maggie says, even though it's not that late. Certainly not as late as it feels. "Sorry. I don't know why I said it like that. Well, have fun. Good night!"

"Good night," Kalli says, and hurries down the stairs.

The central staircase is lit by brass wall sconces. The hallway smells of spices and cinnamon, as if someone spilled a potent herbal tea on the burgundy-colored runner. When she reaches the lobby she hears loud, drunken male voices, and turns in the opposite direction toward the Purl.

The room is dark, but the crescent moon shines in through the big windows. Movement out on the deck catches her eye, and she's surprised to see Belinda, her long white hair blowing in the wind, standing at the balustrade facing the river.

Maggie opens the French doors and steps outside into a chill that cuts right through her sweater. Belinda must be freezing wearing only a flimsy robe, her bare legs peeking out from the mid-calf down.

"Belinda?" Maggie inches closer so she doesn't startle her. Belinda turns and it takes a few beats for recognition to set in.

"Maggie. Can I help you with something?"

"Oh, no, I'm sorry to intrude. I just can't sleep."

A cluster of lights glow faintly from distant riverbank cottages, twinkling like fireflies along the far shore. The moon casts a silvery-blue sheen across the river's surface, and it looks almost like an undulating path of light, stretching and bending with the gentle current. Leaves drift lazily across the surface, carried downstream in slow, languid swirls, their ochre and crimson shapes faintly visible under the glowing surface.

"Well, typically I'd say fresh air is a good cure for that. But it's gotten chilly. So shall we have tea?" Belinda says, not waiting for a response and walking back inside. With one last glance at the shimmering water, Maggie follows her.

Belinda leads her down the hall to a galley kitchen. It has wood-plank floors that are uneven and creek as they make their way to a small table in the corner. The kitchen has soapstone countertops, a ceiling rack of hanging pots and a farmhouse sink.

"You can *feel* the history of this place," Maggie says. "How old is the original building?"

"The original footprint dates back to 1871—the place began operating as a hotel in 1906. Then during Prohibition it was a speakeasy. The previous owners preserved the side door with the peephole, and we still have it here on the property."

This is news to Maggie.

"This is one part of the inn we didn't spend much time renovating," Belinda says, filling a copper kettle with water and setting it on the stove. "I'm not much of a cook, and we really only need it for breakfast."

"It's adorable. Really lovely."

Belinda motions toward a dozen Harney & Sons tea tins lined up on the counter. "Take your pick," she says, and Maggie selects Hot Cinnamon Sunset. Belinda passes her a heavy handcrafted mug to steep it in.

They sit at the table waiting for the water to boil, making small talk until the kettle lets out a shrill whistle. Belinda jumps up to tend to it and then brings the kettle over to fill both of their mugs. The scent of cinnamon fills the air.

"Is this your favorite time of night—when the guests are in their rooms and you have the place to yourself?" Maggie asks, wrapping her hands around the hot mug.

"No, not at all. I love having people around. But tonight, I can't seem to quiet my mind, either."

"Well, I don't mean to be presumptuous, but I'm happy to listen."

Belinda shakes her head. "I've talked enough tonight," she says. "I want to hear more about *you*. What do you do in the city?"

Maggie tells her about Denim, and Elaine Berger—that Elaine is from the area and is the one who told her about the retreat. They talk about retail, and a little more about Belinda's experience owning a knit shop.

"Where do you buy your yarn in the city?" Belinda asks.

"I mostly order it online. My neighborhood knitting shop closed a few years ago."

"Oh, that's a shame. So much is lost when you can't buy in person."

"I know. I really miss it. Sometimes I go to one in SoHo, a place on Mercer Street. But it's expensive." And more, it fell short of the things she loved most about her old knit shop. There'd been a community at Hattie's Knits. Hattie herself offered Maggie a job once. It had been tempting, but she could never leave Elaine. When she declined the knit shop offer, she accepted the probability that she'd be working at Denim until the day Elaine closed it down. A day she hopes never comes.

"I haven't seen a yarn store in town," Maggie says. "Do you have one?"

Belinda shakes her head. "We used to. Closed a few years ago. I miss it. During retreats, I used to take everyone there for a little field trip." She shrugs. "Things change. We adapt. That's why I started hosting my own yarn pop-up."

Things change. We adapt.

Maggie isn't ready for things to change. She doesn't want to adapt. But she has to face the fact that her twenty-three-year-old daughter is going to get married. And nothing will ever be the same.

This knitting retreat weekend is their last hurrah. What was she thinking making plans with that guy Aidan? Time is precious. She's not going to waste a minute of it. Hopefully, by morning, he'll change his mind or forget about it.

She certainly plans to.

Saturday

New Hope Knitting Retreat: Day 2

Breakfast: 8 a.m.–9:30 p.m. at Bucks Tavern

Course Offerings: Intro to Crochet; Intro to Knitting; Tunisian crochet; Estonian Lace; Beginner's Brioche; Repairing Holes in Your Knitwear; Crochet: Cables & Post Stitches

Evening Activity: 5 p.m. Sip & Stitch in The Purl

Chapter Eighteen

BREAKFAST AT THE TAVERN IS served buffet style, on long wooden tables decorated with pumpkins and gourds and set with carafes of steaming coffee. Piper's first decision of the day is choosing between farm-fresh scrambled eggs or steel-cut oats topped with dried cranberries and brown sugar.

Beside her, Maggie pours maple syrup over pumpkin bread French toast and fills two mugs with coffee. Together, they find a table near the windows. The only other knitters in the room are Kalli and Laurel, who briefly look up from their conversation to give them a wave. The rest of the restaurant seem to be a mix of tourists and locals. Two guys from the bachelor party walk in, one she recognizes as Cole's cousin. She thinks about her conversation with Cole in the lobby, and she's still resolved to be more appreciate of her mother today.

She finds the workshop schedule on her phone and turns her screen to Maggie. "So . . . which of these are we registered for?" Maggie had told her the Saturday agenda yesterday when she wasn't paying attention.

"Piper, I just have one last thing to say on the topic of Ethan. Try not to overthink things. I'm certain you don't have anything to worry about."

"Mom," Piper says, reaching across the table and touching

the back of her hand. "I'm not going to let this ruin our weekend." She turns to the course listing on her phone and says, "I think I want to do the Shetland Hap workshop."

She looks up and finds a man approaching the table. She doesn't recognize him, but he's looking at Maggie as if he knows her. He's tall with auburn hair and broad shoulders and thick brows. He's handsome.

"Good morning, Maggie," he says, his deep voice accented in a local Pennsylvania dialect she's starting to recognize. Cole speaks the same way. "I hope you're still up for the challenge."

Her mother smiles tensely. Piper is confused. When it becomes clear Maggie's not going to introduce her, she stands up and offers her hand.

"Hi—I'm Piper. Maggie's daughter," she says. Before he can reply, her mother jumps up too.

"Actually . . . Piper and I have a full day of workshops," Maggie says. "Sorry about that. I really thought we were just making conversation." She gives a forced laugh.

"So you're welching on the bet?" the man says.

She looks at her mother, who's now red in the face. Piper is so confused.

"How do you two know each other?"

"We met last night before dinner," Maggie says quickly.

"Your mom seems to think knitting is more challenging than outdoor survival skills," Aidan says. "And we bet on it."

"I see," Piper says. And she does: Her mother has a little flirtation going on. Good for her!

It's only recently, in the past few years, that Piper has given some thought to Maggie's love life—or lack thereof. Growing up, it seemed normal. Preferable. It was the two of them against the world. But now that she herself is older than Maggie was when she became a mother, things are beginning to look different. Sometimes, she feels responsible for her mother's happiness. In a way, she has always felt that way. Maggie, to her credit, never acted like a martyr. Still, Piper's always been aware of Maggie's selflessness. Even now, first thing this morning, Maggie is worried about Piper's relationship. She wants to talk about Ethan, to fix it for her. But it's not her problem to fix. She needs to start thinking about herself. And this attractive man is a good place to start.

"So what's the bet?" Piper repeats. When Maggie stays silent, Aidan fills her in on their conversation from last night. "So we join you on one of your bushcraft outings, then you take a knitting class?"

"That's right," he says. "I'm Aidan, by the way."

His handshake is strong.

"It was just talk—"

"Mom, a bet's a bet," Piper says, sharing a conspiratorial glance with Aidan.

"I'm not missing the lace class starting in a half hour," Maggie says. Then, to Aidan, "When's this thing happening?"

"Not until the afternoon. Unless you want to head out with us right now for compass training. I wouldn't want to be accused of having an unfair advantage after you two lose."

"Unfair advantage? I learned how to use a compass in fourth grade," Maggie says.

"The afternoon it is, then," says Aidan.

When he's gone, Piper asks, "Did you really learn to use a compass in fourth grade?"

"It was the eighties. I don't remember a thing, but I think there's an app for that now anyway."

Piper smiles. That's the spirit. Now the weekend is starting to feel like an adventure. Like the two of them against the world.

Like it's always been.

ESTONIAN LACE IS a high-level craft. Maggie once read that an Estonian lace shawl is so delicate, even a large one can fit through the circumference of a wedding ring.

But instead of focusing on the workshop, she's still buzzing from the unexpected breakfast encounter with Aidan Danby. Waking up that morning, she doubted he even remembered the conversation, or gave it a second thought. She was fully prepared, if she happened to run into him in the lobby, to simply give a friendly hello and leave it at that.

"Welcome, brave few who dare to tackle this centuries-old knitting tradition," Belinda says. They're only a group of six, including Kalli, Laurel, and Sheila. Each place at the table is set with a skein of delicate white fingering-weight yarn, a pair of thin bamboo knitting needles in size seven, stitch markers, tapestry needles, a notepad, and a printout of patterns. A finished lace shawl is displayed in the center of the table.

Today Belinda's wearing a turtleneck with intricate colorwork and blue jeans decorated with hand-embroidered hems. "Estonian lace is part of a historical craft tradition, with symbolic meaning often tied to the patterns."

Maggie loves that idea. Beside her, Piper is already taking notes. Maggie watches her scratch away at the notepad, her hair falling forward and obscuring her face. She knows her so well, but her daughter can still surprise her. What on earth made her so enthusiastic about the bushcraft challenge?

Belinda talks about the qualities of fingering-weight yarn and why it's the right choice for this particular knitting style. Maggie uses one of the notepads to write that down, trying to keep herself in the moment.

"First we're going to go over some key techniques," Belinda says, holding up a shawl. "Most of what you're looking at here can be accomplished with yarnovers and basic decreases."

Belinda uses a swatch to demonstrate stitches. Maggie leans over and whispers to Piper, "You surprised me at breakfast."

"How so?"

"Your enthusiasm for the bushcraft bet," she says.

Piper, her eyes on Belinda's demonstration, says quietly, "Mom, that guy clearly likes you."

Maggie shakes her head. No way. She didn't get the sense that Aidan was hitting on her. Maybe he's bored with the family weekend, or he wants to mix things up for his son so he stays more involved. He'd practically said so, right?

"You've got the wrong idea," Maggie says.

"I don't think I do. And, for the record, good for you."

Maggie frowns. "I'm not here to hook up with some guy. This is *our* weekend."

Piper works her needles confidently, barely looking over. "Mom, stop putting so much pressure on that, okay? We're here together. It's our weekend, sure. But that doesn't mean you can't meet someone."

Maggie doesn't know where this attitude is coming from. She decides that the only explanation is Piper would rather play matchmaker for her than deal with her own relationship uncertainty. Maggie would never say this to her, of course. If Piper doesn't want to talk about Ethan any more this weekend, that's just fine with her.

Maybe the bushcraft bet is the distraction they both need.

Chapter Nineteen

WHEN BELINDA TEACHES A KNITTING class, the rest of the world recedes. She falls into a state of flow that's like the meditative act of knitting itself. She needs that flow this morning, but halfway through Estonian Lace, she's still waiting for it. The conversation with Max last night was troubling. Sure, they'd discussed accepting the offer on the inn. It was certainly worth *considering*. But she never viewed it as a foregone conclusion. Now Max is acting like there's nothing left to talk about. She never should have entertained the idea for even a second. But how could she have known Max would dig in like this?

"Knit into the same stitch five times, leaving loops on the needle, and purl them together on the next row. This creates a 'nupp,' a key Estonian feature that adds texture."

Of course, the financial aspect is seductive. But she knows that she'd regret it the second she let the inn go. Max would too. She truly believes that.

"Remember to relax the tension in your yarn."

Maggie Hodges, sitting next to her daughter at the table, is busy working her needles, her brow furrowed in concentration. Last night, upset about selling the inn, Belinda experienced an unexpected urge to confide in her guest. She's glad she resisted; knitters are there to relax, not give her emotional support. No, that should be her husband's job. But sometimes that's just not possible. So Belinda keeps a lot of emotions to herself. There's even a part of her history with Max that she'd never told anyone about, not even her closest friends.

Belinda and Max had been married eight years when he had an affair with a copy editor at the newspaper. And when Belinda found out, she did what a lot of women do: she blamed herself. Running the knit shop required long hours. Sometimes, she felt like she spent more time at the store than in her own apartment. Meanwhile, Max was constantly on the move, running on adrenaline chasing the next big story that would break out his career. It was just enough of a chasm for someone else to step into.

When Belinda confronted him, he didn't deny it. In fact, he admitted having feelings for the woman.

"Are you in love with her?" It was the most painful question she'd ever asked.

"No," he said. "I'm not. But I'm in love with how much she cares about the things I care about." Belinda understood what he meant—sort of. And she'd heard once that infidelity has less to do with sex and more with other needs not being met. So she tried to think of something they could undertake together, something to bring them closer and keep them that way.

They talked and talked but as long he worked at the same place as the woman he'd cheated with, they couldn't move past it. His only other job offer came from a small paper an hour north in rural Bucks County. They drove out for a visit, took a detour to New Hope, and the rest, as they say, is history.

She checks her phone, mindful of the time. This particular workshop tends to go over, but she wants to keep things on track so everyone has some free time to explore the town in the afternoon.

"Great job, everyone. As you continue to practice, don't be intimidated by mistakes. There's a reason stitches can be unraveled! As you continue practicing your technique, embrace the imperfections. Lace is as much about the process as the result."

The door opens, and Max walks in and with him, the delicious aroma of chocolate. It's the first she's seen of him today; Still a bit stung from the conversation last night, she left their bedroom before he was awake this morning.

"Sorry to interrupt," he says. "Genevieve's Hot Chocolate Cart is in the lobby." That's when Belinda hears the distinctive tinny bell of the infamous traveling treat-mobile. Genevieve, wife of the local candymaker, has a roving hot chocolate van where locals line up, food-truck style, on the street or she brings a rolling cart by appointment. If Genevieve is in the lobby, it's not a coincidence; it's Max's way of apologizing for last night ending in tension. Or maybe it's to acknowledge her sadness over selling the inn, to show that he cares.

Max is great with grand gestures. It's the subtler, everyday relationship upkeep that gets tricky for him.

Once the room empties out, she turns to him and says, "You shouldn't interrupt a workshop."

"Then you shouldn't have left without saying a word this morning."

He's right. That wasn't a relationship-positive thing to do. But she'd felt hurt.

"I think this decision should be more of a conversation," she says.

He holds up his phone, showing her an email, an update to the offer on the inn. It's *more* money. It's a debate-ender. So she says nothing.

"This is our retirement, Belinda. I'm sorry, but I can't imagine a more important priority."

Maybe he's right again. Maybe sentimentality is getting the best of her. She's gotten set in her ways.

Still, when he leans forward to kiss her on the cheek, she feels her body stiffen.

Really, she can't blame herself for not giving more pushback to the idea of selling when he first brought it up a few months ago. They'd been having such a carefree summer. After years of ups and downs, they'd finally settled into a relationship that was the perfect balance of comfort and a lingering spark of passion. Each year that passed gave them more history, more shared memories. So of course, when he brought up the sale and the move, her first impulse was to say yes. To be agreeable.

Agreeability has always been her impulse. And now she's wondering if it's time to change.

AIDAN AND COLE stand on the riverbank, the morning sun casting a golden glow through the canopy of vibrant foliage. Crimson, amber, and fiery orange leaves reflect off the water's surface, creating a patchwork of color. The air is cool, with a mist wrapping the landscape in an ethereal haze. Aidan can barely see the rest of the guys searching for their own fishing spots nearby.

He's thankful for a quiet few moments with Cole. Last night, he heard from Ritchie that Cole never joined up with the other guys, so he stopped by Cole's room to say good-night but he didn't answer the knock. It seemed early for Cole to be going to sleep, but since he'd been on edge all day, maybe that was exactly what he'd needed.

When Aidan woke up that morning, his first thoughts were about the conversation with Barclay at the bar. He's now concluded that there isn't anything strange about Cole not confiding in him; he's a private person. Aidan understands, because he's the same way. That's why it's been so challenging for him to get serious with any woman. By definition, it would involve going public with his son and the Cavanaughs. And he couldn't do it. Now Barclay's telling him that somehow contributed to Cole's bad relationship judgment? He's not sure he buys it. And so, although he promised Barclay he wouldn't betray their conversation, he feels compelled to say *something*.

Cole's first cast sends the line arcing gracefully over the water, landing softly in a pool where the current slows. Aidan follows with his own line, and they wait for any sign of movement. The river's stillness is interrupted only by the distant call of a heron and the rustle of a squirrel foraging in the underbrush.

"So, are you gonna tell me what's going on between you and your cousin?" he says.

"There's nothing to tell," Cole says.

"That's not how it seemed yesterday. Why didn't you say something about having a beef with him heading into this weekend?"

"Because it's not 'beef.' He's just pissing me off. I showed up this weekend for you. And Grandpa. But no, I don't want to team up with him for these activities."

He wants to be supportive of Cole. If he can't talk to him about the problem, he can at least do something about it.

"Well, here's the good news: We won't be partnering with Ritchie and Scott today."

"Thank you."

"Instead, I lined up some new partners for the afternoon. To mix things up a little."

Cole looks skeptical. "You did? Who?"

"Remember the woman who was upset with our table at lunch yesterday?"

"You mean, the one who freaked out for absolutely no reason?"

"Yeah. That one. Anyway, I ended up talking to her at the bar last night. She actually believes that knitting is harder than outdoor survival skills. So I challenged her to build the fort with us."

"You've got to be kidding me," Cole says.

"Nope. Not kidding. Totally serious. We have a bet. Fifty bucks."

Cole shakes his head. "You can't just invite a random person along."

"They're not random. They're staying at the inn."

"Who's *they*?"

"She's here with her daughter."

Somewhere in the distance, Barclay and Ritchie hoot and holler over a catch.

"Does Grandpa know about this?"

"Not yet. But you know your grandfather; he loves to mix things up."

Cole narrows his eyes. "Dad. You better not be trying to set me up with someone. Because I will save you a lot of trouble and tell you that is not happening." Then, something seems to dawn on him. He looks at him closely. "Unless . . . you're setting *yourself* up. And you need me as your wingman. In which case—no problem."

"Absolutely not," Aidan says, starting to get annoyed. He knows Cole is probably just teasing him, but it makes him uncomfortable. Even if he did find Maggie Hodges attractive—which, objectively she is—he wouldn't be so tasteless as to pick up a woman at his nephew's bachelor party. He has discipline when it comes to his personal life. Unlike his son, apparently.

He feels a tug on his line and gives a subtle pull to set the hook. Once he reels the fish from the water, he sees it's a brown trout, its shimmering body a blur of golden-hued spots and stripes. Aidan admires it for half a minute before gently releasing it back into the river.

"No one's setting anyone up," he says. "I just thought a friendly competition would lighten the mood."

Cole raises an eyebrow. "Sure, Dad. Let me know if Grandpa buys that."

Chapter Twenty

AFTER LUNCH, MAGGIE DRIVES PIPER to the wilderness clearing where Aidan told them to meet. The ground is covered with a mix of rust- and gold-colored leaves freshly fallen from the towering hardwoods surrounding the clearing. Oaks, maples and birches line the edges, their branches half bare.

"It's so beautiful here," Piper said. "It makes me realize we don't fully experience autumn in the city. At least, not like this."

Maggie feels the warmth of contentment rush through her.

The air is crisp and carries the earthy aroma of damp leaves mixed with the faint sweetness of ripe wild berries that dot the undergrowth. In the center of the clearing, wild grasses and late-season wildflowers like goldenrod and asters sway gently. A white-tailed deer stands nearby, cautiously observing.

"So how do we find him?" Piper says, hands on her hips as she surveys the area.

"He dropped a pin," Maggie says, squinting at her phone screen in the bright sun. "But now I think we're walking in the wrong direction."

Piper reaches for Maggie's phone.

"Let me help. Why didn't we plan to meet him outside the inn and follow in our own car?"

"Because they had to meet up with the others first," Maggie says.

"Who's *they*?"

"Aidan and his son."

Piper puts the phone down to her side and looks at her. "What son? You didn't say anything about a son."

"Say anything? You agreed to this so fast this morning I couldn't get a word in if I'd tried."

It was true. And by the time they were immersed in their first knitting workshop, it slipped her mind. Before she can explain this, she spots Aidan. He's with a tall, good-looking young man with sandy-brown hair. His son? The young guy smiles at Piper as if he knows her. When they get closer, Piper says, "What are *you* doing here?" She's unmistakably pleased.

"You two know each other?" Maggie glances at Aidan. Is Aidan in on this? Is it some sort of setup after all? But no, he seems surprised too.

"We met yesterday," Cole says.

"Twice," says Piper, and they recount a story of Cole borrowing her phone. "Your cheek looks better, by the way," Piper says.

He replies with some sort of inside joke, and Piper laughs. How can they have an inside joke already? Somehow, Piper had a whole new friend she knew nothing about. A handsome young man. Ethan wouldn't be happy. Although she has no doubt Piper's interest in this young man, however attractive, is strictly platonic.

"So what's the plan here?" Maggie says.

"The plan is, we have two hours to see how far we can get building a shelter. It's a competition—the rest of our group is paired up. The team who gets the most done during the allotted time wins."

"So . . . the rest of the bachelor party is teamed up and you two have . . . us?" Piper says. "I hate to break it to you, but you're gonna lose."

"Piper! What kind of attitude is that?" Maggie says. "We've got this."

Aidan meets her eyes and it gives her a little jolt. "You think so?"

"Yes," she says, sounding more certain than she feels. She's never built anything in her life, unless you count the Lego sets when Piper was little.

"We already started gathering material. When we're done, we need to get these larger branches propped up for an A-frame, then start weaving in the smaller branches and vines," Aidan says.

"We're gathering materials, not building the actual fort," Cole says to him.

"I know. But if we construct a sample of how the elements we collected work, it shows we know what we're doing."

Cole nods, and Maggie wonders how seriously they're taking their own intra-team competition. She suspects they're not at all concerned about the one among the four of them. They think they've already won.

"I'm ready. Let's go!" Maggie says. Piper shoots her a look like, *Calm down.*

"Cole, you grab the other end of this log for me. Maggie, you and Piper can start stringing together those vines so that when the frame goes up, we can fill in the openings quickly."

Does he presume she and Piper aren't capable of doing heavy lifting?

"Hold up—here comes Grandpa," Cole says.

Maggie recognizes the man heading over. She saw him at the lunch table yesterday. He looks like he's in his late seventies, trim with a nearly full head of gray hair. He's wearing black sunglasses and an olive-green all-weather jacket zipped up, camouflage cargo pants, hiking boots, a tactical belt, and a wide-brimmed hat.

"Hello, boys. Just wanted to meet the guests you told me about, Aidan. Howdy, ladies."

"Barclay, these are our friends Maggie and Piper," Aidan says.

The man lowers his sunglasses and looks at her.

"Aren't you the gal who scolded us yesterday at lunch for being too loud?" he says.

Maggie feels her face flush. Piper turns to her and says, "Wait—what did you do?"

"Nothing," Maggie says. Then, to Barclay, "Yes, that was me. Sorry about that."

"Bygones," he says. "I'm just glad to see you've found a more productive outlet for your aggression."

Aidan takes a step forward.

"Dad, we're all good over here. Everything's under control," he says.

"Not so fast: Since you're now a foursome, you're a new team. Gonna call you Team Boyce, after the great outdoorsman William Dickson Boyce."

"Fantastic. In it to win it, Grandpa," Cole says.

"Wait—what are the other teams?" Maggie says.

"Glad you asked, little lady," says Barclay. "We have team Daniel Boone, and team Davy Crockett—the team the Barclay boys seceded from."

"Seceded might be an overstatement," says Aidan.

"Yeah, Grandpa. We can probably do without the Civil War references."

Maggie is still recovering from "Little lady." She can't believe people still talk like that.

"Well," she says, "since our team is half female, we should be named after a woman."

She feels Aidan looking at her, and Barclay clearly doesn't know whether she's serious or busting his chops. Either way, he's smiling.

"Like who?" he says.

Maggie actually has no idea. She tries to think of outdoorsy women. Jane Goodall? She's a conservationist. Does that count? Bindi Irwin? She's more of a zoologist. An image comes to mind of knee-high Wellies and a pack of corgis. A hike in the Scottish highlands . . .

"We're Team Queen Elizabeth," she announces.

Barclay shakes his head no. "That's missing the point, sweetheart. The theme is outdoors. Wilderness."

"I know. Queen Elizabeth was a huge outdoor person—hunting, fishing, you name it. I bet she could have out-bushcrafted every one of us here. Including you, Barclay."

He seems about to say something, then reconsiders. "Not so sure about your logic, but as an admitted Anglophile, I'm willing to go with it. So, Team Queen Elizabeth, you have an hour and a half left." He pulls something from his bag, something copper and small, and hands it to Cole. It's an old-fashioned compass.

"What did I tell you earlier?" Barclay asks him.

"Never walk into the woods without a tool for getting out."

"Exactly! Ladies, I don't want you picking up any bad habits from these two. You cannot—and it's impossible to stress this enough—you cannot rely on your phone in an emergency scenario." He looks at Maggie and she nods as if she knows exactly what he's talking about.

She looks at Aidan and he mouths "Sorry." She smiles. Barclay makes his way over to a pile of branches, hands on his hips.

"This is your insulation material?"

"That's it," Cole says.

"Not enough." Barclay shakes his head. "Cole, you and your friend there—go gather more vines. These brittle little twigs won't do squat."

Piper looks at her, shrugs, then walks off alongside Cole without another glance in her direction.

Okay then.

Aidan smiles at her and says, "So. I guess it's just the two of us."

It's merely a statement of the obvious, but it gives her a shiver of excitement.

"I'm sure they'll be back soon," she says, though she's sure of no such thing.

Adian, dressed in a weathered flannel shirt and sturdy cargo pants, exudes a sort of charisma that makes it clear he's perfectly at ease in the wilderness. He picks up thick branches and heavy rocks like they're nearly weightless. He seems like someone who is used to manual labor, to getting his hands dirty. She can't help but imagine what he'd be like in bed.

Stop it.

"So, what do you do when you're not hunting and gathering?" she says. She's starting to feel overheated. She's wearing a wool turtleneck sweater under her bomber jacket. Lifting and balancing branches like some giant Jenga game was the most rigorous workout she's had in a long time. Sweating and breathing heavily, she takes a time-out to shed her jacket. She folds it and leaves it on the ground, feeling self-conscious that Aidan is watching her.

"Are you asking me what I do for a living?" he says.

The way he asks shames her a little, but why should she feel embarrassed? It's a perfectly normal question in her day-to-day life. Maybe in that moment, in that setting, it was too personal. Or like she's looking for criteria by which to evaluate him.

"I own a chain of food markets here in Bucks County. Expanding soon to other areas. Cole's in charge of the expansion."

"Oh, that's so nice that you work together." God, she'd love working with Piper. It would be so much fun.

"How 'bout you?" he asks.

She tells him about the clothing store. "I started there when Piper was a baby. I never intended it to be my career. It just turned out that way."

"I can relate. When I started working at the local supermarket stocking shelves I was maybe twelve years old. Did it for pocket money. Never imagined I'd go into the business for real one day. Life, right?" After a minute, he adds, "Taking off for this long weekend was a bigger deal than it should have been. I probably need to manage my time better."

"You don't get out much?" she says.

"I get out about as much as I want. But according to my friends, that's not enough."

She nods. "I hear you on that. I hate to give in to the knitters stereotype, but I'm perfectly happy to be curled up with a ball of yarn or a good book any night of the week. Although, my boss set me up on a blind date two nights ago. I think she was trying to show me what I'm missing, but it had the opposite effect."

He shakes his head. "Blind date? Ever hear the phrase 'just say no'?"

She gives a little laugh. "I should have. Believe me. I left before we ordered and ended up eating dinner with Piper."

Now he's the one to laugh.

They continue pushing log-like tree branches into place. Maggie is tired, but doesn't want to give Aidan the satisfaction of admitting that. She takes on the job of dragging branches from the pile over to Aidan so he can lift them and prop them up. She's not sure she's helping so much as adding an unnecessary step.

"Well, it looks like our kids hit it off. Not only that, seems we're late to the party," he says.

"I know." She wonders why Piper didn't mention that she met someone from the bachelor party.

"You sure she's got a boyfriend?" he says.

"Yes. A serious one, unfortunately."

He looks at her sharply. "You don't like the guy?"

Maggie really just wants one sliver of the weekend where she doesn't have to think about this. But she's the one who brought it up. "I do. But I also think she's too young to settle down."

"You couldn't have been much older when you settled down."

"There was nothing 'settled' about my life at that age. I was alone with a toddler and terrified. I want more for Piper. I want her to have all the freedom and opportunity I missed out on."

"Understandable," he says. "That's probably a universal parenting feeling. We all want better for our kids. Or at least for them to be as happy as possible."

She nods. It feels good to have her feelings validated.

Sometimes, Maggie misses having a co-parent—not just as a father figure for Piper, someone not only for Piper's sake, but for her own. Someone who understands the roller coaster of parenthood—someone to share the good times and the bad. Sure, she can talk to her friends and to Elaine. But that's far from *sharing* the experience with someone.

"Yes, we do," she says.

"So, I have to admit I wish Piper wasn't taken."

"That's sweet, but she is," Maggie says. "In fact, right before the weekend, he told me he wants to propose to her."

"Maggie, that's a big deal. Congratulations. To you and to her."

She wishes she could accept the congratulations and move on, but now she's stricken with guilt. She couldn't talk to Piper about this last night, but now's a chance to confess to someone impartial. After all, she'll never see him again after the weekend. She has nothing to lose.

"Well, I might have accidentally screwed it up."

Aidan stops stacking branches and turns to her. "I find that hard to believe."

Here it goes. "Well, he came to me in a sort of 'can I have your blessing?' way. And I discouraged him. Well, I should say I *encouraged* him to wait."

"Oh. Can I ask . . . why?"

"What I was saying before—about her being so young. I just think she needs to be focused on work right now. I know it sounds bad. Admittedly, it was the wrong thing to do. But honestly, my intentions were good."

Aidan nods and continues with the branches. "I know I joked—well, half joked—about fixing Cole up. But the truth is, I stay out of that part of his life. He's private, I'm private—it's for the best. I don't mean to overstep here, but maybe you need to distance yourself a little. Know what I mean?"

No, she doesn't. Distance herself? From Piper? Never. It feels like she and Cole have been gone a while. She texts Piper:

You doing okay? Coming back soon?

But the text doesn't go through. Her battery probably died.
"Can you text Cole? I can't reach Piper," she says.
"Are you worried? She's with Cole, she's fine," he says.

"I'm not *worried* about her," she says. "I just planned to be spending the weekend *with* her. It's kinda the whole point of being here."

"I get it. I felt the same way about Cole. He works in the business with me, but we don't see each other every day, and even when we do, it's mostly work talk. So I thought this would be great bonding time."

"Great. So text him."

"Relax, Mama Bear: I can't," he says. "Barclay confiscated his phone—all the younger guys' phones—before we headed out. Otherwise, they won't learn anything."

The idea that she can't reach Piper makes her anxious, and it must show on her face. Aidan stops walking and puts a hand on her shoulder. "Please don't worry about Piper. I'm just teasing you about the Mama Bear thing. I wish Cole had a little more of that protective maternal energy around growing up."

Maggie smiles. "Thanks. And for what it's worth, you seem to have done a fine job all by yourself. Though I know, from my own experience, the one thing we can't be is two people."

Aidan looks at her. "Exactly. That's exactly it."

They share a look, and she feels a surprising sense of connection to him. Twenty-four hours ago, she didn't know he existed. The feeling isn't unpleasant, but it makes her uncomfortable.

"Do you think Cole and Piper are talking about us the way we're discussing them?" she says.

He smiles. "No doubt. Who do you think is getting it worse—you or me?"

"Definitely you." She grins, and feels a lightness she hasn't experienced in a long time.

She drags an oversized branch toward Aidan, and realizes that she's no longer in such a rush for Piper to return.

Chapter Twenty-One

*C*OLE DANBY SEEMS UTTERLY AT home in the woods. He stacks branches and gathers smaller vines with fluid, assured movements that make Piper feel clumsy. She stumbles around the uneven, leaf-covered ground beside him, trying to distinguish what makes one stick or branch usable and another not. And all the while, she feels guilty for running around with this strange guy, even though it's completely innocent. She wonders if the unsettled feeling is more about her relationship with Ethan than any attraction to Cole Danby.

She checks her phone for messages and finds she had no reception. It's hard to believe she kissed Ethan goodbye only yesterday. Everything that happened before the weekend feels long ago, as if time itself had stretched and bent. Could anxiety have that effect on her?

An occasional gust of wind sends the leaves fluttering all around them. If she were with Ethan, it would feel terribly romantic. Her mind drifts into a brief fantasy of the two of them in those very woods, and he tells her to look under a tree branch and there's the ring box. He gets down on one knee and asks her to marry him. Or maybe they're here on their honeymoon, like Dove and Lexi. And they stroll through the woods holding hands and planning their future.

Then she feels stupid for letting thoughts like that detract from the arguably perfect day she's having. She and her mother are away on vacation, something they talked about but lately hadn't made the time to actually do together. She really wishes she hadn't found the ring in the first place. It was messing with her head.

She checks her phone. No signal.

"Damn," she mutters. Then, to Cole: "Does your phone work out here?"

"Yeah. But my grandfather takes our phones before every activity," he says.

"So neither of us have a working phone?" She looks around, trying not to feel irrational panic.

"That's the spirit of bushcraft, isn't it? The whole point of you knitters venturing out of your safe little shell?"

"Forget I mentioned it," she says. "No phone, no problem."

After a minute, to redirect the conversation, she says, "Your grandfather seems like a character." She scoops up a branch shaped like a pitchfork.

"My entire family are characters. Not always in a good way."

"Do you spend a lot of time with them?"

"Well, I see my grandfather mostly on holidays. But I see my dad all the time—we work together." He tells her his father owns a big grocery chain in Bucks County.

"Where's that?" she asks.

He laughs. "Here. This is Bucks County. I grew up fifteen minutes from here in a place called Doylestown."

Piper is distracted by something on the ground, a faint flicker of movement that catches her eye. She walks slowly in that direction then bends down to look more closely. There, nestled in a shallow bunch of leaves, is a baby sparrow.

"You okay over there?" Cole calls out.

A few hatchlings had been brought into the shelter during the time she worked there, and she'd learned the first thing to do was check and see if the nest is nearby. If so, it was best to place the baby back where its mother would return. It was only a myth that an adult bird would sense the baby had been handled by humans and rejected.

"I found a baby bird."

He hurries over and peers at the baby. It's very still and one leg seems to jut out unnaturally.

"Is it injured?"

"I'm not sure," Piper says. She wishes she knew enough to make some sort of determination about its condition.

Her love of animals had been intense and deeply ingrained since the time she was a small child. One of the few issues she and her mother clashed over was having a pet. Maggie never wanted the responsibility, even though Piper insisted she'd help. At six or seven years old, she didn't understand that she couldn't walk the dog or run to the store to pick up cat food. The compromise was that Maggie sent her to a place called the Art Farm every summer, a day camp on East 93rd Street that had a little indoor zoo. By the time she was a teenager, old enough to take care of a pet on her own, she was so busy with school and jobs and friends she no longer pushed for it. Thoughts of veterinary school were replaced by accessible ambitions. That's when she started working at the Union Square Animal Shelter.

"Can you help me look for its nest?" she says.

They check the nearby tree branches, but don't find anything. Cole pulls out a pair of binoculars.

"Impressively well-equipped," she says.

"Well, what would a bushcrafter be without binoculars?"

"I can't imagine," she says dryly. "Your grandfather would be impressed."

He spots something and points: The nest is very high up and out of reach. So that's not an option.

"Is there a veterinary office or shelter nearby?"

"There's a wildlife rehabilitation place in Chalfont," he said. "Go get your car. I'll wait here with the bird."

"I can't drive," she says.

"What do you mean, you can't drive?" he says.

"I'm from New York City."

"And what—you thought you'd never step foot outside of it? So much for your survival skills," he says.

She can't argue with him on that. He offers to go get his truck, but she refuses to wait behind. "I'll never find you." She dumps out her tote filled with twigs, bends down and lines the bottom with dried leaves, and slips the bird inside, making sure to hold it loosely and open so it can get air.

"I have some banana boxes in the back of my truck," he says.

Perfect.

It's a ten-minute drive to the Bucks Animal Rescue and Rehabilitation, or BARR. Cole spent a lot of his childhood summers at their camp, and she tells him about her summers at the Art Farm. "You'll like this place," he tells her.

Cole pulls the car up a long driveway that leads to a farmhouse-style building. A gravel parking lot winds around to an expanse of horse stables and a field populated by wild turkeys. He walks around to the passenger door to help her get out of the car with the bird box, then leads her up wood-plank stairs to a wraparound terrace. Inside the building, they're met by a middle-aged woman at a small table holding a small laptop and a few clipboards of paper. Shelves and bulletin boards display informational flyers and cute photos of rescued animals.

"Hey, stranger," the woman says, standing to give him a hug. "I thought I recognized your truck coming up the drive."

Cole introduces Piper to the woman, Denise, and she hands over the bird box. Cole fills out paperwork on a clipboard, while Denise pulls on a latex glove and sets the box on the table. She cautiously opens the lid and gently retrieves the bird.

"Oh, aren't you a cutie?" she said, giving it a quick once-over.

Piper's heart feels full. There's something so moving about holding a tiny, fragile thing like that. She wishes she could stay and help.

"Can you . . . Is there a way to let us know what happens to her?" Piper said.

"Sure—we're assigning her a case number. That's it right there on the paperwork. Give us a day or so and feel free to call and check in."

Cole, noticing Piper's reluctance to leave, offers to give her a tour of the place. The sounds of chirping, squeaking and rustling come from distant rooms, and she hears the bustle of people moving around and talking, the ringing of a landline phone. She's curious to see more, but she realizes she should get back to her mother before she starts to worry.

"We should get back to our parents," she says. She thanks Denise on her way back outside. Cole follows her.

"What's the rush?" he says. "Let my dad and your mother run around trying to build a lean-to shelter. This was their big idea."

True. And yet . . . "I feel like I'm ditching her."

"You're not ditching her. She found a friend her own age. It's good for them. For both of them."

They reach the truck and when they're both back inside she asks, "What do you mean, good for them?"

He shrugs, starting the ignition. "Maybe there's more going on here than a bushcraft challenge."

Oh. Cole said the quiet part aloud. "That's what *I* was

thinking when I first heard about it. But I don't know. I think we're projecting."

"Wishful thinking?" he says.

"Probably."

"Well, maybe we can nudge them along."

"How? Trust me, it'll take a lot more than a weekend in the woods to get my mom interested in some guy. Especially when she came here to spend it with me."

"So give her the best of both worlds; come to our campout tonight."

Is he flirting with her? And does she want him to be?

"I don't like camping," she says. It's true. And also, she might not be thrilled with Ethan at the moment, but that doesn't mean she'd cheat on him. Even flirting with someone else feels wrong.

"What if our parents are hitting it off? Sometimes you gotta take one for the team."

Maybe he's right. What if they are? It's bad enough Piper can't take advantage of the setting and have a romantic weekend. If Maggie can instead? Well, she's all for it.

Chapter Twenty-Two

AIDAN APPRAISES THEIR STASH OF shelter-building materials, and has to admit it's not his best showing. But in fairness to himself and his teammate, Maggie, they're short-handed. Also, he's distracted. By Maggie.

"What do you think?" she calls out from behind him. He takes a moment before turning around. The more time he spends with her, the more he recognizes their chemistry.

"I think we nailed it," he says once she reaches him.

"Really?"

She smiles so earnestly he regrets his sarcasm. "No. Not really. But in our defense, we have been down two team members."

The sun is noticeably lower, creating a dappled pattern on the ground. The interplay of light and shadow lends an intimacy to the moment that makes him uncomfortable. Because he knows it's not just the pretty autumn backdrop; it's Maggie Hodges. He likes her. More than likes her—he's attracted to her. But these are inappropriate and very inconvenient feelings given the family trip he's on.

Just then, walking from the direction of the roadway and parking area—not the woods—Cole and Piper appear.

"Finally!" Maggie says. Aidan feels a little stung at her exuberance. He'd been enjoying their time together.

Cole is empty-handed.

"We got unexpectedly sidetracked," Cole says, and the two of them launch into a story about a hatchling and a trip to the local animal refuge. As they recount their little adventure, there's a lightness in Cole he hasn't seen since the weekend began. It's exactly what he'd hoped for when he suggested the foursome meet up.

"How's it going there, team?" Barclay appears, his cheeks ruddy from the cold. Aidan is starting to feel the chill too. He'd been too busy to notice until now. He looks closer at Maggie, and though her cheeks are pink, she doesn't seem at all deterred by the dropping temperatures. He resists the urge to put an arm around her shoulders.

"Great," Maggie says.

Barclay surveys their work. "Great?" he says. "Little lady, I hate to break it to you, but you're group is officially in last place."

"Who won?" Cole says.

"That would be Team Crockett. Cole, your cousin bested you. Time to up your game," Barclay says. "You have a chance to redeem yourself tomorrow." Then, to Maggie: "Young lady, if you've learned anything from today's exercise, I hope it's that wildlife survival is a man's work."

"That's exactly my takeaway," she says, giving Aidan a playful wink.

Barclay walks off, calling over his shoulder for Aidan to be in front of the inn at "sixteen hundred hours." When he's out of earshot, Aidan says, "I don't think he gets your sarcasm."

"That's okay," Maggie says. "As long as you do. And like Barclay says, get ready to *up your game*. Because now it's time to knit."

AIDAN DIDN'T THINK through the part of the bet where he'd end up in a knitting class. The truth was, he didn't think it would actually get that far. He figured that Maggie would make it for about an hour out there in the woods, then duck out on them. Or if she stuck it out for the whole fort-building exercise, he'd concede defeat and pay her the fifty dollars to make good on the bet. But—surprise, surprise—not only did she stick it out with him until the (pitiful) end of the fort outing, he welcomed the excuse to spend more time with her.

So here he is, in a class about brioche stitch, which in his world is a type of bread. Aidan's legs are already cramped under the low table. Maggie looks equally uncomfortable, though he suspects it's for a different reason: The whole room is sneaking glances at them. The only one who doesn't seem to find anything unusual about his appearance in the workshop is Belinda.

He was surprised how readily Cole agreed to join them. He seemed genuinely interested in who else would be there, asking Piper about the other knitters. Now Cole is sitting directly across the round table, next to a brunette with beautiful dark eyes.

"How do you two know each other?" the brunette asks Piper. Aidan learns her name is Kalli.

"We met yesterday," Piper says.

"Welcome to our visitors from the bachelor party," Belinda says, standing in front of the large windows and framed by the changing light of the sun sinking lower in the blue-gray sky. Her acknowledgment of Aidan and Cole elicits more curious looks from the rest of the group. "I've never had walk-ins at a retreat before. But I understand it's all in the spirit of competition."

Belinda looks at Maggie, and there's a pause before Maggie realizes Belinda is prompting her to explain, and she stands.

She looks around the room, and all eyes are on her. "Hi, everyone. So, yes, we actually have a little bet going. What's harder: bushcraft or knitting. So . . . that's why they're here." She quickly sits back down.

Her announcement triggers a cascade of conversation. He can't tell if the knitters are amused, outraged or a little of both. It takes a full minute for Belinda to quiet everyone down, leaving only a few lingering glances in Aidan's direction.

Belinda instructs them to "cast on," and all around the table hands start moving in a flurry of activity. Aidan, unable to follow the first step in the knitting process, leans closer to whisper to Maggie.

"I thought you said this was a beginner's class."

"It is: Beginner's Brioche." Her fingers move so fast they're almost a blur.

"You're aware there's no way in hell I'm going to get this yarn on those needles, aren't you."

"I told you that at the bar last night. You didn't believe me." She smiles, and when he leans closer he smells good—like the outdoors, but also something spicy and sweet, like nutmeg.

"I should leave now and preserve whatever shred of dignity I have left," he whispers. "Do you accept Venmo?"

She smiles. "Nope. I'm not letting you get off that easily."

He has to admit, he was hoping she wouldn't. The knitting, he could take or leave. But he's in no rush to leave Maggie.

Belinda is talking about things that might as well be in a foreign language: slipped stitches and yarnovers and some indecipherable instructions. But she's interrupted when an Asian woman on the opposite side of the table stands up. She's dressed in jeans and a half-buttoned black cardigan with a Lana Del Rey T-shirt underneath.

"I'm sorry, but I can't just move on to knitting. Not after the sexist little bomb that was detonated in this room." Her hands are on her hips, and she looks around the table as if challenging anyone to disagree with her. Or maybe she's waiting for people to agree with her.

Regardless, no one speaks until Belinda says, "What's on your mind, Lexi?"

"The bet is offensive. It implies the devaluation of a historically female craft. I'm willing to bet that any one of us knitters can keep up with whatever these guys are doing outdoors—but not a single one of them could knit a stitch."

"Okay, babe. We get your point," says the slight, pale woman next to her.

"No, there's an important distinction to be made here: Knitting is a craft. It takes a certain type of intellect and patience. But survival skills? We're born with those. Like any animal." With this, she looks directly at Aidan, challenging him.

He turns to Maggie, and she shrugs.

"You could be right," he says to the woman.

"Don't patronize me." She crosses her arms.

Now the rest of the table is staring at him. "I wasn't patronizing you." And then, feeling compelled to say more, to defend his feminist bona fides, says, "In fact, you're welcome to join us later." He doesn't really mean it, and he hopes the woman isn't interested in the offer.

"Challenge accepted," she says.

"What?" he says.

"I'll take you up on that. Whatever you guys have planned next, I'll be there."

"Lexi, no," says the woman next to her. "Drop it."

"Why? I know he doesn't think I'm right," Lexi says to her. Then, turning back to him: "And I'll put my money where my mouth is. How much is the bet?"

"Fifty dollars," Maggie says. He glances over and sees she's enjoying this.

"Double it," Lexi says. "Then it's almost a respectable bet. Plus, I could really use an extra hundred bucks."

PIPER GLANCES OVER at Cole; he's smiling. He thinks this whole situation is funny. And more importantly, her mother does too. She seems happier, lighter somehow. She hopes Cole's right about the potential for a love connection. It reminds her of that old Lindsay Lohan movie *The Parent Trap*. Getting Maggie and Aidan together is now her weekend goal.

Kalli stands up suddenly. "I agree with Lexi—I'll put up a hundred dollars, too."

"All right!" Lexi says. "We've got a betting pool. I'm good with that. Anyone else want to contribute to the pot?"

Kalli turns to Cole. "Why don't you ask your friends out there in the woods if they want in? Let's see how big we can make the pot, and then winner takes all."

Laurel pulls at her arm and hisses at her to sit down.

Cole has a strange, uncomfortable expression on his face. "Not sure that's a good idea."

"It's a great idea," Lexi says. The entire table is talking. Sheila reminds everyone that she's been to every knitting retreat since the beginning, and "This is a first and I'm loving it." But two people at the table are clearly not loving it: Dove reminds Lexi they're on their honeymoon, and Laurel is furiously whispering to Kalli.

Belinda resorts to waving for everyone's attention.

"While I applaud the spirit of competition in this room, we only have an hour and a half to get into brioche—a style of knitting I could devote an entire weekend to if we had the luxury."

"That's a future retreat idea," Sheila says.

Belinda doesn't acknowledge the suggestion. Maybe she didn't hear it.

"Knitters, I start today's class advising you this: Brioche, like many of life's challenges, requires a shift in thinking. And once that's achieved, it will become a favorite technique. But getting there takes persistence."

Piper's phone buzzes with another call from Gretchen. Again, she lets it go to voicemail. Her phone translates the voicemail to text across her screen and she catches the words *huge opportunity* and *ASAP*. She looks over at Maggie, who's busy writing on her notepad. Her mother would be appalled if she knew Piper was ignoring Gretchen's calls.

"Let's talk materials: For brioche, wool is ideal because the elasticity enhances the squishy texture that's the hallmark of this style. Today, we're working with Malabrigo Rios, a worsted-weight yarn that will give you excellent stitch definition."

In the center of the table a basket is stuffed with yarn in shades like apple green, midnight blue, rose pink, and a few neutrals like putty and gray. They're all prewound with the labels tucked back inside. Something about yarn just makes her itch to hold it, to get her hands moving. But Gretchen's call nags at her.

She'd convinced herself The Fall was the end of her career. And while it stung that Gretchen dropped her, it gave her a convenient excuse to bow out of modeling. But if Gretchen wants her back, then the only way out is to actively quit. Something she's not sure she can do. She's not a quitter—no matter how unhappy she is. Plus, Maggie would be so disappointed.

Belinda tells everyone to choose a yarn from the center of the table. Cole, beside her, seems disinterested until Kalli chooses a skein in midnight blue and hands it to him. While everyone picks through the options, Piper takes the opportunity of everyone's distraction to slip out of the room.

It's time to be an adult and call Gretchen back.

Chapter Twenty-Three

PIPER FINDS A SPOT TO sit halfway down the hall, a carved wood and green velvet settee under a framed oil painting. She can see the closed double doors of the Purl from her seat, but she's far enough away that she's free to talk. She calls Gretchen's cell, hoping she'll get voicemail but no, her (former) manager answers on the first ring.

"There you are!" Gretchen says. "You avoiding me, lady?"

"Um, you fired me as a client."

"It was a momentary lapse in judgment. And I totally respect your hard-to-get vibe, but can we put a pin in it for now? Because, Piper, you were right. The fall *worked*."

"What do you mean, 'worked'? It was an accident."

"Well, whatever you want to call it, thanks to that clip going viral, I have tons of go-sees for you—including print jobs. The real deal. My assistant will follow up with an email, but I wanted to get this on your radar ASAP. Can you swing by the office Monday morning?"

Piper feels cornered. Trapped. "Actually, I'm on vacation."

"Piper," Gretchen says, her voice dropping to convey gravity. "I say this for you, not for myself: Don't miss your moment. We have a short window to capitalize on this. Seize the day and all that. Let's get you in front of these people and make some real money."

"I need some time to think," Piper says.

"Well, don't think too hard," Gretchen says. "You're lucky to have this second chance."

And she abruptly ends the call.

Piper sits and stares at the painting hanging on the wall directly across from her. It's another oil painting, this one a Revolutionary War scene. She replays the call in her mind, then she picks up her phone again and FaceTimes Ethan. When the video appears on her screen, she can see he's in Central Park.

"Hey," she says, smiling.

"Hi! You have a break in the action over there?"

"Yeah, I guess you could say that." It's so good to see him. He's wearing his college hoodie with an army-green coat she hasn't seen since last winter. His big brown eyes are bright and his fair skin is ruddy. His lips are red and chapped, and she misses him with a sharpness that's almost physical.

"I miss you," she says.

"I miss you too."

She glances down the hall at the Purl. "I only have a minute because I ducked out of a workshop. But the weird thing is that Gretchen called me to say the viral post of my fall is getting me job offers. So she wants me to come in on Monday."

He smiles and shakes his head. "So now the fall is a good thing?"

"I know. It's ridiculous. And I told her I need to think about it. Since she fired me, I've been kinda relieved."

"You have?"

"Yes. I want to quit, but there's no way to justify it to myself, or to my mother, especially. And I think that's what's been making me so anxious the past few months. I think it's why I fainted on the runway. It was like . . . subconscious self-sabotage."

"You don't want to model anymore?" he says.

"I don't know. Maybe not. But I can't just quit. What if now's my chance to actually start making good money doing this?"

"The money isn't worth it if you're miserable. And does Maggie know you feel this way?"

Not if she can help it. "No."

"Maybe you should tell her."

"Why?"

He's quiet for a few seconds. "Let's talk about this when you get back."

About *what*? "No, let's talk about 'this' now."

He backtracks, tells her it's nothing. Tells her he loves her. And she knows he does. But she also knows it's not nothing. Why's he in such a rush for her to talk to Maggie about work? He knows she's just going to push her to stick with it. Maybe that's what he thinks deep down, and doesn't want to be the one to tell her.

The doors to the Purl open and Laurel bursts into the hall, her face flushed and her fingers tapping furiously on her phone. She barely looks up in her rush towards the lobby.

"Piper, try to just enjoy the weekend. I'm glad you have some space to think about the whole Gretchen thing, away from the city. Don't let her pressure you."

He's right. Still, she thinks it was strange for him to suggest she talk to Maggie. Typically, she gets the sense that he wishes she and mom had more boundaries, not less. But, heading back inside the Purl, she pushes aside her unsettled feelings. Instead, she thinks of something positive: Cole's potentially brilliant parent trap idea.

BELINDA FINDS LAUREL on the front porch alone. She's sipping from a Bucks Tavern takeout coffee cup and staring out at the direction of Main Street.

There's a moment in almost every retreat where Belinda goes from teacher to den mother. Sometimes it happens on day one. Sometimes there are tears at the farewell breakfast. This weekend, it's the brioche workshop.

"I heard reports of a runaway knitter," Belinda says, sitting in the wicker chair beside her.

"Sorry for walking out like that."

"No need to apologize. I just want you to know I'm here if you need anything."

Laurel fixes her gray eyes on her and sighs.

"You ever care about somebody so much, but at the same time want to strangle them?"

"Of course. I've been married over thirty years."

Laurel gives her a half smile. "Okay. Well, I brought Kalli here this weekend to cheer her up. To support her during a rough time. And it backfired."

Belinda frowns. That's not what she wants to hear.

"She isn't enjoying herself?"

Laurel stays silent for a minute, then says, "She's enjoying herself a little *too* much."

Well, that's a new one. Belinda's there to listen, not talk, so that's what she does. But Laurel doesn't offer anything further. The front door opens and a few of the younger men from the bachelor party head out to the parking area. When the brioche class ended, Aidan Danby invited her to join them for the next activity in the bushcraft-knitting challenge: axe-throwing. She doesn't have time, but the fact that they've constructed this little competition amuses her to no end. Normally, she'd rush to tell Max all about it and together they'd "unpack it," as the kids say today. But she knows all he wants to hear from her is yes, take the offer. And she can't say that right now. Not until the weekend is over. She's giving herself two more days to pretend she has any real argument to make for turning down that kind of money.

Now that she's thinking of it, the bushcraft competition seems to be what set Laurel off.

"I know the outdoors stuff with the bachelor party might be an unwelcome diversion to you, but maybe it will be fun. Maybe it's what Kalli needs right now too."

Belinda's phone buzzes with a message from the staffer at the front desk, but she ignores it. Let him bother Max.

"Kalli isn't making *new* friends," Laurel says. "She already knows Cole Danby."

Belinda is confused. She saw Piper introduce Cole to Kalli, and the interaction was that of strangers. As if reading her mind, Laurel says, "Yeah, that whole 'nice to meet you' thing was an act."

She proceeds to tell her that Kalli had been married to her high school boyfriend for two years when she met Cole Danby and fell madly in love. She tried breaking things off, but it was too late for her marriage. She couldn't go back. Then, when she finally filed for divorce and reached out to Cole, he shut her down. Said he'd been too heartbroken by the whole thing to go back and try again, leaving Kalli completely heartbroken. And so: the knitting retreat.

"I see," Belinda says. And she does: Laurel planned a trip to help Kalli get over a guy, and the guy shows up on the trip. Not good. "But Laurel, sometimes you just need to let people make mistakes. Even people you care about. There's no way through life without a few stumbles, right? As friends, we just have to be there after the fall. And who knows? Maybe this is what she needs to get over the relationship once and for all."

"You think?" Laurel says, looking a little more hopeful.

"Absolutely," Belinda tells her. "A long weekend can work miracles."

Chapter Twenty-Four

IF SOMEONE HAD ASKED MAGGIE where she imagined herself on day two of the knitting retreat, her answer wouldn't have been "Big Al's Hatchet House." But that's exactly where she finds herself, along with Piper, Lexi, Sheila, and the entire bachelor party. Even Belinda decided to tag along.

"Someone's gotta keep Barclay Cavanaugh honest," she said.

The Hatchet House is a cavernous space inside an unassuming, farmhouse-style building a short drive from the inn. It's set up with batting cage–like stalls outfitted with bull's-eye targets. The rest of the space has wood-plank floors, a bar with beer on tap and a merch section selling Al's Hatchet House baseball caps, T-shirts, beer mugs and shot glasses. There's a viewing section with bleachers, and a giant American flag covers nearly an entire wall. Classic rock plays over the sound system: the Stones. Bruce. Bon Jovi.

The bachelors cluster together near the bar, and the knitters are looking at a display of vintage axes.

"I want one of these for our den," Lexi says.

No one asks her why Dove didn't come along, and she doesn't offer an explanation. Laurel, too, made a point of sitting it out. Maggie understands that Dove is frustrated by the distraction on their honeymoon. She's not quite sure what Laurel's upset about.

Barclay ambles over and asks if they have any questions.

"I do," Lexi says. "Does axe-throwing really count as bushcraft? We're not even outdoors."

"Young lady, axe-throwing requires strength, accuracy and precision. All vital in bushcraft. It's also a test of mental focus and discipline. So you can tell me you're not up to the challenge. But that's about the end of this here discussion."

Lexi puts her hands on her hips, widening her stance. "Don't you worry—I'm up for it."

A young man holding a clipboard and dressed in a Hatchet House T-shirt gathers all of them together. He gives a fifteen-minute safety briefing before handing things off to Barclay. Apparently, Aidan's father-in-law is quite the accomplished axeman. Everyone at the place knows him by name, and the safety instructor admits Barclay could "probably teach him a thing or two."

Barclay and the instructors give them tips for finding their grip and maintaining a solid stance. Then Barclay geeks out on them about technique and Maggie's mind wanders. So does her eye.

Aidan is out of her direct line of vision, so she has to pretend to check out the vintage axe display while sneaking glances at him. Somewhere between the last bushcraft activity and the end of the brioche class, she admitted to herself that she's attracted to him. When she looks at him, she finds herself sort of memorizing the color of his eyes, the arch of his brows, the line of his jaw. It's an old habit from the days before iPhones, when she could spend all night talking to someone at a party and then literally never see them again.

Maggie is already thinking of a near-future version of herself, maybe a month from now, when she's forgotten how it feels to be around an attractive man like Aidan. The flutter she feels in her chest, the sense of being acutely awake...it will be like it never happened.

Aidan is looking straight ahead at Barclay, but as if sensing Maggie's eyes on him, he turns toward her. She quickly looks away, heart pounding. She feels like a teenager. If Piper knew this was going on in her mind, she'd tease her. For good reason. Maybe, after the weekend, she'll confess. They'll have a laugh about it driving back to the city together.

"When I use the term 'throw arc,' I mean the final path of your axe once it leaves your hand," Barclay says. "Remember: left-to-right accuracy is far more important than vertical. Even though the targets are circles, your axe landing even a millimeter too far left or right is a miss. Vertically, you have the entire length of the blade that can be in the bull's-eye."

The safety staffer helps everyone select a comfortable axe for themselves. Maggie chooses one with a thin handle with flat edges for grip. When it's time to separate into Team Bachelors and Team Knitters, Lexi says, "How's this scoring system gonna work if the guy team has twice as many throwers as we do?"

"Why don't each of you throw twice?" says Aidan's nephew, the actual bachelor of the party.

"Because then we're going to get tired out twice as fast," Piper says. Maggie gives her a thumbs-up for the good point, and Piper rolls her eyes at her enthusiasm.

After much debate and an embarrassing display of math skills, they figure out a system where only half of the men's throws count toward the tally. To keep score, Barclay oversees Team Bachelors while Belinda maintains the tally for Team Knitters. Maggie's played her fair share of darts games, and that makes the scoring system somewhat familiar to her: Hitting the bull's-eye garners the most points, with each ring decreasing in value moving outward.

Each team forms a short line at the shared target lane. Lexi's taking the first throw for their team, and Aidan is up first for the bachelors.

"Ladies first," Barclay says, and Lexi shakes her head as she steps up to the demarcation line at their lane. Then, using a two-handed grip, she raises her axe straight overhead, leaning slightly forward as she throws. She hits the target near the center.

"Excellent first throw," Barclay calls out.

"Don't be patronizing," Lexi says.

Whiteboards with markers are mounted on each side of the wall, and Belinda hesitates before calculating their team's first points.

"The axe is touching two zones." Belinda consults with Barclay.

"Go by the zone where the majority of the blade sticks. If it's equal, we go with the higher score."

Aidan is up next. Maggie wants to watch, but she's certain her more-than-casual feelings will show all over her face. She makes small talk with Lexi instead.

He lands the bull's-eye. Of course he does.

When it's Piper's turn, she laughs while trying to maintain a good stance.

"Come on, city girl," Barclay calls out. "Do your team proud."

"No pressure!" Belinda says.

"You've got this," Maggie chimes in.

Piper releases her throw and the axe misses the target entirely.

"Do I get to go again?" she says.

Barclay tells her she has three tries before her turn counts as a zero. But she misses each time.

"Okay, I suck," she says, but she's grinning. She's happy.

Maggie won't hesitate to take credit: This trip was a stroke of genius. There's no way Piper would have bounced back so quickly after the professional blow last week if they'd stayed in the city. Remarkably, she seems less affected by it than Maggie, who is still thinking about how to fix things for her. Just because Gretchen was the first person to see Piper's potential doesn't mean she's the only one who ever will. Piper just has to get herself back out there.

"I might be the weak link here," Piper says, returning in defeat. The next bachelor in line steps up for his throw. This time, it's Aidan's nephew.

"Never." Maggie smiles and puts her arm around her. Scott's hatchet lands with a thud, but it's a low-scoring area.

"See? He barely did any better than you," Maggie says.

"Aside from actually hitting the target, you mean?" Piper says. Then, leaning closer. "Listen, I have an interesting idea for tonight."

"Oh?"

She nods vigorously. "Cole invited us to go camping with them tonight. Not for the competition. Just us—for fun."

Maggie is surprised. Piper loves animals, but she's never been particularly outdoorsy. She is, as Barclay said, a "city girl." They've never gone camping together. It never even crossed Maggie's mind. The closest they got was an extremely rustic hotel when they took a road trip to the Outer Banks one summer. She wonders what's going on. If it weren't for Ethan, she'd think for sure Piper had a flirtation going with Cole Danby. But it can't be that. Maybe she's genuinely having a good time and is caught up in the momentum of the weekend. The thought makes Maggie profoundly happy.

And of course, for her own reasons, the invitation to spend more time with the Danbys is appealing. The knitting retreat just got a lot more interesting.

BARCLAY IS NOT happy to see Team Knitters within two points of tying the score after Round One. Aidan huddles everyone together to strategize. Out of the entire bachelor party, only a few of them are significantly better throwers than the women. Ritchie is one of them, but the beer is making his game sloppy.

"Ritchie, we're cutting you off until you rack up some points for us."

"And Cole, no more cavorting with the competition," Barclay says.

Aidan did notice that Cole made a point of helping one of the knitters with her throw: Kalli, the dark-haired, dark-eyed young woman from the knitting class.

"Got it, Grandpa," he says. Then, quietly to Aidan: "I hope you don't mind cavorting with the competition too. Because I invited Maggie and Piper camping with us tonight."

Aidan makes a face like, *ha ha*. Then he realizes Cole is serious.

"Wait. You did? Why?"

"I guess the same reason you invited them to build the fort," he says with a shrug. But Aidan isn't letting him off the hook that easily.

"That was a bet."

Cole gives him a look like, come on.

"She has a boyfriend, you know," Aidan says. "Maggie tells me they're practically engaged."

"What does that have to do with anything?"

"You tell me."

If Cole's attracted to unavailable women, Piper Hodges fits the criteria. Now that Barclay's implying some sort of toxic pattern, he can't help but see it too. And even though Barclay asked him not to, he has to say *something* to Cole. His first responsibility, always, is to Cole.

He almost wishes Barclay hadn't invited him out for drinks in the first place. He didn't need to hear about Cole's relationship, or Barclay's theories on his parenting weaknesses. What's Aidan supposed to do now? He doesn't have a time machine to go back to the past and find a perfect relationship to model for his son. And really, maybe staying single hadn't been a choice so much as an unfortunate inevitability. He never found someone he was interested in, or had enough in common with; not many people in their thirties could relate to being a widower. He'd met women who were divorced, but never one who'd lost her husband. So while he'd had a few decent dates here and there, a few nascent relationships, nothing ever felt like a true connection. At least, not enough of one. So at some point along the way he'd figured, why bother?

"I'm not hitting on Piper, if that's what you mean," Cole says, practicing his arm follow-through.

"Okay. Good. Because chasing unavailable women is a fast track to misery."

Cole drops his arms. "Why do you say that?"

"Because it's true. And I don't want to see you making avoidable mistakes." He glances at the rest of the group to make sure no one can hear them. Between the loud music and the sound of metal hitting targets, he feels comfortable enough to continue. "You're not a kid anymore. Choices you make matter. They can have repercussions that last a long time. Longer than you can imagine."

"So he told you." Cole casts a baleful look in his cousin's direction.

"Don't be upset with Scott. He's concerned."

"Dad, you're right: I'm not a kid anymore. So I don't need Scott's 'concern.' Or yours, for that matter. I don't do my personal life by committee."

Cole walks away just as Barclay calls out for Aidan—he's

up next. Aidan holds up one hand, *gimme five*. Then he looks around for Cole and spots him heading towards the bar. Aidan follows, threading his way through another group. When he's close enough, he reaches out for Cole's arm.

"Hey," Aidan says sharply. Cole stops walking. "Want to tell me what this is all about?"

"Not really. I don't need more negative input."

Aidan frowns. "That's why you're not talking to me about this? Because you can't take a little 'negative input'? That's disappointing—to say the least."

"No, Dad. It's that I don't want to upset you. I don't tell you about all the ups and downs of my relationships because mostly they're not that important. And yes, this relationship was important to me—extremely. But it was a stressful situation because she was married. And I didn't want to put that on you."

Aidan didn't know what he'd expected to hear, but it wasn't that.

"Married? How old is this woman?"

"I know what you're thinking, and no, she's not older and there're no kids involved—nothing like that. We met at a party for mutual friends and it was just one of those things."

"So you weren't only hiding this relationship from me. You were hiding it from everyone."

Cole crosses his arms. "That's accurate."

"Did that feel right to you?"

"Yes, actually. It did. Being with her felt right. And nothing has felt right since. And no offense, but why would I take relationship advice from someone who hasn't had a relationship in years?"

Before Aidan can process the comment—and how it cuts deeper because of Barclay's talk last night—Cole asks him for the car keys. "You can get a ride back with Grandpa."

"Come on. Don't leave."

Cole is stone-faced. Aidan knows how futile it is when Cole's buttons get pushed. It's like a storm he has to ride out. His mother was the same way, and Aidan told him so once.

He gets his jacket from the coat room and hands over the keys.

"See you later?" he says.

Cole turns around. "So far this trip is a little too much family togetherness for me. So let's just call it a day."

PIPER NEVER REALIZED her shameful lack of upper body strength until now, mid–axe throw. And it's humbling. She missed the target the first time around and her shoulder blades already feel like she needs Advil and a heating pad. But more surprising is the rage she feels with each release of the heavy tool. She has to resist the urge to yell out, *Take that!* At first, the burst of anger is accompanied by thoughts of her manager. This, at least, makes sense. Work has been a big source of stress to her, probably more than she'd admitted to herself before now. But then, on her last throw she thinks of . . . her mother. She releases the axe and it finally lands on the target.

What's *that* about?

There's no time to unpack it: Kalli's up next, and Barclay calls out to remind them it's the final turn for each team. Piper watches Kalli then glances at the scoreboard: They need a minimum of four points.

Her phone buzzes with a text from Hannah Elise.

> Hey—every piece I posted you wearing has sold already. Time later to shoot a few more? Lmk xo

Hannah Elise is giving her too much credit. The knitwear sold because it's special. And she doesn't want to shoot any more videos. It feels like work—the last thing she wants to think about. But she'll go tell Hannah Elise in person. She doesn't want it to seem like she's blowing her off.

The bachelor party erupts in shouts and cheers. She turns back to look at the scoreboard, and sees they lost. And although the whole thing was kind of a joke, just for fun, she's a little disappointed.

"Ladies, you lost the battle but not the war," Barclay says. "These men still have to best you at your own game. So what's it going to be?"

Piper looks at her mother, who looks at Belinda. Knitting can't be "scored" like an axe game. What's success in knitting? A project takes days, weeks or months. They need a metric.

"I wish I had a beginner's workshop for the boys today, but I don't," Belinda says. "It's not a fair competition to ask them to keep up with anything more advanced."

"Well, if you can't give our team an arena for competition, I'd say that's a forfeit," says Aidan's brother-in-law.

In the middle of this, Kalli pulls her aside.

"Do you know where Cole went?"

Piper is momentarily confused. Why is Kalli asking her? But then, she gets it: People see them hanging out and think they're hooking up. But if she had an engagement ring, people wouldn't assume that.

"I have no idea," Piper says, looking around. There's no sign of him. "By the way—Cole and I are just friends."

Kalli gives her a weird look like, *obviously.*

"Do you think he left?" Kalli says. Piper repeats that she doesn't know.

"I can text him if you want," she offers. But Kalli backtracks, says she was just wondering. That it's "not important."

By the time Piper turns her attention back to the group, a

solution for the knitting competition has been found: Belinda will add a beginner's workshop to the schedule after all.

"But I need a volunteer to teach it, because I don't have a moment free."

A hand shoots up. Piper is surprised to realize it belongs to her mother. Sure, Maggie's always up for making things more fun. But even for her, this seems impulsive. And Piper suspects this has nothing to do with a desire to teach or facilitate the competition, and everything to do with spending more time with Aidan.

"Maggie. Perfect," Belinda says with a big smile. "As they say: Let the games begin, Or, in this case, continue."

Chapter Twenty-Five

THE ONLY PERSON MAGGIE'S EVER taught to knit was Piper, and that was so long ago. After all these years, stitching is as natural to her as breathing. Now, facing the room full of men, it's hard to get into the headspace of someone who doesn't know a single thing about it.

They're crowded together in a small room on the second floor. The space is packed with bins of yarn and knitwear hanging from a rack, but Belinda's using the Purl for a Shetland Hap workshop. Aidan helped set up a folding table and chairs. The only reason they can all squeeze in is because Barclay and Cole bowed out.

Volunteering to run the workshop had been impulsive, and she holds Aidan Danby entirely responsible. Being around him makes her feel spontaneous. Carefree. It's a dimension of her personality that was dormant during the years of intensive parenting. Now, she feels it still there, humming beneath the surface after all this time.

So now that she's gotten herself into this teaching situation, she tries to remember what helped her learn. Really, most of what she remembers is love at first stitch. She'd tried other crafts before, like beadwork and needlepoint. But knitting immediately felt different. It was an instant source of happiness.

And even though the men sitting around that table are just there for kicks, she feels a certain responsibility introducing them to knitting. Maybe one of them will feel the way she did. She'd find that very gratifying.

"Okay, so starting a knitting project, you have to get your yarn on the needle, and that's called 'casting on.' There're a few methods for this and the one I'm going to teach you is called the long-tail cast-on. The tail is part of what forms the stitches, so you need enough length to cast on all your stitches."

One of the guys asks, "How do I know how much tail I need?

"As much as you can get," Scott says. Clearly, he takes after his grandfather. Ignoring the comment—and the laughs it elicits—she continues.

"A general rule is to estimate about one inch of yarn for every stitch you want to cast on. Okay, so follow what I'm doing here and I'll come around to help after I explain it: First, make a slip knot. Leave a tail that's long enough for your project, then make a loop and pull the yarn through. Place the slip knot on your needle and tighten it a bit—it shouldn't be too tight, or it'll be hard to work with." She's doing the cast-on as she explains it and it's a challenge to go slowly enough for them. "Spread your thumb and index finger apart and drape the yarn over them. The working yarn goes over your index finger, and the tail goes over your thumb. Your hand will look like a Y shape, with the yarn stretched between your fingers."

The most interesting part of the situation is how obvious it is to her that none of the guys are willing to ask questions or admit their mistakes—even though some of them can't seem to get any further than making the slingshot shape with their forefinger and thumb.

"Remember, pick up from the thumb, go around the index finger and pull through."

Maggie demonstrates the cast-on again, walking around

the table and discreetly making individual suggestions to keep the guys on track. If Lexi were there, she knows she'd tell her something like, *You don't have to help them that much. It's still a competition.* But the rest of the knitters are busy taking Belinda's class, and Maggie's not thinking about the competition; teaching successfully would be a personal win.

It's been a long time since she tried something new or challenged herself. Her job at Denim has become rote, and it's been years since she thought about finding work that might be more rewarding. Maybe it was time to start looking again. But then, she couldn't leave Elaine.

This was just her vacation mind getting the best of her. Everyone on vacation thinks, at some point, I wish this was my real life. But that's not how things worked.

"Remember—it's impossible to get better without making mistakes. So if you go through this whole class without making a mistake, then you're not knitting." She remembers hearing this when she was a beginner, and it was liberating. Then, remembering Belinda's advice from the lace class, she adds: "There's a reason stitches can be unraveled."

If only things were as simple to fix in real life.

PIPER MEETS HANNAH Elise by the Adirondack chairs, outside on the lawn between the inn and Bucks County Playhouse. The light is changing, the sun dipping lower and casting everything in an almost violet hue. The fleeting warmth and quicksilver beauty of the moment feels like peak autumn, the perfect backdrop for the knitwear Hannah Elise wants to video. This makes it harder for Piper to break the news that she doesn't want to do any more posts.

"I don't want to sound like an ass, but doing social reminds me of work," she says.

"And that's a bad thing? If I were you, that's all I'd be thinking about out here. I'd trade jobs with you in a second."

"That's bullshit. You're insanely passionate about this stuff. That's why I follow you."

"This ain't my day job, babe." Hannah Elise bends down and opens her pink Away suitcase filled with carefully folded knitwear. She shakes out a cute striped bucket hat and hands it to Piper. "I made it for you last night."

Piper smiles, but shakes her head. "Are you trying to bribe me?"

"Not at all. It's a little thank-you for your help yesterday. No strings attached. And as for being passionate—yeah, I'm passionate about crochet. But you think I want to be spending my weekend with a bunch of middle-aged women looking to party like it's 1999? Mama has to pay the rent."

Piper bobs her head like, *Of course. Totally get it.* But she never imagined Hannah Elise wasn't enjoying herself, and the fact that the weekend is just a J-O-B to her is a letdown.

"But—silver lining: I met you," Hannah Elise says.

It's flattering to hear, but she can't get on board with her cynical attitude towards the retreat.

"I think this place is kinda perfect," she says.

Hannah Elise frowns at her unironic enjoyment of the weekend. Piper feels the need to compensate so she changes her mind about recording. "I guess I have time to do a few videos."

"You're the best," Hannah Elise says. "You don't even have to change into the clothes—just pick something out of the bag and hold it up when I give you the cue."

Piper crouches down and looks through the knitwear, deciding between a pair of chevron patterned bellbottoms and a Granny Square cape. When she straightens up again, she sees Cole walking toward them.

"Hey. What are you doing out here?" she says when he's close enough to hear.

"I need to talk for a sec."

"How'd you know where to find me?"

He turns and points to the second floor of the inn. "I didn't. But I was looking out and saw you two. Sorry to interrupt," he says to Hannah Elise.

Hannah Elise passes him a scarf. "No problem. I could use some male representation. Put this on?"

He takes it distractedly and turns back to Piper. "Listen, I have to bail on the camping tonight."

"Really? I already told my mother and she agreed to go. Did your dad say no or something?"

Cole shakes his head. "It's not him, it's me: I need some space. But I think your mom should still go. But since I'm not, you should hang back, too.

"Why?"

"Because if you go, then there's no chance they'll spend time together. It will be just you and your mom having a romantic night under the starts."

Piper gets it; he's probably right.

"Hey, you two: I'm going live," Hannah Elise says. She tilts her chin up, talking to the phone screen. When she turns the camera lens on Piper, she gets right with the program and holds up the chevron-patterned pants.

"Piper, will you try those on for us later so we can see what they look like with someone actually wearing them?" she says.

On the spot, Piper says, "Sure . . . but in the meantime, everyone can see Cole wearing this scarf." She takes it from his hands and arranges it around his neck.

"For the record, this is nonconsensual audience participation," he says. Hannah Elise keeps going, not missing a beat. Piper tries on a bucket hat, and she and Cole mug for the camera.

Hannah is wrong about the weekend.

She's going to have to find a way to convince her mother to go camping tonight. Without her.

MAGGIE IS DEEP into her explanation of the knit stitch when she hears the distinctive bell of the hot chocolate cart. The guys don't know what the ringing signals and she doesn't volunteer the information. If they leave, she suspects some won't come back. And now she feels invested in seeing how many of them, if any, will leave the class knowing how to get stitches on the needle.

Belinda pops her head in.

"Sorry to interrupt," she says. "But if you feel like a little break, the hot chocolate cart is in the lobby."

The guys run out like kids at the recess bell.

"That might have been a mistake," Maggie says.

"A little sugar never hurt anyone," Belinda says, passing her a hot Genevieve takeout cup. Maggie knows from yesterday it holds the nuttiest, earthiest, most delectably sweet cocoa imaginable. By the end of the weekend, she's going to be addicted. "How's it going in here?"

"I think at least a few of them are getting the hang of it."

"Good!" Belinda says. "But how are you? I actually wanted to give you a break in case you needed it."

"You didn't have to call in the heavy artillery just for me," she says, raising her cup. "But I appreciate it."

"I can't take all the credit. Max summoned the cart."

"That's sweet," Maggie says. "Literally."

"Yes, well, he can be charming. I'll give him that." But she doesn't look charmed. "Do you mind if I sit in for the remainder of the workshop? I won't say a word."

"Oh. Sure." The idea of it makes Maggie feel self-conscious, but she can't say no.

"I just ran into Barclay Cavanaugh. He asked me to officiate this little exercise here—to check in on the guys' progress. He's quite enthusiastic about the competition you've started."

Technically, Aidan started it. "I didn't really expect it to become this whole big thing. I hope you don't mind."

"Mind? It's delightful. You know, I've been doing these retreats for so many years now, but every one somehow surprises me. They're all fun in their own ways, all unique. But today was definitely a first."

Maggie smiles. "I'm glad you're okay with it."

"This weekend is a happy accident. Like I said, the double-booking was a mistake. I'm just relieved it turned out this way."

"Maybe you can plan double weekends like this in the future. It could be a public service to dispel the myth of the granny-in-the-rocking-chair knitter."

Belinda's expression clouds. "I wish I could."

Before Maggie can ask what she means by that, Belinda checks the time on her phone and offers to round up the guys so Maggie can finish the workshop.

"I'll go with you," Maggie says, hoping she might catch Piper. But as they're walking out, Aidan appears at the top of the stairs.

"Do you have a minute?" he asks.

"Um, sure," she says, glancing at Belinda, who reaches over and gives Maggie's arm a gentle squeeze.

"I'll see you in a few minutes."

When she leaves, Maggie turns to Aidan and asks, "What's up?"

"Cole and I had an argument at the axe place. That's why he's not here."

She'd been so caught up in what she was doing, she hadn't noticed Cole was missing. Maybe because Piper didn't come along, either.

"Before that happened, he told me about inviting Piper

camping. But now he's not coming. So I wanted to let you and Piper know the plan is off."

"No camping?" Maggie is surprised by how disappointed she feels. It would have been fun—and Piper seemed so enthusiastic about the idea. It was so unlike her to suggest it in the first place.

"Well, I'm still going with the rest of the guys. But without Cole, I figure Piper won't be interested, and without Piper, you won't want to go. And I get it. The whole plan sort of loses its symmetry."

"Maybe it's not as bad as you think," she says hopefully. "He might just need a reset."

Aidan shakes his head. "I know Cole. He's stubborn."

"You know what? I'm still up for the campout. I'm sure Piper is too." She's sure of no such thing, but it was Piper's idea. "Maybe if we stick with the plan, Cole will come around."

Aidan considers this. "You could be right. That's not a bad idea."

She nods. "Absolutely. We need to set a good example. A plan is a plan." Just like Piper said at breakfast. How could she argue with that?

He smiles. "Okay. I like your attitude."

She likes his too. But that's not why she's going camping tonight. Is it? No. She's going because Piper suggested it, and she wants to keep up the day's momentum. Maybe it's Cole Danby, maybe it's the novelty of the bushcraft activities, but Piper seems less preoccupied about Ethan. Maggie can breathe a little easier. If Piper can just roll with things for a few more days, Maggie will have the chance to talk to Ethan in the city—and take back what she said about waiting to propose.

Crisis averted.

Chapter Twenty-Six

PIPER HAS THE ROOM TO herself while her mother teaches the bachelor party how to knit. It gives her time to strategize about convincing Maggie to go camping without her. It will be a tough sell.

She unpacks her knitting bag, looking for a place to put her practice swatches from the brioche and lace workshops. Then she changes into sweats and a long-sleeved T-shirt and sits cross-legged on her bed against pillows. Looking around the room, she sees yarn is everywhere: on top of the dresser, in bags on the floor, spilling out of drawers. Either the yarn is magically reproducing or her mother has lost all restraint.

Piper reaches for one of the skeins still wrapped in its label. The yarn is hand-dyed merino wool in multiple shades of purple, from eggplant and plum, lilac and lavender. It's buttery soft, and she winds it on her knees.

Her phone rings with a call from Ethan.

"How's it going?" he says, and the sound of his voice floods her with warmth. She decides whatever she was annoyed about earlier couldn't have been that important, because she's forgotten already.

"Hi! Good timing. I just got back to the room. It's been nonstop here."

"Looks like it," he says, an unmistakable edge to his voice.
"What do you mean?"
"I saw your posts."

She stops winding for a moment, wondering what he's talking about. It takes a second or two to realize it's the Hannah Elise videos; she was tagged as a collaborator so they'd automatically show up on her account.

"Oh yeah—she's one of the instructors here. I actually follow her. She's from Brooklyn. Small world."

"And the guy?"

What guy? Oh.

"That's just Cole."

"He doesn't look like a knitter."

Ethan's not usually jealous. But the video must be a stark contrast to the cozy old lady retreat he imagined. Maybe that's a good thing. Maybe he's started getting a little too comfortable in the relationship. Taking her for granted.

"He's not. There's a bachelor party at the inn. Cole's here with his dad. It's funny, actually—we're trying to set Maggie up with him."

Ethan is quiet. "Okay. Well, I'm glad you're having a good time. Did you decide what to do about Gretchen?"

"No. I'm trying not to think about her." She starts winding again. The yarn has an airy, squishy feel to it, and she decides she'll start a blanket. Something simple and meditative. Something she can work on tonight while she's alone.

"So tell me more about the retreat. What's been the highlight?"

She thinks about the cute town, and meeting Hannah Elise, and the great food, and being in nature. And she realizes her favorite experience so far was the surprise trip to the animal shelter.

"I found a baby sparrow in the woods and brought it to an incredible wildlife refuge out here."

"Were you guys knitting outside?"

"No. It's a long story." She hesitates to tell him another story that includes Cole, but she has nothing to feel guilty about. "My mom and Cole's dad made some sort of bet last night at the bar, and so I ended up going with her to build a fort."

"With the bachelor party?"

"No—not the whole bachelor party. Just with Aidan and Cole."

Ethan is quiet for a few seconds.

Then he says, "Maggie's not trying to set you up, is she?"

Wow, he really has a thing about her mother these days. Now she remembers why she was annoyed during their last conversation. "Why would you even say that?"

"I'm joking."

He's not, but she's going to let it go. They're simply a little off this weekend, and she doesn't want to make a big deal out of it. Like he said: They can talk when she gets back. "Anyway, I'm staying in tonight. Alone. Just me and my knitting needles. I think I'm going to make little blankets to donate to the animal shelter."

She hears her mother's key in the door. Piper doesn't want to continue the awkward conversation in front of her. She tells Ethan her mother is walking in and that she'll call him a little later.

Maggie's cheeks are flushed and she's carrying a paper take-out cup.

"Hey there! In case you missed the hot chocolate cart." She puts the cup down on the dresser and tells her all about the knitting class for the bachelors. "I'd forgotten how challenging knitting can be to start—how what's second nature to us can totally trip up beginners. And it was kinda special to see people connect to knitting for the first time. Especially a group of skeptics." She goes on and on about how a few of the guys seemed genuinely pleased with themselves by the end of the class.

"Sorry I missed it," Piper says.

Maggie smiles. "Me too. I wish you were there. Who knows—maybe this won't be the last workshop I ever teach." She turns to the wooden dresser and pulls out socks and sweaters. "Are you packed for tonight? We're meeting Aidan in the lobby after dinner."

Here it goes.

"Yeah, about that: I think you're going to have to go without me."

Maggie stands up. "Why? I know Cole dropped out. But I told Aidan you and I are still up for it."

Piper presses her fingers to her temples. "I have a headache."

Maggie stops her flurry of movement around the room. "Oh no. You haven't been having them since the fall, have you?"

"What? No. No—nothing like that. Maybe it's the change in climate."

"We're two hours from Manhattan."

Piper shrugs. "The fresh air is a shock to the system. It doesn't matter; I'm going to sleep it off. But you should go have fun."

Maggie opens the dresser drawers again, putting the clothes back in.

"What are you doing?" Piper says.

"I'm not leaving you here all alone."

"Oh, yes you are." Piper sits up. "You can't just sit here with me in a dark room for hours." Or maybe she could—but Piper doesn't want her to. "Please just go without me."

Maggie shakes her head. "Absolutely not. I'll keep you company. You'll need dinner, won't you?"

Piper realizes her tactical error. "Mom, I'm fine. I don't even have a headache. I only said that so you'll go without me."

"Why would you do that?" Maggie looks baffled. Maybe even a little hurt.

Piper chooses her words carefully. "Because Aidan obviously likes you. And you like him. So go—have fun. It's a Saturday night."

"But it's our girls' weekend!"

"Mom, our entire life has been one long girls' weekend."

Maggie moves closer, sits on the edge of Piper's bed.

"Do you need space from me?" she asks.

"If I say yes, will you go?" This makes them both laugh for some reason. Maggie looks down at the needles and yarn in Piper's lap.

"You're really just going to stay in and knit?" she says.

Piper nods.

"Okay. I'll go. But if you change your mind, I'll come back anytime."

So it wasn't such a tough sell after all. All she had to do was tell her the truth. That's the one thing that had always set them apart from other mothers and daughters: No matter what, they always kept it real.

That's what makes the whole disappearing engagement ring so upsetting. It's okay if Ethan changed his mind. But she wants him to be honest with her.

The only dealbreaker in a relationship is dishonesty. And she wonders if the only person she can count on for the real truth, no matter what, is her mother.

BELINDA AND MAX traditionally eat dinner out together on Saturday nights. Since they work together and also live at their work, it's especially important that they carve out time to be a couple.

Tonight they go to the Salt House, a gastropub right around the corner housed in a building dating back to the 1700s. Inside, Belinda always feels the history in the small, tight dimensions of the place, and it creates an intimate environment. Like the inn before they renovated it, the first-floor dining room is all exposed wooden beams and stone walls. Belinda and Max, as regulars, score a coveted table for two near the roaring fireplace. They order their usual: fish and chips for her, a burger and beer for him.

Another relationship rule for their Saturday evenings is that they don't talk business. But before their entrées arrive, Max says, "Have you given any more thought to the offer?"

But then, selling the inn isn't just a business decision. It's personal. All too personal.

She shakes her head. "Max. I don't want to think about losing the inn while I'm in the middle of a retreat weekend."

"We're not *losing* the inn, Bee. We're *gaining* some financial security. And a new adventure. I think it's exciting to talk about."

"Well, we'll just have to agree to disagree on this one." She sips her red wine. He nods, recalibrating, knowing it's better not to push.

"Okay. What would you like to talk about?"

She wants to talk about the afternoon, the unexpected turn things took with their knitting-bushcraft challenge and the trip to the axe place. She'd known Barclay Cavanaugh casually for years, but after this afternoon, she considers them friends. His gruff, slightly off-putting exterior hides a delightful, mischievous kid inside. She had so much fun playing yin to his yang with the group, she found herself wishing it was Max leading the charge with the bachelors while she played team captain with the knitters.

Where to begin? "I don't know how it started, but the knitters and the bachelor party have a competition to prove what's more challenging: knitting or bushcraft. So we all went axe-throwing this afternoon, and then one of my knitters taught the guys a beginner's class. They really hit it off."

Max smiles appreciatively. "See? Things tend to work out. You need to worry less and trust me more."

"That's a little self-serving," she says. "Anyway, it was fun. I wished you were there. Maybe if we do something like that again tomorrow you'll tag along?"

He breaks eye contact. "Actually, I was thinking of doing a little housing research tomorrow. The Realtor tipped me off about a great town house for rent right off Chestnut Street. I know you're not free to come along, but I figure if it's promising, we'll go together after the weekend." He notices the upset look on her face and quickly adds, "Unless you don't want me to go without you at all. I just wanted to get a jump on things."

"I don't mind you going without me. But I think it's premature to start looking for a new place to live." She can't even try to hide her dismay. Things are moving too fast.

She knows Max has a restless streak. It's what led him to stray from their marriage in the first place. She thought he'd matured out of that. Apparently, she was wrong.

"We should at least get a sense of the market so we can make educated decisions moving forward. That's why I'm happy to go do some of the legwork on my own."

Belinda doesn't know what to say. They're so far apart on this issue, it scares her.

He reaches for her hand, enclosing it in both of his own. Their eyes meet across the table, and she wants to find reassurance in their connection. She tries. He pulls one hand free and then the other, and he looks something up on his phone. He turns to show her the screen. It's a brownstone in Center City.

"Look at this beauty. Our retirement."

She doesn't want to retire. And she doesn't understand why, after all this time, he wants to go back to Philadelphia. It had been a huge adjustment to leave all those years ago, and under painful circumstances. She convinced herself, long before it was true, that country living suited her. And now it did. And what—he's changed his mind? He wants to walk away from everything they've built together for the past three decades. But what choice does she have? Either she leaves the inn, or she leaves her marriage.

And she decided long ago that she's never leaving her marriage.

Chapter Twenty-Seven

*T*HE SUN SET AND THE temperature fell along with it. But it's still a beautiful night under the stars, with a three-quarter moon shining in a cloudless sky.

The campout, a late addition to the weekend itinerary, was Barclay's idea—a nostalgic nod to all the times he'd taken Cole and Scott camping when they were kids. Making it doubly disappointing that Cole bailed out.

Aidan still hasn't told the rest of the group, hoping Cole will change his mind. Maggie was right: They couldn't indulge Cole's bad mood. Time to lead by example.

He also hasn't yet told the guys that the ladies are joining them. Maybe he'll get shit for it, but ultimately, he doesn't care. Maggie and Piper have been a little silver lining in what otherwise has a been a disappointing weekend.

"So where's my grandson?" Barclay says.

Barclay insisted on helping Aidan pitch the tent. It's sturdy, high-quality, and essentially idiotproof. Aidan can manage himself, but with Cole missing, he's the only one not paired up.

"He'll be here later," Aidan says. "Probably."

"What do you mean, probably?"

Aidan hesitates before saying, "You know he and Scott aren't getting along."

"Well, you need to put a stop to that."

"They're adults, Dad."

It's a good time to tell him about Maggie and Piper—to change the subject. He does, and Barclay raises an eyebrow.

"Something going on that I should know about?" His tone is light, teasing. But it makes Aidan uncomfortable.

"Wasn't my idea," he grumbles.

"Pretty little lady, that Piper," he says. "I'm glad to see Cole moving on to greener pastures."

"They're just friends."

"Friends that go camping on a Saturday night," Barclay deadpans.

Maggie appears, lugging a suitcase and wearing impractical footwear—black leather boots with a heel. She's bundled in a faux-fur coat and a thick knit cap with a pom-pom on top. It's chilly out, but not that chilly.

"We're not sleeping out in the elements," Barclay says. "These tents are insulated."

"Hello to you too, Barclay," she says, unruffled. Her dark hair peeks out from the cap, framing her heart-shaped face.

"Where's Piper?" Aidan says.

"Oh—she can't make it. She has a headache."

Aidan feels Barclay's eyes on him, and he doesn't meet his gaze.

"So . . . just you?"

"It's just me," she says cheerily.

"Humph," Barclay says. Then, putting a hand on Aidan's shoulder, he says, "Friends that go camping on a Saturday night."

"What?" says Maggie.

"Nothing," Aidan says quickly. "Let's get your bags into one of the tents."

THE CAMPSITE IS fifteen minutes from the inn but feels like a world away. Out in the wilderness, in the darkness, gathered with a bunch of—well, let's face it—virtual strangers, Maggie tells herself she can drive back to her room and cozy bed anytime. Then, after a round of whiskey hot toddies around the open fire, she forgets all about that idea.

They're all sitting in a circle, the guys dressed in flannel shirts and hoodies and draped in blankets. Barclay stokes the flame with fresh kindling and Aidan's brother-in-law refills everyone's mug using a thermos. The sky is vast and velvety, a deep, dark blue dotted with countless stars that are unobstructed by city lights. The moon casts a silvery glow illuminating the silhouettes of tall oaks and maples, their branches now half bare.

The guys are teasing one of Scott's friends, calling him a teacher's pet because he was the most proficient knitter by the end of the workshop. A few of them got stitches onto their needles, but he showed a genuine aptitude. She doesn't understand why this should be something embarrassing.

"Knitting isn't a *feminine* thing," she says. "Not anymore. Just look on TikTok if you don't believe me."

Scott opens a package of graham crackers and passes around bars of chocolate. Aidan pops marshmallows on top of sticks and hands one to her.

"For s'mores."

She's never roasted marshmallows over an open flame before, and when she gives it a try she burns it to an inedible charred lump. Aidan shows her how to hold it an optimal eight inches from the flame, and to rotate the marshmallow slowly and steadily.

"I guess my team's lucky this wasn't one of the challenges," she says.

"Hate to break it to you, but you might be the only one

even in your own group who doesn't know how to do this. Roasting marshmallows is a basic life skill."

"I'd be offended if I didn't think you're probably right."

Clouds roll in, obscuring the moon. If it weren't for the fire, they'd be in pitch darkness. If Piper were there, Maggie would scoot closer to her. But she's sitting alone, in between Aidan and Scott. Somewhere in the distance, an owl calls out with a melancholy hoot.

"I think it's story time," Barclay says in a mock-spooky voice.

"The Soldier in the Woods," Scott says. She looks over at Aidan, and he's nodding in recognition.

"That's right: The Soldier in the Woods," Barclay says. "Do you boys know this story?"

Scott's friends tell him no, and a silence falls, the only sound is the crackle of the fire. Barclay starts to speak in a slow, exaggeratedly low voice: "Centuries ago, during the Revolutionary War right here in Bucks County, PA, a young private named James Douglas Finch fled his regiment, desperate to escape the bloodshed. As punishment for desertion, his fellow soldiers dragged him deep into the woods, bound his hands with rough rope, and tied him to a massive oak tree. He begged for mercy, but none came. They left him there to starve, his cries of suffering swallowed by the rustling leaves. Centuries passed, but James Douglas Finch never left. It's said that on nights when the fog rolls through the woods, you can hear the scrape of boots dragging through the underbrush and the creak of a rope swinging from a tree branch. Walkers who linger too long feel an unnatural chill wrap around their necks like cold hands . . ."

He falls silent, and Scott says, "Boo!" making her jump.

"Okay, no more of that," she says. "How about something less nerve-racking?"

"Like what? We got nothing but time out here," Barclay says.

She thinks about sleepovers from when she was a teenager. "How about Two Truths and a Lie?"

"Where's Cole? He'd be good at this game," Scott says, mostly to himself, but loud enough that Aidan hears and says, "That's enough."

Scott stands up and says he's going to turn in for the night. His tent-mates follow.

"Not so fast," Barclay says. "And by the way: I know that's code for going off to smoke the devil's lettuce. But before you leave: a toast."

Maggie turns to Aidan and mouths, *The devil's lettuce?*

Barclay stands up and raises his glass. "I want to take a moment to remind us what we're all celebrating here this weekend: My grandson Scott is getting married. Now, our friendly competition this weekend has been all about teamwork. And what a coincidence: So is marriage. In fact, there's no more important teammate than the person you choose to spend your life with. So, Scott, I congratulate you on taking this step with Ashley. May the fire you two build together burn long and bright."

It's a little corny, but Maggie feels a lump in her throat.

"Hear, hear," Aidan says, standing up. Everyone joins them, and Maggie self-consciously gets to her feet, feeling like an interloper. Drinking by the campfire is one thing. But it's clearly a family moment, and she doesn't belong. Clearly, it's time for her to go to her own tent too.

Chapter Twenty-Eight

PIPER LIES IN BED IN the dark, awake. She called Ethan back, but it went straight to voicemail. She keeps thinking about their last phone call from his perspective. What if he were on a trip having some random adventures with a strange woman? Staying at a romantic little inn? She'd be annoyed. But that doesn't mean she's done anything wrong. And if Ethan is worried about any misunderstanding, about her seeming too *available*, well, that's what engagement rings are for—signaling that you're off the market. She's not going to lose sleep tonight feeling guilty about making a new friend.

At this point, she wishes she'd gone camping after all. She could use the company.

Up above, floorboards creak in Kalli and Laurel's room. She imagines them settling in for the night, having some fun girl talk. The same thing she'd be doing with Maggie right now if she'd gone camping. And since Cole is the one who's responsible for her sitting alone in the room in the middle of her mother-daughter weekend, she figures she can bother him. It seems only fair.

She texts, asking if he really stayed behind all night. When he says yes, she admits she regrets not going out.

Your parent-trap idea better work or I just wasted a whole night of this trip being alone.

He writes back:

Don't be alone - u can hang w/me. I'm watching Don Draper.

She'd love to hang out and binge a show. But again, she thinks of Ethan. The optics are not good. But her need to escape her ruminations wins out. She changes back into her jeans and sneakers. This is strictly a friendly hang.

Cole's room is on the fourth floor, the Ben Franklin. When she reaches it, the door is ajar and the room is fully lit. Cole's still wearing the same clothes from earlier.

A big flat-screen mounted above the dresser is playing *Mad Men*. Piper watched the show with Maggie back when she was in high school. The world it depicts is so outrageously sexist, she found it hard to believe it reflected the reality of any time, ever. But Maggie swore it depicted the era accurately. "And it explains so much about my mother." All Piper could think was that it really sucked to be a woman in the 1960s. "Except for the clothes," Maggie said. "The clothes almost made up for the social oppression." This weekend, experiencing the gender-biased assumptions of the bushcraft-knitting challenge, she sees that as much as things change, they stay the same. So even though the competition is for fun, she wants to win.

"Our room doesn't have a TV," she says. "And I'm in a double."

"I guess they figure if two people aren't sleeping together they won't agree on a show to watch."

"Interesting theory," she says.

She sits in an orange upholstered armchair near the windows, acutely aware of the bed and her proximity to Cole.

"So, how do you think it's going out there in ye olde wilderness?" he asks.

"Hard to say. But why are you talking like it's the 1800s?"

"I figure that's when people spent a lot of time in ye olde woods," he says.

"Another interesting theory."

"I'm full of them."

Their eyes meet and she feels a little spark. Barely noticeable. But it's there. She looks away, pretending to check her phone. This was a bad idea. And Ethan has every reason to be annoyed with her.

"So are we going to talk about this or what?" Cole says.

"About what?"

Cole uses the remote to turn down the volume on the TV.

"So, obviously there's some . . . tension between us."

If she's going to convince Ethan that there's nothing for him to worry about, she should make sure of that. Right now.

"I'm completely in love with my boyfriend." It's true, but she wonders now if there's something wrong or missing. How can there still be room for her to be attracted to Cole?

"I'm not suggesting otherwise," Cole says. "And for the record, I'm in love with someone myself."

"The person you've been calling all weekend."

He nods.

"So . . . end of discussion. We're both on the same page, so to speak."

She's quiet for a minute. "My mother thinks I'm too young to be this serious about someone."

He shrugs. "Maybe we are. But speaking for myself, I know how I feel when I'm not with her. And I don't like it. So that's what I'm going on—not some vague idea of the ideal time or circumstance to fall in love."

She smiles. "I get it. And I agree."

"So . . . friends?" he says.

"Friends," she says, relieved. With that cleared up, she's eager to move on. "So why'd you get into a fight with your dad, anyway?"

Cole extends his arm, clicking the remote to get *Mad Men* rolling again. "Don't get me started. He forgets that I'm an adult now. My whole family does. No one has any boundaries. And I hate that word—it's a cliché. But there's no other way to put it."

"I get it," she says, though she doesn't think Maggie has boundary issues. Not really. Sure, she sometimes gives unsolicited opinions. But it's never been a real problem. Except maybe for the doubt she's planted in her mind about prioritizing her relationship with Ethan over mostly anything else.

Cole swings his legs over the side of the bed and walks to the mini fridge, offering her a beer. She shakes her head no. "We're both burdened with a single parent," he says. "All the pressure to make them proud. To somehow pay them back for doing it all, and doing it alone."

Hearing her own most private thoughts come out of Cole's mouth is shocking. And she realizes it's the first time she's discussed this with someone who can relate. "Sometimes I feel guilty for having my own life. Like, I'll be out with my boyfriend and thinking about my mom home alone."

"Do they get along? Your mom and your boyfriend?"

She considers that for a moment. "I've always thought so. But she thinks we're too young to be so serious. What about your dad and . . . Well, I guess he doesn't know about Kalli?"

Cole shakes his head. "I never discuss my personal life with my dad. Especially not lately. Sometimes, it's just better for our parents not to know. You get what I'm saying?"

She thinks so.

They sit with that for a moment, then he restarts the show and they watch until someone knocks on the door. Cole jumps up and goes to the door, opening it just enough to peek his head out into the hallway. She hears whispers, and then he says something like, "Just come in." Then, more whispers.

Cole steps away from the door, and Kalli walks in.

Piper's confused. Sure, she saw him helping her with her axe throw. But she didn't realize they'd hit it off enough to be hanging out.

"Hey, Piper," she says, giving her a smile.

"Hey," Piper says, standing up.

And then, silence. The air between Kalli and Cole is electric, like they're connected by an invisible forcefield. And then, it all clicks: Cole is Kalli's tragic romance. The man she met while married to someone else.

"Okay . . ." she says, eyes widening. "Well, it's late. I'll leave you two."

"Wait," Kalli says, stepping closer. "Please don't say anything to Laurel about seeing me here tonight."

Piper shakes her head. "I won't. But if this is a problem, why did you bring her along for a weekend with Cole?"

"A weekend with Cole? I didn't know he was going to be here," Kalli says. "Before this weekend, we hadn't spoken in two months. This really was supposed to be a girls' weekend getaway. To forget about him—which I haven't been able to do. And then I show up and he's here."

This really is a small town.

"But why all the secrecy now? I understand it wasn't ideal to meet while you were still married to someone else. But you're divorced," Piper says.

"*Getting* divorced," Kalli clarifies. "And Laurel thinks I need to deal with that—emotionally and legally—before I get involved with someone else."

"And my cousin knows the whole story and came down on me for it," Cole adds. "So no, we're not in a rush to have anyone see us together." He sits on the bed and Kalli moves next to him. He wraps his arm around her shoulders and she leans in close. He kisses the top of her head. "But we're going to prove the haters wrong."

Piper has a lot of questions. "Does this have anything to do with your fight with your dad?"

Kalli turns to him. "What happened?"

"Nothing happened. Except Scott must have told him something, because he started giving me a lecture at the axe place. But I don't think he knows any details, or that it's Kalli." He pauses, then adds, "But maybe that should change."

"Cole, no. Don't start anything," Kalli says.

"I'm not starting something. I wanna finish something. I love you, and I'm tired of apologizing for that." They kiss, and keep kissing, until Piper takes her cue to leave.

"All right guys . . . see you tomorrow."

She shows herself out then stands in the hall for a minute, processing. *I have to tell my mother about this.* Maggie likes to think she has every couple figured out from a mile away. But she didn't see this one coming. Her next thought is more complicated. It's something along the lines of, now *that's* passion. That's commitment. That's forward momentum.

It would be nice to feel a little more of that certainty in her own relationship.

Chapter Twenty-Nine

MAGGIE IS TUCKED INTO HER sleeping bag. Outside her tent, it's quiet. The bachelor party has disbanded, the campfire extinguished. Now she's in the dark, surrounded by virtual strangers. This was a stupid idea.

An animal howls in the distance. A coyote? A wolf? She doesn't know if they have wolves in Pennsylvania. But what is a wolf, really, except an extremely aggressive outdoors dog? She'll be fine.

She grabs her phone and is searching "dangerous woodland animals of Pennsylvania" when it buzzes with a call from Piper. She answers immediately. "I'm so happy to hear from you!"

"I was hoping I wasn't waking you," Piper says.

"Wake me? How can I sleep? It sounds like there are predators out here."

"Like . . . serial killers?"

"No. Wild animals."

Piper laughs. "Mom, it's Pennsylvania, not Tanzania. You're fine. Where's Aidan?"

"He's in his tent. Everyone is in their tents, and thanks to you I'm here alone. My chances of fending off a bear are greatly diminished by your absence."

"Well, try to survive the night. If you're really scared, go find Aidan. I'm sure he'll tell you there's nothing to worry about."

"I'm not going to bother Aidan. I'd rather get eaten by a bear."

"That's rational. All right, Mom. I just wanted to say goodnight—and thanks for this weekend."

Maggie smiles. "I love you, Piper. See you in the morning."

After the call, Maggie pulls the sleeping bag higher up her chest and stares up at the darkness. She hears rustling outside, and she sits up, heart pounding.

"Maggie?"

What's Aidan doing out there?

"Yes?" she says, incredulous.

"Can I talk to you for a minute?"

Okay. She unzips her sleeping bag, kicking it off. "Be right there." She pulls her hair loose from the messy ponytail and shakes it out. It's pitch black out, but she's not taking any chances.

The tent is sealed with a zipper and a series of hand-ties, and it takes her a few seconds to undo them all. She parts the curtain of fabric and steps out into the cool night. She hadn't realized how much warmer it is inside her tent.

"What's up?" she says.

Aidan has a thick blanket around his shoulders. She can barely make out his features in the moonlight.

"I'm checking on you. Listen, I've been camping out here my whole life. There's nothing to be afraid of."

"Oh, I'm not afraid," she says.

"Really? Because I heard you on the phone a minute ago."

He heard her stressing out about the wild animals? She closes her eyes for a second to process her mortification. "Sorry if I disturbed you. I was just talking to Piper. I'm a bit of a night owl."

"A night owl," he says.

"Yes."

"It sounded to me more like you're concerned about night owls. And other woodland creatures." He smiles to show he's not being unkind.

"You have remarkably good hearing."

"Not really. It's pretty quiet out here. And . . . my tent is only a few feet away."

"Right," she says. "Sorry about that."

She's aware of how she's dressed: sweatpants and two pairs of fuzzy socks and her pilled turtleneck over a flannel button-down. As much as she'd like to think it's campout chic, she knows it's more *Little House on the Prairie*.

"Do you want me to escort you back to the inn?" he says. "I don't want to torture you."

The offer is tempting. Except she's not a damsel in distress. She's a strong, competent, independent woman. Isn't that what she told him the first night they met? The campout isn't part of the bushcraft challenge, but there's no question that leaving would be a defeat.

And really, she doesn't actually want to leave. Standing there with Aidan, under the stars in the dark of night, she feels like anything could happen. And she likes it. It's been a long time since she had that sensation—utter freedom but also being without a net. It's like being twenty years old again.

"No, I'm fine. But I wish Piper had come along."

"I get it," he says with a sigh of empathy. "We both got dumped by our kids tonight."

They look at one another. The silence becomes heavy. Excruciating.

"Do you want to come in?" she says.

"To help fend off the wild beasts?" he says. "Sure. What kind of bushcrafter would I be if I didn't?"

"Is wild-beast fending on your itinerary?"

"That's how we traditionally close out these weekends."

They duck inside her tent and Aidan shines his phone so she can locate the small camping lantern next to her sleeping bag and turn it on.

"I feel better with that light on," she says. "I'm going to sleep with it."

"At this point, I'm surprised you actually agreed to do this," Aidan says.

"Me too. But that's how much I want Piper to have a great weekend. I can't say no to her." That doesn't explain why she's still out there. Alone in the tent with him. And they both know it. Sitting there on the ground, facing him a few feet apart in the glow of the lantern, the attraction is so obvious it's embarrassing. In the distance, she again hears the animal howl. But she's no longer afraid.

Aidan leans forward and kisses her.

Sunday

New Hope Knitting Retreat: Day 3

Course Offerings: Fair Isle Hap; Stranded Knitting and Mosaic; Seaming and Blocking; Tapestry Crochet.

4 p.m. Crafting and Tea Time in The Purl

~~**7 p.m. Evening Activity:** Closing Dinner Stitch & Share at Bucks Tavern~~

** updated: We'll be meeting in the Purl for a Sip & Stitch) at 6 p.m. before dinner at 7:30.

Chapter Thirty

PIPER CHECKS HER PHONE AS soon as she wakes up, but there are no updates from Maggie. And so, alone in the room, she sits in bed knitting small animal blankets she started last night.

When the sun comes up, she checks the Bucks Tavern breakfast service hours, and she throws on the jeans she's been wearing all weekend before making her way down to the lobby. She texts Ethan to call her when he's up. Still no word from Maggie.

Since she was alone in her tent when they spoke late last night, Piper assumes there was no love connection with Aidan Danby. Cole will be disappointed. And on the topic of Cole: She's still thinking about Kalli's surprise appearance, and the story of their romance. If they can work out their complicated situation, she has no excuse not to clear the air with Ethan. When she gets back to New York, she'll just confess about finding the ring and ask him if he's having second thoughts. It's as simple as that. If he says he's reconsidered taking that step, fine. It's better to know.

The restaurant is quiet; the only person she sees from the retreat is Sheila, who gives a wave from the self-serve coffee bar. She's dressed in a crochet muumuu with tassels at the ends of her sleeves.

"We missed you last night at karaoke," Sheila calls out.

"Thanks. I probably should have gone with you and the rest of the group. I planned to go to sleep early and that didn't happen."

Sheila shares some details of the evening while Piper navigates the coffee bar. She pours herself a medium roast and stirs in a scoop of brown sugar. Across the room, Cole ambles in and heads straight for a corner table. His hair is mussed like he just rolled out of bed, which is no doubt the case.

"Lexi and Dove will be down any minute," Sheila says. "I think Dove is almost ready to forgive Lexi for spending the afternoon axe-throwing yesterday. And are we finished with that, by the way? Because I don't know if their honeymoon can survive another day of competition." She gives Piper a wink. "But I'm not going to complain about a little male company."

"I'm not sure about the status of the whole bushcraft/knitting thing. But there's Cole Danby over there. I'll ask him."

Sheila adds whipped cream to her coffee. "Okay, doll. Report back."

Piper gives her a thumbs-up that says, *Will do*. She pours a second cup of coffee for Cole and carries it to his table. He's on his phone and doesn't notice her until she's pulling out the chair across from him.

"Hey," she says, slipping into the seat and sliding one of the mugs across the table.

He looks up, his under-eyes the color of a bruise.

"Hey," he says. "Oh—thanks. I need this."

"You look like it."

He yawns. "I didn't get much sleep."

"Spare me the details, please."

He shakes his head. "That's not what I meant. Any word from Maggie this morning?"

"Not yet." She takes a sip from her mug, wondering why

the coffee here tastes so much better. "The last I spoke to her she was in a panic about dangerous animals lurking in the woods. She said she heard strange noises."

"Sounds potentially fatal," he says. "Luckily, my father's out there to fend off any beasts of the wild. Do you know the human brain can't distinguish between love and fear?"

She's never heard that. "No. But if that's true, I'm sorry to say that's the closest she got to love last night. When we spoke she was in her tent—alone."

Cole takes a swig of the coffee. "Not surprising."

"Not surprising? I thought you said you thought there was something happening between the two of them. That was the whole point of you asking me to hang back myself last night."

"Maybe it was just wishful thinking."

She feels a stab of disappointment.

"Look," he says, "my dad met my mother when he was around our age, and that was it. And then after she died, he never even brought another woman around. Not once."

Piper is surprised. "He never dated again? I mean, it's been a long time."

"I'm sure there've been women," Cole says. "I'm not naive. But he never brought anyone home to be part of our family life."

A server stops by to hand them menus. Piper isn't hungry.

"You gonna order?" she asks him. She pulls one of her animal-blankets-in-progress out of her tote. It's still on the needles and she holds it up, careful not to let the stitches slide off.

"Maybe. I'm not a big breakfast person, but there's time to kill until the rest of the guys get back from the campground. What're you making there?"

"It's a blanket to donate to the animal refuge," she says. "I knit a few last night. When I worked at the shelter back home, I used to line the cages with them to make them cozy. I was thinking I could drop them off at BARR sometime before the end of the weekend."

"I'm sure Denise would appreciate that a lot." He checks his phone. "Wanna stop by before everyone gets back here? We can see how your bird is doing."

She'd been thinking about the fledgling. And there's still over an hour before the first class, Flawless Finish. At that point, she doesn't even know if her mother will be making it back in time for the workshop.

"Sure," she says. "Let's go."

BELINDA IS WORKING the front desk because they're short-staffed. Ordinarily, she doesn't mind desk duty, but it's the last full day of the retreat and she hates to miss the entire breakfast hour. And Max can't help out because he headed to Philadelphia to look at the town house she doesn't want.

The front desk phone rings, a caller asking about availability for a spring wedding. Belinda can't bring herself to admit—not to herself, and not to the caller—that the New Hope Inn might not exist in the spring. Who knows what a buyer might do with the place?

"Let me take your information and have our manager get back to you this afternoon." The manager being herself. Really, she has to wonder if he's truly thought this through. Sure, a big move—a big change—is attractive, like a wink from a stranger. But after the novelty wears off, Max will remember how much of their day-to-day lives is entwined with the inn. And by then it will be too late.

Maybe today, the simple act of discussing a spring wedding would be enough to reset the conversation. If money is the sole motivation for the sale, maybe they can explore ways to increase revenue. If he needs more time off, they can work that out too. There must be a compromise to be found somewhere.

"Excuse me."

Belinda looks up to find a fair-skinned woman with inky black hair wearing an eggplant-colored leather trench coat. Her lipstick matches the coat.

"Good morning. How can I help you?" Belinda says. Maybe she's an actress trying to find the playhouse next door.

"I'm looking for Piper Hodges. Can you ring up to her room?"

This gives Belinda pause. She can't disclose guest information. And in all the years she's been at the inn, this policy has never been tested. The dilemma must show on her face, because the woman adds, "I'm Gretchen Lundgren, her manager. She told me she's here."

Belinda tries the Margaret Mead landline, but no one answers.

"I can't reach Piper is at the moment. But you're welcome to have a seat and wait. Or try her cell phone?"

The woman lets out an impatient sigh. "If Piper were answering her phone, I wouldn't be standing here talking to you." Then, recognizing the sharpness in her tone, says, "I'm sorry. But this is time-sensitive business." With that, she turns and walks over to the seats closest to the fireplace.

Belinda reaches for her own phone. She doesn't have Piper's number, but she does have Maggie's. She gives her a call—not for the manager's sake, but for her own.

Something tells her this is something Maggie would want to know about. Immediately.

MAGGIE WAKES UP aching and stiff in her sleeping bag. She can tell, before she even moves, that her back will be punishing her for this. But the night was worth it. Who needs mobility?

She inches up on her elbows and looks over at Aidan. He's still asleep in his camping quilt. Sunshine streams down from the clear plastic skylight in the top of the tent, and she takes the moment to look at him without being self-conscious. For once, she doesn't have to pretend not to notice how handsome he is. She sees the light auburn in his stubble and resists the urge to reach out and touch it.

The minute he kissed her, she realized how very much she liked him, and that the feelings had been brewing since Friday night at the bar. Feelings strong enough that she had sex in a tent. A first for her. It feels like something she might have experienced in her twenties if her life had taken a different turn. The fact that it happened now, at her age, feels like a gift from the universe.

She reached over slowly, careful to avoid any abrupt movements that might wake him, and drags her handbag closer by the strap. When it's within reach, she reaches inside and pulls out her NARS compact. She has bedhead (tent head?) and her lips look red and chapped. That, she knows, isn't from the cold. It's from all the kissing they did last night. She hasn't kissed like that in years. The thought gives her a delicious little shiver.

Aidan stirs and she immediately looks away, concerned that somehow her gaze silently disturbed him.

"Hey," he says.

"Hi," she says.

"We survived the night."

"No bear attacks," she says, smiling. "But thank you for sticking around just in case."

"Well, when you put it that way, I feel a little used," he says, grinning back at her.

Her phone rings. She glances down, certain it's Piper checking in on her. But it's Belinda.

Strange. She mentally runs through the day's itinerary. Is she late for something?

She flashes the phone screen at Aidan, mouthing *odd*, before answering.

"Hi, Belinda," she says. "Everything okay?"

"Yes, I'm actually trying to reach Piper but I don't have her number."

Maggie's confused. "Why do you need Piper?"

"There's a woman here . . . says she's her manager?"

Maggie sits up all the way. "What do you mean by *here*?"

"Standing in the lobby. With a very impatient look on her face."

What the hell is happening? There must be some mistake.

"Can you put her on the phone?"

She hears the thunk of the landline receiver on the hard wooden desk, and then muffled background noise. After a moment, a strange voice says, "This is Gretchen."

After all the years of hearing about Gretchen, after the giant opportunity she gave her daughter, this is the first she's ever spoken to her. She imagined one day when she met Gretchen she'd have the opportunity to thank her. Somehow, she feels like instead she's going to be dealing with something unpleasant and messy.

She texts Piper.

Call me ASAP!!

"Gretchen, this is Maggie Hodges, Piper's mother. Is there a problem?" She keeps her eyes on her phone for a response from Piper. Nothing.

"Yes, there's a problem. I have a job for her, and she's not returning my calls."

What? There must be a misunderstanding. Piper would

never blow off her manager. At least, not on purpose. But then, Gretchen was no longer her manager. None of this makes sense,

Maggie looks at her phone, willing a response from Piper. Still nothing.

"Gretchen, if you can just wait there for a few minutes," Maggie says, already looking around for her jeans. "I'll find Piper."

Chapter Thirty-One

AIDAN SNUCK BACK INTO HIS own tent before the other guys noticed he'd ever left. The one benefit of Maggie having to run off back to the inn so early was that they both avoided a walk of shame.

For someone who always prides himself on being discreet, last night was a big risk. One he surprised himself by taking. Maybe it was the whiskey, or maybe it was just the simple fact that he's attracted to her. She's beautiful, sure. But the world is full of beautiful women. It's more the connection he feels to her, how easy it is to talk about the one aspect of his life that, after all these years, he still feels uncertain about: fatherhood.

Maggie's situation with Piper is different in the details, but similar at the core: Single parenthood is a bitch. It's isolating as hell. Maggie gets it because she's lived it.

That doesn't excuse his behavior last night. The bushcraft weekend is to celebrate his nephew's impending nuptials, not to have a fling of his own.

He rolls up his camping quilt and shrugs off his jacket. The morning is warming up already. Bucks County in the fall is perfection.

"Uncle Aidan, you in there?" Scott calls out. Aidan can see his silhouette framed by sunlight outside the tent.

Aidan unzips the front tent flap and steps out into the sun, shielding his eyes with his hands.

"Morning, Scott."

"My dad's still asleep, but I'm heading back to the inn for breakfast with my friends."

"No foraging? I'm sure your grandfather has ideas about finding some berries or something around here."

"Good one. Nah, we're hunting down some pancakes. But I wanted to talk to you before we go." He looks around the tent. "So Cole never showed up last night."

"No. He didn't. He's just dealing with some stuff. It's nothing personal." He puts his hands on his nephew's shoulders. He hates to think of Scott and Cole at odds. Family is too important.

"This is messed up, Uncle Aidan."

"Like I said—it's not personal."

"I know exactly what it is." He takes a step closer to Aidan, lowering his voice even more. He nods toward the tent. "Let's talk for a minute."

Aidan turns back and opens the entry flap, holding it for Scott. "After you." He follows him inside. Really, he just wants coffee. But he's gotta clear this business out of the way first.

"So, what's on your mind, Scott?"

"Grandpa told you about Cole and the married woman."

"To an extent. I don't know the details and I don't want to know. It's not really our business. From what I understand, Cole did the right thing. The relationship is over. So, let's all just move on. It's certainly nothing for you two to fight about."

"Don't you want to know how I found out about it?" Scott says. Clearly, he wants to tell him. But Aidan's had enough of this. "The only reason I even know about it is because my fiancée works at the same school as the woman he's had the affair with. She's friends with the woman's husband from college."

Aidan is losing his patience. "Again, not our business."

"Well, Cole made it my business. Or maybe it's a coincidence, but I don't buy that. She's here this weekend. She's part of the knitting retreat."

Aidan isn't sure he's heard him right. He has to let that sink in for a few seconds.

"Who?"

"Kalli Dimitrou."

The dark-haired woman. No wonder Cole was so enthusiastic about taking the knitting class. And he's the one who chose seats at that table next to her yesterday.

"Tell me everything," Aidan says.

The coffee will have to wait.

MAGGIE HAS NO idea what Piper's manager is doing in New Hope, but she welcomes the excuse to slip away from the campsite early and discreetly. A one-night stand is not respectable behavior for a mother-daughter weekend. She doesn't need the whole rest of the inn to know about it. She'll 'fess up to Piper, though. That is, if she ever gets to talk to her again. She still isn't answering her phone or the hotel room.

By the time Maggie reaches the inn, she's starting to worry. Belinda is behind the front desk and tells her, "Your visitor is right over there." She nods her head to a seating area just off the main floor, where Gretchen Lundgren sits in a paisley wingback chair next to a wall of framed historical prints. With her stark hair and leather trench, the fashion executive looks more like a futuristic visitor. A character out of *The Matrix*.

Gretchen Lundgren looks up as Maggie approaches and introduces herself. The woman stands, revealing herself to be tiny.

"Apologies for intruding on your trip," she says. "But Piper is ignoring my messages and I need an answer."

Maggie's confused. "I'm sorry, I don't know what you're talking about."

Gretchen looks at her with undisguised irritation. "I'd like to talk to Piper."

"Of course," Maggie says, flustered. "I'm sorry she never got back to you. She might just need a weekend off."

"Don't we all," Gretchen says. "But Piper has a brief window to turn failure into opportunity. I understand she's probably embarrassed, but she's got to dust herself off and get back out there."

It's Maggie's fault. She's the one who insisted on the weekend getaway. She didn't imagine there'd be work for her so soon after falling on the runway.

"She told me you fired her as a client."

Gretchen gives an impatient wave, like batting away an insect, and mutters something under her breath. Maggie again dials Piper's number and it goes straight to voicemail. Gretchen is now also busy tapping away on her phone.

"I'm sure she'll be here any minute," Maggie says. "Why don't we go have coffee?"

"Coffee would be nice," Gretchen says with a tight smile.

Maggie leads her through the lobby to the interior entrance to Bucks Tavern, where she finds the knitting gang at one big table. It seems almost everyone is there except for Piper. And no one knows where she is. Sheila's the only one who saw her this morning, but only briefly.

A host seats the two of them at a table near the self-serve coffee station. Maggie's mind is racing. Maybe Piper is avoiding Gretchen on purpose since she fired her. She's probably distrustful. But when she floats that idea to Gretchen, she says, "I apologized to Piper for my lapse in judgment. And I'll continue to apologize. But in the meantime, there's an opportunity on the table. Real money. And I don't like to lose out on money. I'm hoping she feels the same."

The more she hears, the less any of it makes sense. Why would Piper blow off a second chance with Gretchen? The answer is, she wouldn't. She must be avoiding her phone for another reason, and Gretchen fell through the cracks. Maybe Piper's taking some space from Ethan. That's a possibility.

"I'm sure there's an explanation for all this," Maggie says.

Gretchen isn't listening. Her eyes are locked on something behind Maggie.

"I recognize that woman," Gretchen says. Maggie turns. The only person she sees is Hannah Elise, sitting at the far end of the bar working a pair of needles, a trail of yarn unspooling from her bag. She's wearing a fabulous, distinctly Hannah Elise outfit: crocheted pants of contrasting textures and colors paired with a simple white T-shirt and elbow-length knit arm warmers.

"The knitter? With the curly hair?" Maggie says.

"Yes. She's the one in the videos."

"What videos?"

"Piper's social. Her posts. Do you know her?" Gretchen says.

Maggie nods. "She's an instructor here."

"Can you introduce me?"

Maggie welcomes any distraction while they wait for Piper. Hannah Elise doesn't look up from her crochet even when they're standing right beside her. She's absorbed in her craft, her hands moving with speed and confidence, her posture straight, her face relaxed and content.

"Hi, Hannah Elise—good morning," Maggie says.

She looks up.

"Hey, Maggie. You and Piper coming to my Shetland Hap workshop?"

"Yep. We'll be there."

Beside her, Gretchen clears her throat.

"Um, Hannah, this is Gretchen Lundgren," Maggie says. "Gretchen, this is Hannah Elise, one of the instructors here."

Gretchen extends her hand. "I'm with GMI Management."

Hannah Elise's eyes widen.

"I noticed your video with Piper Hodges," Gretchen says. "You made me want to drop everything and pick up a crochet hook. And I have zero interest in knitting," she continues. "So I checked out your account. You have an impressive following."

Hannah Elise beams. "Thank you!"

The bartender appears with a latte for Hannah Elise. It's embellished with a foam pumpkin design.

"And *you* have a great look," Gretchen says. "Have you ever considered modeling?"

Maggie's can't believe what she's hearing. It's almost as if she witnessed Ethan hitting on another woman. Well, not exactly. But still: Piper doesn't return a few phone calls and Gretchen is ready to move on?

"Excuse me for a minute. I'm going to call Piper again."

She walks briskly back to the lobby and by the time she reaches the front desk she hears raised voices. There, right in the curve of the room just before the stairs come into view, she sees Kalli and Aidan's nephew Scott arguing. She had no idea they even knew one another; it's the first time she's seen them interact all weekend.

Scott isn't particularly tall—certainly not compared to Aidan and Cole. But he still towers over Kalli, and her body language suggests she's shrinking back away from him, her arms crossed protectively in front of herself while she says, emphatically, "It wasn't planned!"

"I don't believe you," Scott says.

"Why is this your business?"

"It's my bachelor party. And he's my family."

Belinda is no longer behind the front desk. So if anyone's going to intervene, it's going to be Maggie. She walks over to the two of them and stands close enough to reach out and touch Scott.

"Excuse me," she says. "Everything okay here?" She looks pointedly between the two of them. Kalli's face is flushed. Scott crosses his arms now too.

"Everything's fine," he says, looking at her. "Is my uncle with you?"

"No," she says, feeling herself blush.

Kalli turns and walks away to the stairwell. Scott shakes his head and walks in the opposite direction, leaving Maggie standing alone and wondering what she just interrupted.

Then she remembers why she wanted to be alone in the lobby in the first place. She dials Piper and it again goes straight to voicemail.

"Piper, I don't know what's going on with you, but you have to call me back. I'm getting upset."

THERE ARE MOMENTS in life that are like highway signs. If you're paying attention, they let you know when to get on or off the road.

At the animal shelter, Piper and Cole check their bags and phones at the door. He chats up another person he's friendly with, while she follows Denise to the back. She's delighted to see all the soulful eyes peeking out from cages, the air marked by the distinct scent of fur and feathers. She experiences a deep twinge, something like homesickness. She experienced something similar yesterday when they first walked in, but hadn't fully understood it. Now she does.

"This is so generous of you," Denise says, unfolding one of the blankets and showing a colleague.

Denise leads her to the birdcage where the baby sparrow is recovering. He hops around a makeshift nest of dried leaves and twigs.

"He's healthy," Denise says. "The leg you told us about wasn't an injury. That's a natural stance for hatchlings this young. But you did the right thing bringing him in—he was completely vulnerable to predators on the ground."

"So tell me what's next for our little guy here?" she says.

While Denise explains the process of easing him back into the wild, Piper's distracted by the movement of a sleek-looking cat roaming a cage. With its leopard-like coat, it appears to be a Bengal. This particular one has eyes like green glass and a penetrating gaze.

"Wow," Piper says. It's only the second time she's seen a Bengal in real life, and the last time hadn't been this close. She's seen one loose in Central Park, the tragic dumping ground for a lot of Manhattan pets. "That's a Bengal, right?" Piper says.

Denise turns to look at the cat. "That's Roxie. Yeah, she's a beauty. A family brought her in last week. They found her wandering near the canal. They tried to keep her, but she was aggressive with the kids."

She walks toward the Bengal and Piper follows her. "It's hard to see her confined to a cage," Piper says. Bengals are particularly high-energy cats, and there's no room in the space for a climbing tree or anything to give it exercise.

"I know. After we rehab her injured leg, we're going to find a home for her."

"Hey there, Roxie girl," Piper says. The cat looks at her

with something like disgust. She stands straight and regal, those remarkable eyes unblinking. Piper feels a strong pull to the animal. It's like that sometimes—a mix of curiosity and affection that gives her an overwhelming need to connect with them.

"When there aren't any other animals or birds loose, I try to let her stretch her legs a bit. We can try that now." Denise opens the cage and the cat emerges gingerly. Piper sits on the ground and makes soft clucking sounds, hoping the creature will come close enough to pet her. It's a long shot, but she wants to try.

"You can give her one of these," Denise says, handing her a cat treat. Piper takes it from her, but before she can unwrap it the cat is walking slowly toward her, pupils dilated, in playful hunt mode. Piper drums her fingers on the floor to entice the cat to pounce on them, and she does. Then Roxie slinks closer to Piper.

"Hi, beautiful girl," she says. The cat walks onto her lap and she finishes opening the treat, and holds the plastic wrapper out so Roxie can lick the creamy salmon concoction. After she devours the first bit, Piper pulls the treat back to squeeze more to the top, and before she realizes it Roxie is in her face taking a big swipe at her. Piper doesn't feel the scratch at first, but when she realizes what's happened she touches her cheek and sees blood on her fingertips.

"Oh! Jesus, let me see that," Denise says, rushing over. "Are you okay? I'm so sorry."

"I'm fine," she says, "Don't be upset with the cat. It was just an accident."

Except: wasn't an accident.

Five minutes ago, she didn't fully understand why she'd been avoiding Gretchen. But it's because she knows she wants to tell her, *Thanks but no thanks.* And a part of her—a big part—is afraid she won't go through with it. So she's doing nothing. Except putting her face in front of that feral cat wasn't *nothing*.

Cole walks in, sees her sitting on the floor and bleeding, and says, "Damn, Hodges. I can't leave you city folks alone for a minute. Let's get you back to the inn."

Chapter Thirty-Two

MAGGIE CHECKS THE ROOM AND Piper's not there. Now she's getting angry. This is just inconsiderate. And fine, yes, Maggie did spend the night out. But Piper basically insisted. That doesn't mean it's okay to go incommunicado. And to ignore Gretchen like that? And also: Why didn't she mention that her manager wants her back? The whole situation is disturbing.

She's mulling all of this while she takes the stairs back down to the lobby—at the same moment Aidan is heading up. Her stomach does a little flip.

"Hey. Sorry I ran off like that," she says. "I've been trying to find Piper."

"No problem. And also, what a coincidence. I'm trying to find Cole."

Their eyes meet. Oh? *Oh.*

"You don't think. . . ." Under normal circumstances, Maggie would never imagine Piper cheating on Ethan. But Piper and Cole both chose to stay back at the inn last night. And now they're both apparently missing from their respective groups. So it's hard not to at least consider the possibility.

"At this point, I have no idea what my son is up to," Aidan says.

His eyes have flecks of gold and burnt umber as if they're reflecting the season itself. *Autumn Aidan*, she thinks. Two days ago, this man was a stranger. And now? What? They aren't together. They'll probably never see each other again after the weekend. But in this moment, at least, it's something. And he must feel it too, because he leans forward and kisses her. It's even better than she remembered from last night.

"Mom?"

She turns around to find Piper and Cole making their way up the stairs. She'd be embarrassed—busted, as the kids say—but she notices something odd about Piper's face. There's a streak of makeup, maybe lipliner. It takes a few seconds for Maggie to comprehend that the bright red mark on Piper's cheek isn't cosmetics—it's a bloody scratch.

"What happened to your face?" she says, aghast. Piper's hand immediately flies up to cover it.

"Where were you two?" Aidan says to Cole.

"Why do I feel like we just got caught breaking curfew?" Cole says.

"I don't know. Why *do* you?" Aidan says.

"Hey, folks," Barclay calls from the bottom landing. "Aidan, I've been looking all over for you boys. Did you lose track of our itinerary? It's time for fishing."

"Excuse us," Maggie says, taking Piper by the elbow and steering her down the stairs, past Barclay, into the lobby. Ignoring Gretchen and then messing up her face? "Are you *trying* to destroy your own career?"

Maggie stops walking. That's exactly it: Piper is sabotaging her career. She's been quiet quitting. Except when her manager shows up on their knitting retreat, it's not so quiet anymore. And now she, Maggie, is involved. And so she's going to fix it.

WHEN MAGGIE AND Piper leave, Cole takes it as his cue to do the same. Aidan follows him up one flight of stairs to his room on the third floor, where Cole doesn't invite him in.

"Dad, not now," he says. "I'm dealing with something." His voice is low in consideration of other guests on the floor.

"I *know* you're dealing with something. Did you invite your girlfriend to come here this weekend?"

Cole's jaw pulses in the way it does whenever he's stressed or irritated. After a pause, he unlocks his room and waves him inside, closing the door behind them. The space is tidy—Cole's always been remarkably neat. He takes after his mother in that way. The thought of Nancy gives him a sense of urgency; he owes it to her not to bungle this conversation.

"I didn't invite Kalli this weekend. I had no idea she'd be here. And actually, it turns out to be exactly what we needed. Except for Scott and his unwelcome opinions. But then, you know that. I assume he's the one who told you about my personal life."

Aidan wants to say, *Why didn't you tell me about your personal life?*

"I think Scott just wants what's best for you. He's getting married. He probably knows a thing or two about navigating relationships, and how hard it can be under the best of circumstances. Why make things harder for yourself getting involved with an unavailable woman?"

"She *is* available." Cole shakes his head. "This is why I didn't tell you about her months ago. I didn't want to upset you."

Aidan doesn't buy that for a second. Cole knows he's handled a lot tougher things than a relationship he might not approve of. This is something else. Cole is embarrassed by the situation he finds himself in.

"I think you didn't want to tell me because you didn't want to admit you were doing something wrong," Aidan says.

Cole gives a small laugh. "It never seemed wrong to me. I'm sorry you haven't met anyone since Mom. Maybe you forget what it feels like to fall in love."

That stings. Aidan feels a flash of defensiveness. But then, Cole might be right. Regardless of all that, he's still not happy with the way this all unfolded.

"I'm troubled you think I'd judge you over your relationship. I might not always agree with your choices, Cole, but I want you to feel you can talk to me."

Cole looks skeptical. "And what would you have told me if I said I was in love with a married woman?"

He's never heard Cole use the word *love* about a girlfriend.

"Well," he says carefully, "I would have told you that I just don't want you to get hurt. I know we can't always control who we have feelings for. But some choices are less likely than others to lead to a good outcome."

"No one knows what's going to lead to a good outcome," Cole says. "Look at you. You did everything right. I can't imagine finally finding the right person, marrying them, and then losing them."

Aidan feels stricken. The last thing he wants is for his son to feel sorry for him.

"Yes, it was difficult. But Cole, that has nothing to do with my concern for your relationship choices. Any parent would feel the same way."

Cole shakes his head. "Dad, I get it. Hell, I'd want to play it safe after all that too. But that's not my approach. I'm willing to get hurt. To me, with Kalli, the upside is worth it. I don't expect you to agree or understand, and I'm sorry if it upsets you. So I'll respect your choices if you can respect mine."

"I'm not playing it safe," Aidan says. He's reeling. It's like someone just held up a mirror to his face, he looked into it, and the reflection is not his own. He doesn't like the feeling. Not one bit. And he's going to do something about it.

MAGGIE IS WALKING through the lobby so fast Piper needs to trot to keep up with her. They pass Lexi and Dove on their way to the Purl, a workshop that at this point Piper and Maggie will miss.

"You two coming?" Lexi calls out.

Maggie doesn't slow down, leaving Piper no time to answer. She just gives a half wave, half thumbs-up, and keeps walking a step or two behind Maggie.

Piper really wishes her mother would back off.

"This doesn't need to involve you," she says.

"That would be a lot more convincing if your manager hadn't crashed our weekend," Maggie says.

"Ex-manager."

"Not according to Gretchen," Maggie says. Piper follows her around the corner into the wide stone hallway leading to Bucks Tavern.

"So now you're on her side?"

That stops Maggie right in her tracks. She turns to look at Piper.

"Since when are there *sides*? I don't know what's going on with you, but I'm not going to let you throw away this opportunity."

"It's not your choice!" she says, louder than she intended. The words just burst out before she could modulate her voice. And the effort to contain them leaves her shaking.

Maggie looks hurt and shocked as if Piper smacked her across the face. Worse, she says nothing. They just stand there looking at each other for what feels like an eternity. Piper can't take it anymore and continues walking without her.

"So you're quitting?" Maggie says from behind her. "Just like that? I have to say, Piper, that's extremely disappointing."

Piper turns around, her heart pounding. "Well, I knew that was coming."

"What's that supposed to mean?" Maggie crosses her arms, her expression stony. Piper can't remember the last time she had an argument with her mother, and she'd do anything to hit the pause button, to save both of them from the painful and unfamiliar experience of being in conflict. But she can't. There's only one thing to do, and it's something she should have done when she first met Gretchen, and that's be honest with her mother—and herself.

"It means, from the moment I told you about meeting Gretchen, I knew on some level I'd end up disappointing you. Because I never wanted that job. I did it for you."

"Don't put this on me! You're the one who doesn't even appreciate the opportunities you have in front of you."

"I *do* appreciate opportunities in front of me. I'm simply not choosing the one *you* would choose. And you have to learn to deal with that instead of trying to control my life."

She brushes past Maggie to find Gretchen. She can't wait to tell her she's done.

Chapter Thirty-Three

*B*ELINDA DECIDES THAT SINCE THE Cavanaugh party is joining the group tonight, she'll host in the lobby instead of in the Purl. She's always wanted to throw a big celebration in that space. And now, since there isn't a single guest at the inn who isn't also coming to the party, it's the perfect chance to experiment with transforming the space from functional to festive. Maybe her *last* chance.

She pushes that thought away.

The lobby doesn't have the dramatic water views of the Purl, but it has the grandeur of its history. She strings lights along the mantel and railings, sets out a few baskets of pumpkins and gourds, and programs a playlist with songs from Norah Jones, Jackson Browne, the Lumineers. The corner just past the front desk is a perfect space for a self-service bar, with a side table that can serve as a nice little station for mulled cider and cinnamon sticks.

The front door opens, bringing a gust of fresh cool air—along with Max's return.

Belinda stands from the crouch position she'd been in, arranging a garland of faux autumn leaves around the lobby stair's banister.

"I'm surprised to see you back so soon," she says. She

doesn't mean it to come across as negative, but Max looks mildly wounded.

"Well, one of the places I was going to look at fell through. But the place on Chestnut is in mint condition. There's no way it will still be on the market by the time we're ready to make an offer. But it's good to know things like that are out there."

She turns back to the garland, willing him to stop talking. She doesn't want to hear any more. He'll ruin her weekend if she allows it.

"So, the good news is, I can come to your shindig tonight after all," he says.

She stops weaving the garland in between the wooden slats, her body going still.

"You really don't have to. I shouldn't even have brought it up," she says. There's a beat of silence, but she keeps her back to him.

"Well," he says finally. "I want to."

Belinda stares straight ahead at the stairs, blinking back tears. "I actually don't want you to come. It's just going to remind me what's going on with this place . . . the sale . . . everything I'm trying not to think about."

Behind her, she feels him move closer until his arms encircle her. She lays her head back against his shoulder, trying to feel connected. But the simple joy she felt decorating a moment earlier is gone, replaced by a sinking sense of dread.

Someone calls out her name. She and Max move in tandem, turning around to find Hannah Elise standing near the front desk.

"Sorry to interrupt," Hannah Elise says.

"No—no, not at all." Belinda straightens her cardigan and crosses the room to be closer to her. "I'm glad you stopped by before things get busy. Change of plan: We're still having the Sip & Stitch but the bachelors are coming too . . ."

Hannah Elise looks tense. "Belinda, this is really difficult for me to say, but I have to leave."

"You mean . . . out to lunch?"

"No, I mean I have to leave the retreat. I'm really, really sorry."

"Are you okay?"

In all her years of hosting the retreats she's never lost an instructor in the middle of a weekend.

"Yes. It's just . . . I have an opportunity I can't pass up. I've been recruited by a talent manager and she wants me in New York for a casting—like, now."

Belinda can't make sense of what she's saying. How did this come out of nowhere?

"It's Sunday. Do you have to respond today?"

"Well, yes—she's here, actually. And she'll give me a ride back to the city."

Hannah Elise rattles off some story about Piper Hodges's manager. Is that why the woman showed up at the inn? "She wants me to go back with her. I feel terrible about this, but you know I've been trying to grow as a knitting influencer, and this will take me to a whole other level."

Belinda glances at Max, who's busy fiddling with the sound system wiring and pretending not to listen. But she knows he hears every word. She feels embarrassed for some reason, as if Hannah Elise quitting undermines the value of her entire endeavor. As if it's a sign that Max is right and she's holding on to something unreasonably.

"Can this wait a few hours?" she says.

Hannah Elise runs her hand through her mass of loose curls, looking at her with doe eyes and saying something about not sure if she can get a train ticket for later in the day and her return trip tomorrow is too late. "I'm so sorry, Belinda. I just hate my day job so much and this is a big opportunity for me. And I don't expect to get paid for the weekend, obviously."

The money is the least of Belinda's concerns. Hannah Elise has two workshops left on the schedule. Belinda has a thought: Maggie Hodges. She did a fine job teaching the bachelors' intro class. She was patient, methodical and inventive with her troubleshooting tips. And Belinda liked the way she made a point to show how a mistake could, in a different pattern, turn out to be a useful technique.

Belinda can really use Maggie's creative problem-solving right about now.

PIPER WALKS ALONG Main Street, the bustling and vibrant brick paths dusted with gold and crimson leaves fluttering from old maples and oaks. The door to a nearby bakery is propped open, and she smells cinnamon and freshly brewed coffee. The contrast between the bucolic town and her state of mind is jarring.

She keeps mentally replaying the scene with Gretchen, who looked at her with disgust. *Your face! Is that why you've been ignoring my messages? If so, you should have just told me. I wasted a whole day coming up here.*

People stroll along the sidewalks, wrapped in cozy scarves and wool coats. The rhythmic clink of bicycles passing by reminds her to pay attention, not to get completely lost in her thoughts. She walks past the canal, water reflecting the amber hues of the trees that line the banks. A street vendor calls out to her, trying to sell her on caramel apples, warm cider and jars of local honey. Piper stops for a cider.

She turns left, onto the street with the vintage shop. The familiar path reminds her of how she felt two days earlier when Gretchen first left a voicemail. Arguably, Piper is in a better place now, forty-eight hours later. She's been honest with herself and with Maggie. She ended her business relationship with Gretchen. So why doesn't she feel more relieved? She sits on a wrought-iron bench across the street from the vintage shop. She's wearing the Doc Martens Maggie bought for her. And she regrets her harsh words during the argument back at the inn. She knows her mother isn't trying to control her life. She was just lashing out because of the pressure she put on *herself* to make her mother's years of sacrifice worthwhile.

She checks her phone and sees a missed call from Ethan. They haven't spoken since their awkward conversation last night about Cole. She tries him back and is relieved when he answers.

"Hey—sorry I missed your call," she says.

"No problem, but I'm on the subway so I might lose you," he says.

"I miss you too," she says quickly, then realizes that's not what he said.

"You doing all right?"

"I'm fine," she says unconvincingly. Then she tells him about Gretchen's surprise appearance, and quitting, and the confrontation with her mother. But she feels bad telling him about the fight with her mother since he's been knocking her all weekend.

"I'm proud of you."

"For what?"

"Making your own decisions. Living your own life."

"I was mean to my mom."

"Piper, I'm sure you weren't. Telling her something she doesn't agree with isn't being mean. Having boundaries isn't mean. You were just speaking your truth."

She looks around. Couples push strollers and college kids are taking videos and a guy on a bike is decked out in gear like he's peddling in the Tour de France. And she thinks, sure, Ethan applauds her truth when it's directed at Gretchen and Maggie. But how much would he like it if she vented her frustration with *him*?

"Ethan, did you change your mind about us planning a future together?"

"Why would you ask that?"

Should she admit to finding the ring? Not now. Not on the phone. So instead, she says something else that's bothering her. "I've felt really disconnected from you all weekend."

"Is that why you're hanging out with that guy Cole?"

Piper feels bad he'd even think to ask that. "Absolutely not."

He's quiet. Doesn't he trust her?

She swallows hard. Everything in her life feels uncertain. She'd thought two things were rock solid: her relationship with her mother and her future with Ethan. Now that foundation seems cracked.

"Ethan?" The call's been dropped. They've lost their connection.

Literally.

MAGGIE WAITS IMPATIENTLY for Hannah Elise to show up for the Fair Isle Hap workshop.

A "hap" is a traditional Shetland Shawl, and the technique originated in the Shetland island north of Scotland. She learned it herself years ago, something she'd discussed with Belinda at the opening-night dinner. But she'd been looking forward to seeing Piper try it for the first time. Now it seems that isn't going to happen: Piper's a no-show. Maybe she should have expected as much after their argument.

Where had Piper gotten it into her head that Maggie gave

up her dreams for her? She'd never said that—never suggested it or even thought about it, really. She's sure of it. Sure, it was thrilling for her to know that her daughter was walking in shows for designers she herself admired. And yes, Piper's fashion career feels like a form of delayed gratification; Maggie ended up with a connection to the fashion industry after all. Piper's career is a precious, unexpected consolation prize.

And how was she supposed to know that Piper was unhappy modeling? She distinctly remembers watching the movie *The Devil Wears Prada* together. They both agreed with Meryl Streep during that last Paris scene, when her character turns to Anne Hathaway and says—of the absurdities and sacrifices of life in fashion—"Don't be ridiculous, Andrea: *everyone wants this*." They had agreed! And so no, she doesn't think she missed some big clue. If Piper had been unhappy, she'd hidden it from her. The realization gives Maggie a sense of deep loneliness.

When is this class going to start? She checks her phone for the time and sees a text from Aidan.

> I hope things went better between you and Piper than with me and Cole. Time for a drink tonight? Before the festivities?

It's tempting. She can confide in him. Tell him what's going on without the risk of judgment. Aidan, of all people, can relate. But she can't commit to slipping away for some time with Aidan. She has one night left to salvage what's left of their mother-daughter weekend, and that's her priority.

Belinda walks into the room, apologizing for the delay, assuring everyone the workshop will start in just a few minutes. Then she turns to Maggie. "Can I talk to you for a minute?"

"Um, sure."

What now? Maggie thinks, following her out into the hall. Had Belinda witnessed her argument with Piper? Or maybe she ran into Piper and saw she was upset.

"What's going on?" she says anxiously.

"I know this is a big ask," Belinda says, wringing her hands. "But can you teach this workshop?"

"This one as in here, now?"

"Yes."

"What about Hannah Elise?"

"It appears Piper's agent stole her away from us."

It's surprising, but not as surprising as it should be. After all, Maggie had been the one to introduce them. Maggie presses her hand to her forehead. What more could go wrong?

She wants to help out—she feels partially responsible for Gretchen Lundgren showing up in New Hope in the first place. But she's not sure she's capable of teaching something as advanced as the Shetland Hap.

"I don't mean to put you on the spot," Belinda adds. "It's your vacation."

"You're not putting me on the spot. I'm just not sure I can do a good job."

Belinda reaches out and puts a hand on her shoulder. "I'm willing to take that chance. If you are."

Sure. Why not? What's the worst that can happen? With knitting, even when she messes up, she knows how to fix it.

If only life were more like knitting.

Chapter Thirty-Four

THE GLOW OF THE FIREPLACE casts flickering shadows on the lobby's stone walls. Belinda takes a moment to look around the room, and it confirms what she's come to expect over the years: The Sip & Stitch is the moment when the group of former strangers becomes a sort of knitting family. Anyone peeking in at the party wouldn't be able to tell who'd just met three days ago and who'd arrived already friends. And everyone is dressed in their handiwork: Sheila wears a floor-length Granny Square cape, Laurel sports a knit jumpsuit and Maggie is dressed in dark blue jeans and a jewel-toned crewneck sweater.

As planned, the bachelor party hasn't yet joined them. She wants a few minutes alone with her group. She taps the old bell on the front desk to get everyone's attention and then waves them to gather around.

"I just want to say, you've been a special group this weekend. It's my twenty-fifth knitting retreat, and the first that incorporated axe-throwing . . . so thank you for that." They laugh, and she feels the love in the room, and now she wishes that she *had* asked Max to come. To show him that running the inn isn't a job to retire from, that it's a lifestyle: surrounding themselves with people during peak occasions of their lives, helping them make memories. Giving them the place to do that. And creating their own along the way. "I always use the last night of the retreat to unveil the group portrait, so here you go," she says, holding up the framed print. "Hot off the press."

She passes it around, and while everyone's looking at it, she texts Max.

Can u stop by the lobby for a minute?

"I hope everyone feels they've learned something they can take home with them after this weekend. But remember: Knitting, like life, is never something you can master. Mistakes will be made. Projects will fail. It's a process. Embrace the process, and you will always have a source of joy." The group applauds. She has mixed feelings, knowing that she herself is struggling with the process of life at the moment.

"That was really special," Maggie says, walking up to her. "This whole weekend has been special."

"Thank you so much for teaching the classes. You got rave reviews!"

"I enjoyed it. And really, by going through the process of explaining things aloud I think it's going to make my own technique better."

She nods. "I've found that to be true." She sees Max across the room. Excusing herself, she makes her way over to him, stopping to pour herself a mug of their spiked cider: Captain Morgan, apple cider, star anise, orange and ginger root. She takes a sip and it fortifies her.

"That was quick," she says. "Thanks."

"You know I wanted to be here. I'm glad you changed your mind about it."

"Can I talk to you for a minute?"

She leads him from the lobby to the corridor outside the dark tavern, closed on Sunday nights. She sees through the doors' windows the chairs are upside down on the tables. Even from outside, she can smell the restaurant's lemon-and-pine cleanser. Here, away from the fireplace, the stone walls hold a chill.

"This feels very cloak-and-dagger," Max says.

She looks at him. "I don't want to sell." She presses her fingers to her temples to ward off the stress headache she feels building. "I'm sorry. I said I was okay with it, and I wanted to be, but I'm not."

"Bee, I realize I shouldn't have brought this up during your retreat. I understand you feel sentimental. But we work practically around the clock, three hundred and sixty-three days a year. I can't do that much longer. Maybe you can keep up this pace, but I'm telling you I don't want to. This offer is our retirement."

The cider turns sour in her throat. "And I told you, I don't *want* to retire."

"I understand that. But you can't ask me not to take this golden parachute. You can find new work in Philly once we move. I'm not stopping you." He puts his hands on her shoulders and looks her in the eyes. "I need you to get on board with this."

PIPER WAITS UNTIL the last possible minute to go down to the Sip & Stitch. She wants it to be crowded so she can easily avoid her mother. By the time she leaves her room, she can hear the undercurrent of chatter and the clinking of glasses from two floors below.

The lobby is warm and welcoming, the air rich with the scent of crackling firewood and something sweet, like baked apples.

She takes a small plate from a side table and loads it up with crostini topped with fig jam and brie and a few slices of pear. Then she heads over to one of the couches, where Dove and Lexi sip from mason jars. The drinks are garnished with orange wedges and cinnamon sticks.

"Hi, Piper," Dove says, scooting over to make room for her. "We missed you at Shetland Hap."

She sits, offering some excuse about needing to get exercise. And it's true, she did take that walk into town. She's still thinking about the phone call with Ethan—what he said about her listening to her gut.

In all the confusion of the weekend, one thing is clear: She wants a future working with animals. She's not sure exactly what that will look like, but she knows the next step is going back to school to finish her degree so every option is available to her.

"Also, your mom did a great job teaching the workshop," Lexi says.

"Mom taught the workshop?" Piper hasn't spoken to her since their argument. "What happened to Hannah Elise?"

Lexi shrugs, and Piper scans the room. She doesn't see Hannah Elise, but she spots her mother talking to Belinda. She turns back to Lexi and Dove and changes the subject.

"So, how's the first week of married life?" She's pretty sure she remembers them saying they'd gotten married just last Monday—at Philadelphia City Hall.

They look at each other, smiling in an intimate, connected way Piper recognizes. It gives her a pang.

"Great," they say in unison.

"What made you decide to do the City Hall thing?"

"It was the only way to make certain it was fully ours," Lexi says, and turns to Dove for affirmation.

Dove nods, adding, "We wanted to avoid the hassle of dealing with our parents. They haven't been that supportive."

"You're so lucky to have Maggie," Dove adds.

At this, Piper reflexively looks across the room. And sees her mother making a beeline toward her.

MAGGIE SEES PIPER across the room, her high blond ponytail like a bright flag. The scratch on her face is still visible, though a less angry red.

Had she somehow pushed her daughter into a career she didn't want? Had Piper felt that the only way she could justify quitting was to mess up so badly she didn't have a choice? If so, she knows she owes her an apology, but she doesn't know where to start. She can only trust that once they start talking, she'll find the words.

Maggie interrupts Piper's conversation with Lexi and Dove, putting a hand on her shoulder. "Can I talk with you for a minute?"

Piper pulls one of her nervous ticks, yanking the ponytail holder out of her hair and then redoing it with a quick twist of her hands. But she agrees and follows her to a quiet corner of the room.

"I owe you an apology," Maggie says.

"You're apologizing?" Piper crosses her arms.

"Yes. It wasn't my place to come down on you over what happened with Gretchen. It's your career. Your life."

"Well, thanks for saying that," Piper says, unsmiling. Unhappy.

"I honestly never imagined you didn't love the work. It never crossed my mind."

Piper sighs. "There were times when I did. Just not enough to give up certain other things."

"But what did you have to give up? The plan was always that you'd go back to school later if you wanted."

"I'm giving up my time. I could have had my undergrad degree by now. I'd be that much closer to a long-term career."

"Okay. Like what?"

"Like . . . animals. I think I want to go to veterinary school."

"Veterinary school." This shouldn't be such a surprise, not if she really thinks about Piper. Piper is not an extension of herself. "Okay. I get it. But I still don't understand what I did or said to make you feel pressured to go into fashion. I mean, I told you it was a great opportunity, and it was. But I'm getting the feeling it's more than that. Is it my shopping habit?" She gives a smile to lighten things up, and Piper smiles back.

"It wasn't something *you* said. It was something Birdie said."

Birdie? The minute she hears her own mother's name, she knows this won't be good. And sure enough, Piper tells her about the time when she was a kid that she told Birdie she wanted to be a veterinarian, and Birdie told her she better not get pregnant and drop out of school like her mother.

Maggie shakes her head. Leave it to her mother to say such a thoughtless, destructive thing. It was exactly the type of cruelty Maggie ran away from in the first place. A reason she maintains distance from her mother still.

"I wish you'd told me about that when it happened," Maggie says. "It's not true. I didn't lose my career because of you. I chose you because what I got out of being a mother was more than a career in fashion could offer me. It gave me unconditional love and a best friend. It wasn't even a contest. I guess fashion meant as little to me as it means to you. Because I walked away from it for something bigger and better."

Piper steps closer and Maggie folds her into her arms. Piper tightens her arms around Maggie's back, and she can feel her mother's heart beating against her own.

"We've been so busy with my drama, I never got to hear about your night," Piper says as she gently pulls back from Maggie's embrace.

"What *about* my night?" Maggie says, trying to keep a straight face but feeling her expression betray her with a mischievous smile that tells Piper all she needs to know.

"Uh-huh. So the wild animals weren't so bad after all?"

"Let's just say I'm a bit of an animal lover myself these days."

"Mom! So you like him!"

The sound of the party gets markedly louder. Even from their secluded spot, it's clear the bachelors have arrived.

"We should go back in," Maggie says. She starts to turn, but Piper grabs her arm.

"Mom, I just want to say how much I love you. You're my best friend. Thank you for this weekend."

Maggie's eye tears up. They hug again as someone clangs a utensil against a glass for attention. She didn't realize how loud it was until the room falls silent. The only thing left is the music, an Ed Sheeran song. And then Barclay calls out, "All right, ladies and gents. It's the moment of truth."

"I guess we should go back in," Maggie says. Piper throws her arm around her shoulder.

The mother-daughter retreat was exactly what they'd needed.

Chapter Thirty-Five

*T*HE HUG FROM HER MOTHER feels so good. She just wants things between them to get back to normal.

Back in the heart of the lobby, it's clear the party hasn't had time to gel. It's like a middle school dance, with the boys on one side of the room and the girls on the other. In the center, Barclay stands alongside Belinda. He's not dressed in his usual outdoorsy clothes, but instead is wearing khaki pants and an argyle sweater. Belinda is wearing an aubergine cable-knit sweater dress and white opaque tights and furry low boots. Her white hair is in one long braid down her back. She's beautiful, exactly the way Piper hopes to look when she's an older woman.

"We want to commend you all on the spirit of competition that you brought to this weekend," Barclay says. "And we know there's a bunch of cash on the line, but Belinda and I chewed it over, and it's hard to pick a winner when it's clear both groups stepped far outside their comfort zone. And I have to say, that's what bushcraft is all about."

"And knitting!" Belinda adds.

"You gotta face your fears," Barclay continues. "You gotta learn by trial and error. Do things badly before you do them well. As long as you let yourself experience these things, you're a winner. So instead of cash exchanging hands, we hope you'll accept these tokens as reminders of what you all accomplished this weekend."

Some of the guys hoot and holler. Piper can't tell if they're being ironic or they're genuinely excited as Barclay and Belinda hand out little gift bags tied with twine. The bachelors' bags are silver foil; the knitters' are red. Piper glances at Cole and he walks over.

"Did you know about this?" he asks her.

"No! How would I know about it?"

They turn to Maggie.

"Don't look at me," she says. "I lost control of this thing the second Barclay and Belinda got involved."

They open the gift bags; Cole's contains a knitter's starter kit, complete with straight bamboo needles, a prewound skein of wool and a tape measure. Piper's holds a small wooden hatchet and a "Nature's Fire Kit" of pine cones, twine and wax. The room is buzzy with conversation—some of the guys are still arguing that they won, and Lexi's loud voice rises in defense of the knitters. Amidst this clamor, Scott stands up on a chair, raising a tumbler of whiskey in the air.

"You guys are the best," he says, his words slurred. He continues, his words running together and trailing off. Aidan is waving him down, and he wraps up with: "Thanks for the best bachelor sendoff any guy could ask for. And Cole—dude, no hard feelings. I just want you to be happy."

Piper feels all eyes in the room turn in her direction since she's standing with Cole, and then he walks toward the spot where Scott made his speech.

"Scott, you're the closest thing I have to a brother. And even though we haven't seen eye to eye lately, that doesn't mean

I'm not wishing you and Ashley a long and happy marriage. And as for me—don't worry. I'm good. Better than good." He raises his glass. "To Scott."

Everyone raises their glasses and echoes with a chorus of, "To Scott."

Then Cole does climb up on the chair. This time, he turns his back to the cluster of bachelor partiers and looks toward the back of the room, where his eyes settle.

"One more thing: Kalli Dimitrou, I love you. And I promise, our bumpy start will have a happy ending."

Piper looks at Kalli. Everyone looks at Kalli. But Kalli's eyes are locked on Cole, and she walks to him. As soon as she's close enough, he jumps down and hugs her.

Piper turns to Maggie, who's sharing a glance with Aidan. The intimacy of the look between them suggests to Piper that whatever happened last night was more than a hookup. Good for her mother.

The room erupts in chatter, but Piper is still able to hear her phone ring in her bag. She fishes it out and sees it's Ethan calling.

"Hey—it's kinda loud in here. I'll go to another room and call you back," she says, covering one ear with her hand and walking toward the Purl.

"Come outside," he says.

She stops in her tracks.

"What do you mean?"

"I'm here. At the inn. On the front porch."

Is this real? She looks around, as if anyone in the midst of the merriment has any clue what's going on. They don't, of course. It's remarkably easy to slip outside unnoticed.

He's sitting on the porch swing, bundled in his navy peacoat and a black hat she knit for him two winters ago.

"Ethan! What are you doing here?"

He stands up and she runs over, throwing her arms up around his neck, pressing her body against his. He holds her tight.

"Something I should have done before now," he says. She steps back just enough to look at him and he drops to one knee. Before she can say something, the ring she thought was gone is in his hand.

"Piper, I'll never forget the expression on your face the first day I saw you at the animal shelter. You were so defensive on behalf of that cat. I thought, *This is a woman who cares*. A lot of people don't. As I got to know you, I realized your compassion runs even deeper than I imagined, and you're even more beautiful inside than out. I've loved you for three years now, and I'll always love you." He pauses, and she feels like she's suspended in midair. "Piper, will you marry me?"

This is actually happening. Piper tears up, nodding and saying yes as he slips the ring on her finger. He hugs her and she clings to him, eyes shut tight. But then she has a troubling thought. She steps back.

"Wait. You didn't drive out here and propose to me because of Cole, did you?"

Ethan smiles and shakes his head. "No. But I can see how the timing looks like that. Piper, the truth is I was planning to ask you this weekend all along. But between you having a rough time with the show, and what your mother said—"

"Hold it right there," Piper says. "What, exactly, did my mother say?"

MAGGIE FEELS BUBBLY and light, as if she'd had a few glasses of champagne. But she's sober and simply lit up with the joy of the moment. She sits with Aidan on the sidelines of the improvised dance floor, where the younger people are dancing to the seventies song "Funkytown." Cole's dramatic little announcement was like the uncorking of a champagne bottle: a big pop and the party really gets started.

"You know, I gotta hand it to Cole. The timing of going public with their relationship was a pro move," she says. "It's like a politician waiting until five o'clock on a summer Friday to announce they were 'consciously uncoupling.' A few seconds of attention, and then a collective shrug."

"I have to admit, I'm surprised," Aidan says. "That was a very un-Cole-like thing to do. And I'm still not sure about this whole thing."

"Well, the headline here is that Cole took a big stand tonight. Critics be damned."

"Critics be damned? I'm afraid that includes me."

"Well, in the words of Lenny Kravitz: Let love rule."

"You did not just quote Lenny Kravitz."

"I did. You're not just talking to another single parent; you're talking to a fellow Gen Xer."

"I knew there was something I liked about you."

He seems about to put his arm around her, then changes his mind. Cole might be ready to go public, but clearly Aidan is not. And that's just fine with her. She just liked spending time with him.

"And things with Piper are all patched up?" he says.

"Completely." She and Piper not only resolved the tension—they're closer than ever. This weekend was exactly what they needed. Maybe they can make an annual tradition out of it—return every autumn for a New Hope Knitting Retreat.

Aidan hands her his gift bag.

"Trade you."

"Are you complaining about your knitting kit? Because you should be grateful."

He looks dubious. "How do you figure?"

"You got out of paying me fifty bucks." This gets a smile out of him.

"So you think you won?" he says.

In that moment? Definitely. "Yeah. I do," she says.

Their eyes lock. She has the surprising realization she's happy. Just happy in the moment. But then he says, "Do you want to hang out later?" And she feels her smile fade. Last night was one thing. But if they spend time together again, like that, it will open up the question of keeping in touch. And where's that going to go? Her life is in New York.

"Aidan, I like spending time with you. A lot. But I'm really bad at this."

"Parties?"

"No. Relationships. I've gotten comfortable with a simple life. Just work and being a mom."

"I get it. I have too. But maybe it's time to get uncomfortable," he says. "Cole and I had a conversation earlier. I told him what I thought about his precarious relationship status, but it turns out he had some things to say to me too."

"Such as?"

"He seems to think I play it too safe."

Maggie understands that in sharing this, he's saying that Cole is right. And that maybe it's something she needs to hear too.

"I guess . . . since I don't even live around here . . . it's harmless. Well, maybe not completely harmless. I mean, what fun would that be?"

He leans closer, and she wants to touch the auburn stubble along his jaw.

"Listen," he says, "I'm feeling a little partied out. So I'm going to call it a night."

She feels disappointed, but then he hands her one of the inn's brass room keys and says, "I'll be up for a while. If you get partied out too."

He leans over and kisses her cheek before leaving.

Maggie flushes and glances around the room to see if anyone witnessed what just happened. She looks for Piper—to say good-night and don't wait up—but doesn't see her anywhere. She asks around, and Lexi tells her she saw her leave the room. She walks out to the lobby, looking around, and only sees Max behind the front desk.

"Hi, Max. You didn't happen to see my daughter, Piper, did you?"

He nods. "She was just here. She went outside."

Odd.

She thanks him and hugs herself, bracing for the cold outdoors. The front door creeks as Maggie opens it, and she meets a bit of resistance from a gust of wind. At first, she doesn't see Piper. Then she turns to the far side of the porch and nearly loses her breath. Piper isn't alone.

"Piper?" she says.

Ethan and Piper both look over. Piper's eyes look extra blue from crying. Her pale face is red and blotchy.

"I don't want to talk to you," she says. "I can't even look at you!" Her lower lip trembles, the way it always has when she's agitated. It was so adorable when she was a little girl, Maggie had to sometimes fight to keep from smiling inappropriately at her tantrums. But there's nothing to smile about now.

"What happened?" Maggie says.

"You! You happened," she says.

"I'll wait in the car," Ethan says. When he's gone, Maggie tries to reach for Piper, but she pulls away from her.

"What's going on?"

"You can drop the act. I know you told him not to propose. This whole weekend, I've been wondering if maybe he changed his mind about us. And I *told* you about it. You said nothing to me about your conversation with him. Nothing!"

"Piper, I can explain."

"Save it. I'm leaving."

She turns and walks away into the darkness. In the near distance, Maggie hears the rumble of a car engine.

She stands stunned for a few seconds, then realizes she has no time to waste. She has to get her things and go after her.

Chapter Thirty-Six

AIDAN CHECKS HIS PHONE. IT'S close to eleven, but still no Maggie. He wonders if the party could possibly still be going on. So he texts Cole and asks him.

It's beginning to feel ridiculous to still be dressed in his pants and oxford shirt. But changing into his sweatpants feels somehow inappropriate.

There's a knock at the door. He jumps up and opens it, trying to keep his smile low-key. But he's thrilled, like he's a teenager again.

It's not Maggie.

"Hey, Dad," Cole says, walking in. "Didn't want you to be all lonely in here by yourself."

"What makes you think I'm lonely?" Aidan says, peeking down the hall before closing the door. No Maggie.

"Well, your text for one thing. But also, I wanted to say I'm sorry if my speech made you uncomfortable tonight. I'm guessing that's why you left the party early."

"That's not why I left early." The truth was, he left the party because he felt weird celebrating with the Cavanaughs while he's falling for a new woman. He doesn't care how much time passed, or how much Barclay himself signaled that maybe he wasn't doing Cole any favors by remaining single. It still elicited complicated feelings.

"Well, like I said: I'm sorry if it made you uncomfortable."

"It didn't make me uncomfortable. If you're happy, I'm happy."

Aidan doesn't know what else to say, so he steps forward and gives his son a hug. When they separate, he says, "I look forward to getting to know Kalli after this weekend. So go— enjoy the rest of your night."

"I don't want to ditch you. I know you wanted a bonding weekend and I haven't been a great partner in that."

"This . . . right here. That's all I could ask for. So go! Don't worry about me." It's time to break the habit of pretending like there's no one in his life but Cole. Barclay is right about that. "Actually, I'm not going to be alone. Maggie Hodges is stopping by after the party."

Cole frowns. Aidan wonders what he said wrong. Was that too much sharing?

"Dad, I'm pretty sure Maggie left."

"She left the party?"

"No—she left the inn. Left town. Piper texted me she had to run back to the city and that it was a long story. And then someone at the party said they saw Maggie leaving with her bags."

Aidan is embarrassed. He wished he'd never brought it up.

"Go have a good night," he says. "It's a relief, actually. I'm beat."

Maggie just took off like that? Without a word? Well, if that's the way she is, better to find out now.

He changes into his sweats.

MAGGIE EXITS THE GW Bridge at the Henry Hudson Parkway to reach the West Side instead of her home on the Upper East.

During the two-hour drive back from New Hope, she replayed the scene on the porch over and over, like a bad dream she could defang if she just thought about it rationally. And then she tries to remember what, exactly, she'd said to Ethan the evening he showed up at the store. Had it been that bad, really? That an engagement would put pressure on Piper? It was true.

But in the end, Piper just quit her job anyway. Just like that—as casually as if she were canceling her Netflix subscription.

Every thought she has hurts more than the last. She wants to get home, crawl into her own bed, pull the covers up high, rewind to last week and not say a word to Ethan. *You said nothing to me about your conversation with him. Nothing!* Maggie wished she could unsee the disappointment on Piper's face when she spat out the words, but she's afraid it's indelible.

Maggie should have told her about her conversation with Ethan the minute Piper confided in her about their argument that first night at the retreat. *That* was what she'd done wrong. And she'll be the first to admit it—if Piper gives her the chance.

It takes Maggie ten minutes to find parking that's in reasonable walking distance to Ethan's apartment. The building is close to Columbus, and has a gate with a latch, a short flight of stairs, and then a heavy wrought-iron door that opened to a vestibule. The vestibule has an old-fashioned call-up intercom with the tenants' names and apartments listed. Beyond that, a locked door.

Driving through the inky darkness of New Hope had felt like the middle of the night. But here, on the streets of Manhattan, people are still walking back from dinner, from the theater, from a run to the corner bodega. She presses the apartment buzzer, and after a few seconds of crackling static she hears Ethan's voice over the intercom. "Hello?"

"Ethan, it's Maggie. I need to talk to Piper."

"I'm sorry, Maggie. Piper doesn't want to talk right now. It's late. Maybe you two can—"

"This can't wait," Maggie says. Silence. And then:

"Leave me alone!" Piper yells so loud the metal frame of the intercom seems to vibrate.

Maggie shrinks back. She stands alone in the vestibule, under the punishing fluorescent light of the wall sconce.

The door opens and a couple walk inside with a rush of cool air and smattering of dry leaves skittering across the floor. They're in their thirties, maybe a little drunk, holding hands and very definitely into each other. The guy unlocks the door, then turns to Maggie. "You need to come in?"

She wants to go in, but she doesn't want to infuriate Piper any further by disregarding her boundaries.

"Um, no. Thanks."

The couple disappear into the building, and when the entranceway door clicks closed behind them, Maggie feels shockingly alone. Her daughter is right beyond that locked door. But she might as well be a million miles away.

Maggie walks back outside. She's in no rush to get back to her car, or to her empty apartment. So she sits on the stoop, uncomfortable with the strange feeling that there's somewhere she's supposed to be.

And then she remembers: Aidan. She stood him up!

Mortified, she looks frantically through her bag for her phone, then realizes she's still holding it. *Please, still be awake!* She dials his number and paces in front of Ethan's building. The call goes straight to voicemail. But wouldn't he have called or messaged her to see if she was still coming? She checks the hip pocket of her jeans, feeling the room key tucked inside, and her stomach sinks.

Well, no wonder he didn't text her. He thinks she flaked

and is probably annoyed. She presses her face into her hands. But it's just as well: Now that she's back in the city, she can see she'd just gotten caught up in the bucolic little bubble of the weekend.

The only thing that matters is fixing things with Piper. But clearly, that's not going to happen tonight.

Chapter Thirty-Seven

IN THE MORNING, THE LOBBY has changed from chariot back to pumpkin. Belinda works side by side at the front desk to manage checkout. Lexi and Dove are first in the queue, their luggage bulging with yarn and fledgling projects. Dove exchanges hugs with Sheila with murmured promises to reunite at a future retreat. At that, Belinda's stomach drops. She glances over at Max, but if he heard the comment, he gives no sign. He's busy juggling key returns and printing out paid receipts.

"Exceeded all expectations," Lexi says, sliding her key across the desk to her. "Five stars!"

Belinda hands out the gift bags: a New Hope Knitting Retreat tote filled with two skeins of hand-dyed yarn from a local producer, a copy of Saturday night's group photo, a bag of coffee beans from Bucks County Roasters and a recipe card for the Bucks Tavern's hot toddy.

"I have to say, this weekend is the best swag yet," Sheila says. "Although I can't imagine where I'm going to put that hatchet."

Laurel and Kalli are up next, and Laurel takes a moment to lean forward, over the ledge, and say to Belinda, "Thanks for listening yesterday. I guess it all worked out."

Belinda smiles at her, trying to think about what she'd said in those few minutes after Laurel left the class in a huff over Cole showing up. *A long weekend can work miracles.*

She realizes she'd been hoping for one herself. But every conversation with Max leads to the same dead end: selling. Still, if there has to be a final weekend, one last retreat, she couldn't have asked for a more interesting one. She especially enjoyed meeting Maggie and has a parting gift to thank her for stepping in to teach: a luxurious blanket she knit using a beloved and discontinued British yarn called Jaeger.

She scans the group to see if she can pull her aside for a moment now, but the bachelor party seems to have descended on the front desk all at once, loud and rowdy, still riding the wave of last night's revelry. Aidan and Cole look a little bleary-eyed, clutching bottles of water and to-go coffee. Scott is loudly recounting a particularly wild moment—"And then the tent collapsed and we could have sworn just before it happened we could make out the silhouette of a bear"—while Barclay, dressed in pressed trousers and an army-green all-weather coat, leans against a stuffed luggage cart. A cascade of beer pong balls rolls out of a half-zipped duffel bag.

"Belinda, I was just telling your hubby that it was another great stay," Barclay says. "The New Hope Inn never disappoints."

She smiles. "I'm so pleased you enjoyed. It means a lot that you chose to have your family celebration here."

"Well, I have to admit your knitting ladies added a little spark to the festivities. Admittedly, not entirely welcome at first. But in the end, everyone's happy. So that's all that matters, right?"

She'd forgotten his little run-in with Maggie the first day at lunch.

"Yes, all the kids learned to share the sandbox," she says. "Speaking of: Have you seen Maggie Hodges this morning?"

Barclay shakes his head. "Can't say that I have."

"Actually," Aidan says from behind him. "Maggie left."

"What do you mean?"

"She took off last night. Piper, too."

That can't be. Belinda turns back to Max. "Did Maggie turn in the keys for Margaret Meade? Are they checked out?"

Max looks confused. "Well, yes. Is that a problem?"

Why would Maggie leave without saying goodbye? There must be some mistake. She checks the metal lockbox on the wall where they keep the room keys, scanning the rows of brass hooks. Sure enough, two keys dangle from the Margaret Meade spot.

Meanwhile, Max is handling Aidan's checkout.

"I'm actually short one key," Aidan says.

"It happens. Do you know if you lost it here inside or somewhere off-site?" Max asks.

"I didn't lose it. Maggie left with it."

Belinda's ears perk up. This is news to her! Even more reason to wish Maggie hadn't left so abruptly.

"Is that so?" Barclay says, letting out a low whistle. Aidan ignores him.

"Thank you for the wonderful stay," he says, his voice tight and his tone stiffly formal. Then the bachelor party clears out, and Belinda is left alone with her husband.

"I'm really surprised Maggie left without saying goodbye," she says.

"Bee, I hope you can take this in the spirit in which it's intended," he says. "She was just a guest. These are customers—not your life. The two of us—that's real life. So let's move on and see where that life goes next."

"The inn has been our *life* for the past thirty years," she says. "You can't deny that just because you want a change."

Max puts his arm around her. "I'm not denying anything.

But nothing stays the same forever. And part of being happy is not resisting change."

As much as she hates to admit it, maybe he's right.

"Okay, Max. You win."

Their eyes meet. "I'm not trying to win, Bee. This is a good thing. You'll see."

He steps forward and kisses her on the forehead.

The knitters are clustered near the front door, exchanging patterns and final hugs and promises to keep in touch. She doesn't want them to leave. She's not ready to move on.

As Max said, she has no idea where life would take her. All she knows is that she doesn't want to go.

AIDAN HANGS BACK while Barclay hands out cigars in the inn parking. Ritchie suggests he save it for when Scott becomes a father.

"Well, getting married is the first step so consider this a prefatherhood celebration," Barclay says. He's just trying to keep the party going, the freedom of the weekend before getting home to his wife. Mary is a sweetheart but she runs a tight ship.

Barclay claps Aidan on the back, offering him a light.

"Nah, thanks, I still don't smoke," Aidan says.

"Where's Cole?"

"He's saying goodbye to Kalli." He checks his phone. Cole should have been outside ten minutes ago. Ritchie's not the only one prolonging the weekend, reluctant to get back to reality.

"I hear he's not the only one who had a little action this weekend," Barclay says.

"Oh, no?" Aidan says, pretending he doesn't know what's coming.

"So Maggie forgot to return your room key, eh?"

Aidan shakes his head. "It's not like that." Even though it is—was. But the night at the campfire was a fluke. He should have left it at that. There was a reason he was still single after fourteen years of being a widower, and a reason she'd never married. They liked it that way.

"*Sure* it's not," Barclay says with a wink. Aidan feels a flash of annoyance, and Barclay must sense it, because he stops with the innuendo and claps Aidan on the back. "Aidan, I'm just busting your chops. And I feel like I can do that, because we're family. Now, you know that Nancy was the apple of my eye—I loved that girl more than anything. And I like to think I knew her pretty damn well. And from what I know of my girl, she'd want Cole to have a good relationship example to model after, and she'd want you to be happy."

Aidan nods. There's some truth to what he's saying.

"Barclay, I appreciate that. And I'll think about it."

Maybe Aidan should start taking dating more seriously. But that doesn't mean he should be more serious about Maggie Hodges: What happens during bachelor party weekend stays in bachelor party weekend.

The New Hope Inn isn't *The Love Boat*, after all.

Chapter Thirty-Eight

MAGGIE WALKS TO DENIM BEFORE the store opens. Lexington Avenue is bustling with the early-morning frenzy of people getting to work and school. Cars clog every side street, buses line the avenues, and everywhere people are walking dogs. A street-cleaning truck whirs noisily by just as she reaches the shop, and she ducks under the awning to avoid the dirt and dust it kicks up in its wake.

Through the glass door pane, she spots Elaine already at the counter lining the store's branded shopping bags with colorful tissue paper. The door is locked, so she knocks. Elaine looks up, surprised.

"Welcome back," she says, opening the door. "I wasn't expecting you until tomorrow."

"We left the retreat early." Maggie bursts into tears. "I'm sorry. I didn't get much sleep last night."

Without another word, Elaine locks up, makes sure the closed sign is outward-facing and leads Maggie to the back of the store. The stockroom is more of a large closet, shelving and racks lining the walls. Transparent, stackable bins house accessories like scarves and belts. There's a tiny table, the surface of which is covered with spare barcode scanners. Elaine pulls out a stool tucked away in the corner and insists

Maggie sit. She herself remains standing, arms folded in front of her chest.

"Tell me everything."

Maggie does: starting with Ethan showing up at the store as she was closing Thursday night, and their conversation about the proposal and timing, and going through the way the whole thing snowballed over the course of the weekend.

"And now she won't even take my calls. Can you imagine? Piper won't speak to me."

Elaine nods sympathetically. Then she reaches out and clasps one of Maggie's hands in both of her own and looks her in the eye.

"Maggie, I've known you since you were younger than Piper is now. And I can tell you, in case you've forgotten, that you never planned to make this store your lifelong career."

The comment is so off-topic, she assumes Elaine is just trying to distract her.

"What's that got to do with anything?"

"Just an observation. Would you agree?"

Sure, there's some truth to it. Working in the clothing boutique isn't her dream job. But most people don't get to make their living in the way they want. Sure, some people do: like Belinda and her knitting retreats at the inn. While others, like Piper, throw a once-in-a-lifetime chance away because it's not *their* dream. But there's no sense thinking about that now.

"Are you trying to cheer me up or make me feel worse?"

"Neither." Elaine toys with the spectacles on a chain around her neck. "I'm trying to convey a point: It's important in life to take a chance sometimes. To leap before you look. And sure, you think it's easy for me to say. But I practice what I preach. I started in finance, then I opened this place, and I'm always investing in new businesses and opportunities. The key is to keep pushing forward."

She stands up and takes deep breaths. Talking to Elaine isn't helping one bit.

"Maggie, come sit for a moment. Last week, after Piper had the little mishap during the fashion show, what did I tell you?"

Again, she's not following her. But she tries to play along, tries to remember. That morning was five days ago already, and it's a blur. She just shakes her head.

"I told you: Even things that look terrible in the moment are actually paving the way for something good to happen."

Now she remembers. It seemed like an empty platitude then, and even more so now.

"How can something good come out of Piper not talking to me?"

"She's taking some space. But she's also *giving* you some space."

"I don't want space!"

"Well, maybe you should reconsider that. Never underestimate the value of space," Elaine says. "And once you don't mind it so much, I guarantee that's when Piper won't need it anymore."

The front door buzzes.

"That's my scarf delivery," Elaine says, reaching out and patting her knee. "Think about it."

Maggie is disappointed that Elaine, her stalwart, confident mentor and—let's face it—substitute mother figure has so little to offer in this moment of need. But really, what did she expect? The only thing that will alleviate her misery is Piper's forgiveness.

She's going back to Ethan's, and this time she's not leaving until she speaks to her daughter.

PIPER WAKES UP and reaches for Ethan, but he's already gone from their bed. She looks at the ring on her finger and sighs with contentment. It's so cozy in the warmth of the comforter, she feels she could stay there forever. Then she sits up with a start: Maggie.

She jumps out of bed. Seven hours of sleep hasn't alleviated her anger. If anything, she feels worse. Maggie's transgression becomes more and more damning the more she thinks about it. She doesn't want to be bogged down in this negativity; this should be one of the happiest weekends of her life. So she turns things over and over in her mind, looking for some angle that gives her an emotional exit ramp, a way to just let it go. But she keeps coming back to this: The one thing she always knew for sure was that she and Maggie never lie to one another. But her mother did lie. She did!

Even if Maggie genuinely thought Ethan would somehow be putting pressure on her with a marriage proposal—and Piper still doesn't understand that logic—that misbelief should have ended Friday night when Piper confided in her. She should have told Piper the truth.

She finds Ethan in the kitchen, his back to her while he rummages through the refrigerator. She plans to walk right over and put her arms around him, but stops short, her attention caught by a vase of towering white lilies, their heady, intoxicating scent mixing with the aroma of fresh coffee.

"What are these for?" she says, kissing Ethan on the cheek. He's freshly shaven and dressed for work. He doesn't answer, but takes her hand and leads her to a chair at the table in their tiny little corner breakfast nook.

"I know you're upset with Maggie. But I don't want that to overshadow the joy we should be feeling."

She kisses him. "It's not. And I want to keep it that way." *We wanted it to be ours.* Piper can hear Lexi saying the words that she didn't fully appreciate at the time. But now she understands them completely. "So I have a request," she says, stepping back just enough to look him in the eyes. "I don't want a big wedding. I want to elope."

Ethan frowns. "Really?"

"Yes. It's the only way to get married on our own terms."

"Let's see how you feel in time. I know you're upset right now, but I think you'd really regret excluding your mother."

"I won't. I'm thinking about a lot of conversations I had with people this weekend. I'm not the only one who feels this way. In fact—you know Cole?"

"Don't remind me," Ethan says, but smiles. They can laugh at his jealousy now that they've come through the weekend.

"Cole hid an entire relationship from his father just to avoid upsetting him. And it all came out over the weekend, and it made me realize how questionable some of my own choices have been. Like, how much am I doing because I want to, and how much have I chosen to make my mother happy? No more of that. It's you and me."

She can tell by the expression on his face that he thinks she's being reactive, but he won't push for now. He just kisses her cheek, takes her hand and suggests they go grab breakfast at Barney Greengrass before he heads into the office.

They grab their coats and take the stairs down to the first floor. She stares at the ring as she walks. After all the time she spent thinking about it, now it's on her finger. She feels a little foolish for all her worry. All this time, Ethan was never the problem. It's been her relationship with her mother.

The lobby, as always, smells like their first-floor neighbors' cigarette smoke, and one of the overhead lights is out, making the narrow space dingier than usual. Also unusual is someone sitting on the vestibule bench . . . knitting.

And that someone is her mother.

"What are you *doing* here?" She glances back at Ethan, who holds up both palms as if to say, *Calm. Easy. It's okay.*

Maggie jumps up, her face tense and determined.

"I understand that you're upset with me. But Piper, you can't just refuse to talk. And I'm not leaving until we do."

Piper shakes her head. Beside her, Ethan says, "I have to get to work, anyway—"

"*No*," Piper says sharply. "We're going to have breakfast."

"I'll wait for you outside," he says. Before she can object, Ethan is off down the corridor, the heavy front door opening with a groan and then slamming shut behind him. Her mother grabs hold of Piper's left hand.

"Are you—"

Piper turns back to Maggie and shakes her hand free. "Yes. We're getting married," Piper says.

"Oh, sweetheart. Congratulations."

She moves to hug her, but Piper takes a step back.

"*Congratulations?* You told him not to propose. This only happened in spite of you."

"I understand how you feel. That's why I want to talk it through."

"Mom, you can camp out in this lobby all day and night. But that's not going to change anything."

"So what will?" Maggie's eyes are wide. "Tell me how to make this right."

Piper feels bad, but she's not the one who created this situation. And so she only has one answer for her mother. At least, for now. "I need you to leave me alone."

Chapter Thirty-Nine

*B*ELINDA STANDS IN THE MIDDLE of the Purl holding the framed group knitting retreat portrait in one hand, a nail and hammer in the other. She walks to the portrait wall, rests the new frame on the ground and strikes the nail into the first empty space she can reach. She's efficient with a hammer, and the nail is secured with just two quick strikes. But it feels so good to beat something into the wall, she keeps hammering until the nail is embedded up to the head. Then, just for fun, she hammers in another. And then another.

"Bee? What are you doing?"

Max stands in the doorway.

"I'm hanging the retreat picture. Like I always do."

They look at each other, and it feels like a standoff.

The past twenty-four hours, they've done nothing but bicker. And last night, they had a big argument, and now she can't even remember what it was about. It was probably over something trivial. Everything Max says and does sets her off.

He rubs his jaw. "Why are you putting it up just to take it down again soon?"

It's a logical question. Max is nothing if not logical.

Selling the inn makes sense at their stage of life. People downsize from houses to apartments. They retire. Belinda knows she is not the first person at age seventy to have decisions to make, to confront the difficult reality that things change. And she would have to admit, if someone had asked her back in 1998 if she planned to be running a hotel for the rest of her life, she would have said absolutely not. And maybe that's still true. She's just not feeling good about making the change right now. But Max is, and rational thinking is on his side.

"If you want to sell this place for financial reasons, I won't hold you back. And if you move to Philly, that's your prerogative. But I'm not sure I want to go with you."

MAGGIE SLIDES INTO her usual booth at Gracie Mews diner just as the sun sets. She's not hungry, but if she has dinner, she can view the day as over. And she wants to end the day as soon as possible. More than that, she wants to forget the day ever happened.

Across the aisle, the old woman who used to scold Piper as a child is in her usual spot, eating soup, alone. Her rouge and eye makeup look bright and hopeful even though her expression is, as usual, miserable. The old woman has witnessed countless dinners over the years shared between Maggie and Piper. Now, Maggie has the strange urge to slide into the seat across from her and say, *You won't believe this* . . .

Would Piper have called to tell her about the engagement if she hadn't shown up on her doorstep? No. She would not have. That's clear from the conversation they'd had in that airless little vestibule.

Maggie lets this sink in: Her daughter got engaged and had no intention of telling her. It would be unthinkable just forty-eight hours ago.

A server comes by the table, and it's not Dimitris. She's relieved. She doesn't want to do the usual "breakfast for dinner" banter without Piper. In fact, before the server's finished delivering her order to the kitchen, Maggie knows she's going to have a hard time eating.

It feels very warm and loud in the room. In addition to the booths and tables, the diner has a busy horseshoe-shaped counter. Behind it, servers run around in constant motion, pouring drinks, swapping out dishes and distributing checks. And just beyond the counter is a semi-open kitchen from which waitstaff move back and forth, back and forth, in an endless churning of meals.

Maggie's stomach churns, and she considers canceling her order. She looks around for her server and instead spots Dimitris on the other side of the counter. She tries to get his attention with a wave, and when that doesn't work, she gets up from her table. Walking toward the counter, her shin hits something hard, and she loses her footing, toppling over onto the hard terrazzo floor.

What the hell just happened? She sits up.

"Look where you're going!" the Dragon Lady scolds. Meanwhile, her metal cane is jutting out from the floor underneath her table.

"I tripped over your cane!"

The old woman purses her crimson lips before saying, "There's absolutely nothing in your path. You fell because you're not paying attention."

She *is* paying attention.

Maggie, giving up on the idea of canceling her order, walks back to her table—a little shaky but otherwise fine. She ignores the stares and whispers, and soon she's forgotten as everyone gets back to their meals and conversation. The Dragon Lady stands from her table and takes a long time getting into her coat. Maggie watches her leave.

There's absolutely nothing in your path.

She knows the woman said that just to cover her ass for letting her cane nearly break someone's neck. But to Maggie, the words take on a bigger meaning. *There's nothing in your path*: You have no future. Or is it encouragement? *There's nothing in your path*: There's nothing stopping you from being happy. But there is: Her daughter isn't speaking to her, her own boss basically told her that her job is meaningless and the one guy she's fallen for in as long as she can remember ignored her texts, probably assuming she's a flake.

Is some of this her fault? Absolutely. She made some mistakes. Fine, a lot of mistakes. But she could fix them. Wasn't that what she said over and over this past weekend? You can't get better if you don't make mistakes. If it's true for knitting, why can't it be true for life?

When Maggie sat in that diner with Piper less than a week ago, she'd been so certain that what she and Piper needed most was togetherness. Now she understands that what they need is the opposite: They need time apart to be the fullest versions of themselves. And in order to accomplish that in a genuine, lasting way, Maggie has to find a way to make her own life and work meaningful. But she doesn't know how to do that. Everywhere she looks, she sees through the lens of herself and Piper. She doesn't know how to experience the world differently.

Maybe that's because she needs a new world.

The Dragon Lady passes by on her way out the door. Her rheumy blue eyes meet Maggie's, and she holds her gaze. "For the record," Maggie says. "I *am* paying attention."

Chapter Forty
Friday

*I*T'S LATE MORNING ON HER day off when Maggie arrives in New Hope. A mist still hangs over the river. Last night, she left a message for Belinda that she would be coming to town, that she'd like to see her.

Maggie parks at the inn, the same spot she pulled into one week ago exactly.

Inside, the familiar scent of the lobby hits her hard: Notes of cedar and coffee and pine give her a sharp pang of longing. And it's a specific longing . . . for Aidan. The intensity of the feeling is disturbing. She doesn't have the emotional bandwidth to deal with that right now.

Belinda is behind the front desk. She's dressed in a red-and-black plaid cardigan with pearl buttons and bell sleeves. She looks up and offers a small smile.

"Oh, dear. Maggie, I owed you a return phone call."

"No, I owe *you* an apology." Maggie feels better just seeing her. "I didn't mean to leave without saying goodbye."

"No apology necessary," Belinda says. She doesn't ask what she's doing back in town.

"I was hoping we could get coffee. But since you're busy, I can always walk around until—"

Belinda holds up one finger. She picks up the desk phone

and dials. "Max, I need you to relieve me at the front desk." There's a pause, and then she says to him, "Really? Well, I have things to take care of too!"

Maggie is taken aback by the sharpness in her tone. She hasn't heard Belinda raise her voice—not to Max, not to anyone. Belinda hangs up, looks at her and says, "Where to?"

"We can just go to Bucks Tavern if that's easiest."

"I've a better idea. Let's have a change of scenery."

Maggie follows her outside, through the parking lot with a right turn onto Main Street. The last time Maggie followed that path she was on the walking tour with Piper. How had that only been a week ago?

Two blocks down they reach Ferry Market, an old freight station that's been converted into a buzzing food court. Belinda leads Maggie from vendor to vendor, pointing out her options: Brazilian. Mediterranean. Pizza. A candy stall. Yet another charming spot in New Hope. Maggie feels a surge of excitement.

She can't wait to tell Belinda her idea.

PIPER CLASPS ETHAN'S hand, hoping she's doing the right thing. New York City Hall is a grand-looking building in lower Manhattan, but the corridor in the Office of the City Clerk is dull and colorless. Rows of gray cushioned benches line the walls for waiting couples. The only decorations are municipal plaques and civic posters.

It's not the place Piper envisioned them getting married, but in the wake of her mother's toxic overinvolvement, the priority is moving forward. She's wearing a simple shirtdress she bought for their first date. Next to Ethan, who's wearing a suit and tie, she feels underdressed. They seemed to have dressed for two entirely different events. She wonders if she's depriving him of a traditional wedding, something she never knew he might care about. And it strikes her that she still has things to learn about the man with whom she'll be spending the rest of her life, and vice versa. It's okay, it's normal, and they'll figure it out as they go. Together.

Two days earlier, when they got their marriage license, he'd seemed excited about their decision. But now that they're waiting in a blockish vestibule that feels like they've been summoned to jury duty, he's clearly having second thoughts. But she's not having second thoughts, and so she doesn't acknowledge the way he's looking around as if trying to find an emergency exit.

"Inside the clerk's office will probably be nicer," she says. She reaches for his hand. "After today we can plan a party or ceremony to include your family. Maybe right after New Year's?"

"*My* family?" he says. "What about *your* family?"

She shakes her head. "Ethan, we're here. We've talked about this. It's fine."

He looks unconvinced, but squeezes her hand. Then he stands up, phone in hand. "I'll be right back."

THE FERRY MARKET seems like it's always been there. It's not shiny or artificial. Everything in New Hope seems just right. And she imagines her future knit shop nestled on one of those intimate side streets, a building with black shutters and a plaque at the front door detailing its history as a blacksmith's. Some of the original loading dock remains, converted into cozy nooks with benches and tables where Maggie and Belinda sit having coffee.

"This place opened eight years ago, but still feels new to me. At the time, some people weren't happy about it."

"Why not?"

"It was symbolic—the changing identity of the town."

"This town is a special place," Maggie says. "Belinda, again, I'm so sorry for running out like that on Sunday night. Things with Piper just blew up and I had to deal with it."

"Maggie, you certainly don't owe me an apology," she says, taking the lid off her cup and blowing gently into the steam. "I was just hoping nothing was terribly wrong."

"To be honest, things have been better."

Belinda's hazel-gray eyes are focused on her with kindness. And it gives her hope.

"I need to make some changes in my life, and realizing this, I thought of you and what you've accomplished by building your life around your passion. I admire that so much. It hasn't been something I've ever been able to do. And so instead, I put all my focus into Piper. And I realize now I need to stop doing that. For both our sakes."

Belinda sighs. "I appreciate that, but I think you're giving me too much credit. I never had children, so I was never torn between two things. You're probably being too hard on yourself."

Maggie's phone rings. She glances at it with her persistent and unrealistic hope that Piper will reach out after all. She jumps up: It's Ethan.

"Belinda, I'm sorry—I have to take this."

She holds up her finger to emphasize she'll be just one minute, then walks outside of the clamorous food court, ducking around the corner of the neighboring bookstore and pressing the phone to her ear.

"Ethan? Is everything okay?"

"Hi, Maggie. Everything is fine. But the thing is, we're down at City Hall. Piper wants to get married today. So, here we are. And I just think that in spite of what's going on between the two of you, she's going to regret not having you here."

Maggie's stomach drops. She's two hours away, and her mind shifts into high gear, searching for a way Ethan can possibly hold Piper off until she gets there. But then she stops herself: If Piper wants to get married at City Hall today, Maggie needs to respect that.

"Ethan, it's incredibly kind of you to call me about this. And I know it's not for me—that you're doing it for her." That's love. What more could a mother want for her child? "But Piper knows what she wants. Trying to interrupt that would be a mistake. I learned that the hard way. So don't you worry about it. Just . . . well, congratulations."

"Are you sure?" he says.

She is sure. Although, when she ends the call, her heart is so heavy she's momentarily disoriented. Despite what she said to Ethan, she still wants to run back to New York. Instead, she goes back inside the marketplace where Belinda is waiting.

Maggie hasn't even had a chance to tell her the idea yet.

"Sorry about that," Maggie says, slipping back into her seat. Piper is getting married.

Piper is getting married!

Belinda sips her coffee, then leans forward.

"Maggie, whatever you're dealing with back home, let me assure you that no one has life completely figured out. Certainly not me."

Maggie shakes her head. "Please, let me finish or I'll lose what little nerve I've mustered." She takes a breath. "I'm thinking about moving to New Hope. I want to do something with knitting . . . maybe open a yarn shop. That might be a ways off, but in the meantime, I'd love to teach at your retreats if you'll have me. And then, if I'm able to open a yarn shop, we can find a way to create synergy between the store and your retreats. We can expand your class offerings, even do some off-site at the shop. I just think the possibilities are so exciting."

A strained silence settles over the table.

"Maggie," Belinda says. "We're selling the inn."

She's not sure she heard her right. "What do you mean?"

"Max wants to move back to Philadelphia."

She's shocked. It takes her a moment to recover.

"Is that what *you* want?"

"No," Belinda says. "But there's an offer on the table, and we could retire comfortably on it. Max doesn't want to work forever. It's not fair for me to ask him to."

"Have you tried?"

"Maggie."

"I'm serious. What about your retreats? You've built so much here. It means everything to people. I saw it myself. Sheila's been coming here for years. Kalli and Laurel are going to make a tradition out of it. I was only a part of it for one weekend and I saw the community you've built."

Belinda sighs. "To be honest, I did try talking to Max about other options. But money is money, and I can't hold him back."

"So . . . you're leaving New Hope."

"I really don't know, Maggie. Like you, I find myself at a crossroads. So, as you see—I don't have things all figured out after all."

Maggie pushes her plate away. She can't eat. As bad as she feels about the news, she imagines Belinda feels worse.

"I can't believe this," Maggie says.

"Well, for what it's worth, I like your knit shop idea. You'd be great at it. And it would be wonderful for the town."

Maggie shakes her head. "The knit shop idea doesn't work without you."

Belinda reaches out and pats her hand. "That's very sweet. But of course it does."

Maggie can barely swallow from the lump in the throat. She sees that Belinda too has stopped eating. Whatever Maggie has lost with this news, Belinda is losing more.

"Are you okay?" Maggie asks gently.

"No," Belinda says, her eyes glassy. "But I'll make do."

Now Maggie feels just awful. "I didn't mean to upset you," she says.

"You're not the one upsetting me," Belinda sniffs. "Please . . . stay over tonight. I know this isn't what you came here expecting to hear. But we can have a nice dinner together and I'm hoping you won't feel the trip is a total loss."

How can she refuse? But she has work tomorrow. And yet Elaine is the one who pushed her to start thinking in this direction. Plus, Elaine is from New Hope. She knows of the inn. She's the one who told her about the retreat in the first place. If anyone will understand, it's Elaine.

"Sure," Maggie says. "I'll stay."

PIPER IS GETTING anxious. She knows that getting anything official done in New York City is a bureaucratic nightmare, but it had been so easy getting the marriage licenses, she'd hoped they'd just be in and out—Mr. and Mrs. before noon. She's eager to say *I do*.

The waiting vestibule is getting more crowded with couples. Behind them, a baby wails in its stroller. A cell phone rings despite the signs saying Please Silence Your Phones.

A nearby door leads to the ceremony room, and every so often, various clerks step out to call out names. Piper has been keeping track, and she's fairly certain they're next.

"It's starting to feel real," Piper says, and Ethan squeezes her hand.

She hopes someone can take their photo—something better than just a quick selfie. It would be ironic if she had countless photographs of herself wearing clothes that meant nothing to her but not one of her in her bridal outfit. If she could even call it that.

Behind them, the door to the clerk's office opens and someone calls out in a raspy voice with a heavy Brooklyn dialect, "The Brandt-Hodges party?"

Piper and Ethan stand, and when she turns toward the office, she's surprised to see a familiar face.

"Hannah Elise?"

"Piper?"

"*What are you doing here?*" they say in unison.

"You two know each other?" Ethan says.

So this is the bureaucratic day job Hannah Elise refused to talk about.

Hannah Elise steps out of the doorway, joining them in the waiting area. She's wearing plain black pants and a striped button-down shirt, her strawberry curls tamed in a bun. Only the silver nose ring reflects anything about her personal style.

"We met this weekend," Piper says. "Hannah taught some of the workshops."

Until she ran off with Gretchen. That was a whole story she hadn't even gotten around to sharing with Ethan.

"You didn't tell me you work at City Hall," Piper says.

"You didn't tell me you were getting married."

Fair point. A gray-haired man pokes his head out of the clerk's office door and barks at Hannah Elise to keep things moving.

"All right, let's get you hitched." Hannah Elise looks around the room. "Where's Maggie?"

"Couldn't make it," Piper says.

Hannah Elise looks skeptical. "I thought you two were, like, best friends."

The words are a blow. Up until this weekend, she thought so too. Anyone who'd spent time with Piper and Maggie at the retreat would think the same. She wants to go back to the way they were before Sunday night. But there's no going back. And really, she doesn't have to explain herself to Hannah Elise, or anyone. Still, she looks at Ethan. They're doing the right thing, aren't they?

Seeing her moment of hesitation, Ethan says, "Can you excuse us for just one minute?" He takes her by the hand and leads her out of the room, back into the bustling, wide external corridor. He stops after a few feet and says, "I called your mother."

She was not expecting this news and is taken aback. "I hope you're joking."

"No. I'm serious. A few minutes ago—when I took that walk. I called her, and I told her where we are and what we're doing."

Piper's heart starts pounding. "And?"

"And she said she respects your decision and if this is what you want, she won't get in the way."

"No, she didn't."

"Yeah. She did. I wasn't going to say anything to you. But if you're on the fence about getting married this way, I thought you should know: We don't have to rush because you think Maggie's going to interfere or make it all about her. She's not going to. So, I'll ask you one last time: Do you want to go through with this today?"

Piper doesn't need to think about the answer. "I don't."

He's right. There's no real reason to rush. She needs to take a breath.

She needs to talk to her mother.

Chapter Forty-One

AIDAN CAN'T STOP CHECKING HIS phone. He knows it's inexcusably rude, especially on a date. Aidan finally took his vegetable purveyor, Beverly Cricket, up on her lunch invitation.

He'd gotten the message from the weekend loud and clear: He needs to make his personal life more of a priority. But he's going to take baby steps, unlike Cole, who is fully committed to a future with Kalli. Aidan thinks he's rushing—they've never had a normal, out-in-the-open relationship. There's still a lot to learn about one another. But at least now Aidan and Cole can talk about it.

"Everything okay?" Beverly asks.

They're having lunch at the Grape Seed, a restaurant housed in an ivy-covered redbrick colonial on Mechanic Street. She told him to pick the place, and he chose to dine out in New Hope instead of Doylestown for two reasons: one, it's arguably the best date town in Bucks County. But also, it's not in his neck of the woods, so local gossip can be avoided. It's win-win.

"A cheese delivery didn't show up," he says with a contrite smile, slipping his phone back into his pocket. "Heading into the weekend without gouda and brie is a problem."

Beverly smiles with understanding. She's an attractive

woman in her forties, petite with wavy blond hair to her shoulders, round cheeks, and a small gap between her two front teeth that he only just now notices.

"I get it," she says. "This time of year, things start to get crazy. You wouldn't believe the demand for pumpkins . . . It would blow your mind."

"I can imagine. I can't keep them in the stores."

He looks out the window, cracked open to let in the fresh air. The early-afternoon light filters through the branches of maples and oaks, casting dappled shadows across the sidewalk. Families with kids in tow stop to look in shop windows, while a few cyclists pass slowly, wheeling their bikes beside them. A breeze rustles the fallen leaves, sending a swirl of crimson and gold skittering along the ground. Couples stroll leisurely, bundled in scarves and light jackets, occasionally pausing to read the plaques on the historic buildings. Somewhere in the distance, a street musician plays an Ed Sheeran song.

There is one downside to his choice of location, one he didn't anticipate, but probably should have: It makes him think about Maggie Hodges.

He'd been hurt when she stood him up. But then he told himself it was a blessing in disguise—at least he didn't get in any deeper with her. She was clearly erratic. And she lived two states away. Wrong for him in those big ways, and probably many others he would discover in time. Bullet dodged.

It was good he accepted Beverly Cricket's invitation. He should have done it sooner. Maybe now he'll be able to stop thinking about Maggie.

EVEN AFTER BELINDA'S terrible news about the inn, Maggie feels compelled to visit the yellow storefront—the one she discovered during the walking tour that first day of the retreat. The spot has been on her mind since the moment she had the idea for a knit shop in town.

But she never, for one second, considered a New Hope without Belinda. The sale of the inn changes everything. Because she realizes now she doesn't actually want to move to New Hope just to open a knitting shop; she wants to move to New Hope to build something with Belinda. If Belinda is leaving New Hope, what's Maggie's plan B?

Everything she sees along the way reminds her of Piper, and it hits her: Piper is married. But if she had to get married this young, at least it's with a decent man who loves her. Maggie won't forget the call Ethan made to her today. And as her now son-in-law, she has plenty of time to make things up to him. And she will.

Maggie turns at the corner. She sees a man who reminds her of Aidan, and this brings back the odd longing she'd experienced when she walked into the inn lobby. Then she realizes the man doesn't just look like Aidan, he is *actually Aidan*. And he's not alone.

She has about four seconds to process this before Aidan sees her too. The diminutive blonde beside him is talking, gesturing broadly. It's clear from how close she walks to him, arms grazing, and the way she looks up at him, that she isn't simply a business associate or a pal.

"Maggie?" Aidan says. Is that disbelief in his voice? Annoyance?

"Hi," she says, her brain filled with static. The only thing that's clear is her urge to reach out and touch him, while a grasp of basic conversation eludes her. After "hi," she's got nothing.

"What are you doing here?" he says.

"I'm here for the weekend. Belinda and I are . . . working on a project." Well, it's half true.

Aidan looks quizzical but, given the circumstances, doesn't ask her to elaborate. He introduces her to his "friend" Beverly.

"How do y'all know each other?" Beverly asks with a smile.

"We met this past weekend," Aidan says.

The woman's smile becomes a lot less friendly.

"His son and my daughter hit it off," Maggie says to fill in the blanks. She turns back to Aidan. "I came back here to apologize to Belinda for running off like that." It's true, if not the full story. "I feel terrible about leaving so quickly and not saying goodbye." This part is directed at him, and a barely perceptible nod tells her he understands that. "I had a crisis with my daughter," she explains for Beverly's sake.

"I hope that's resolved," Aidan says.

"I'm working on it."

"Always best to bury the hatchet," he says, and she looks up sharply, wondering if his choice of wording is a nod to their weekend. Their eye contact, the heat between them, is her answer.

Beverly, maybe picking up on their more-than-passing acquaintanceship, says archly, "I'm *so* glad I never had kids. The world's overpopulated. We need more food, not more people. That's why I focus on my vegetables."

Maggie nods, not knowing what her vegetable focus is, exactly, and not wanting to prolong the encounter by asking.

But then Beverly says, "And what do *you* do, Maggie?"

The question feels like a challenge—as if Maggie now needs to prove her own worthy contribution to society (since she contributed to overpopulating it). And something about the pause she takes to consider this makes her answer it more for herself than for Beverly.

"I'm a knitter," she says.

That's the bottom line. She's a knitter. That's her answer. And it's been there this whole time.

"I need to go," she says, telling Beverly it was nice to meet her while avoiding meeting Aidan's gaze. It's too hard to look at him.

She turns and walks back toward the inn, waiting until she feels certain she's out of sight to make a phone call. Elaine doesn't answer her cell, but she picks up the store landline.

"I need a favor," Maggie says. "Two, actually. First, I know it's last-minute, but I've been thinking a lot about our conversation on Monday and I need the day off tomorrow."

After a beat, Elaine says, "What's the second?"

"I need you to meet me in New Hope."

Chapter Forty-Two

THERE ARE MANY THINGS BELINDA could be doing since returning from coffee with Maggie: answering emails, calling the linen vendor, paying the florist bill. But she does none of these things. Instead, she's standing in the middle of the Purl contemplating the portrait wall.

She's troubled by the conversation with Maggie, and so she minimizes it by telling herself that everything Maggie said was just talk. And she reminds herself that it's often like that for her guests in the days following a retreat: They can't quite let go of the weekend. And if she's done her job right, they shouldn't want to. She'd always hoped she could at the very least teach people about knitting, and at the most, maybe something about themselves. And so yes, she's fielded calls from guests asking for the name of a Realtor. Or asking about the elementary schools. Sometimes they just call to book a return weekend, this time with their significant other. They all want to keep one foot in New Hope.

But deep down, she knows it's different with Maggie, and Belinda would have liked nothing more than to encourage her. She wishes she could plan a retreat with Maggie as an instructor. It would be a dream to have a new knit shop in town, and to find creative ways for them to work together. But now, none of that is possible.

"So this is where you've been hiding," Max says behind her and standing in the doorway. "You're not answering your phone."

She turns and walks closer to him. "I didn't hear it ring. Why?"

"Maggie Hodges just picked up her room key at the front desk and asked for you. She's here for the weekend again?"

"Yes. She surprised me today with a visit."

"Oh, that's great. But . . . you remember that I'm going to be in Philly, tomorrow, right? I'm just reminding you so that if you're planning an outing with Maggie you have someone to cover—"

"I don't need anyone to cover for me," she snaps. She'd considered maybe she and Maggie could spend some time together tomorrow afternoon since she's here, maybe go antiquing across the bridge in Lambertville. But she hadn't thought it all through.

"Are you sure you don't want me to reschedule this appointment for a day when we can both go?" he says.

She already told him no—she's not interested in looking for a new home. That she has a home. "You're on your own with this one," she told him.

"Am I on my own *finding* the new home, or will I be on my own *living* in it?" he presses.

She doesn't know how to respond.

"Can you please tell Maggie she can find me back here?"

When he leaves, she returns to the portrait wall and looks at herself standing amidst the group. She's in the center, sitting beside Sheila, wearing a big smile, one she knows that in the moment was genuine. But it wasn't genuine. Had she been deeply happy for even one minute since agreeing to sell the inn? Why on earth had she said yes so easily? The knitting retreats mean so much to her. How could Max ask her to give that up?

"Belinda?" Maggie says from the doorway. "Do you have a minute?"

Belinda waves her in. "I'm so glad you stayed in town. I want to tell you: The knitting shop is a great idea. I believe in you, Maggie. Don't let my situation change your ambitions."

"That's the thing, Belinda. My ambition isn't necessarily a knit shop. It's to continue what I experienced here last weekend. Not just the knitting, not just the inn, not just teaching, not just you—but all of it, together. I believe it can be just the beginning of something special."

"Maggie, you need to let this go. You're making it more difficult for me. I appreciate the idea, and that you want to work with me. I obviously felt the same way getting to know you last weekend. But then there's reality. Some things can't be fixed."

"I don't agree," Maggie says urgently. "What if I find an investor to buy out Max? The inn is half yours, right? So if you want to keep it, you just need someone to compensate Max for what would be his half of the sale."

Belinda digests this, then says, "Is this for real? You know someone who would want to do this?"

"Possibly. It's worth a shot. The woman who owns the clothing store where I work was born and raised here. She moved to New York before you took over the inn, but she's the one who told me about the knitting retreat in the first place. She was in finance for the first part of her career and now she invests in things all the time."

Belinda nods. "Okay. Sounds promising. How do we make this happen?"

Maggie needs to get Elaine under Belinda's roof. She remembers the New Hope Inn from decades ago, but that wasn't *Belinda's* inn. "I don't know when she was last here, or what she envisions when she thinks about this place. And I want her to see it the way I experienced it this weekend." It will be a challenge to re-create the energy of the knitting retreat, but she'd like to figure out a way to try. She'd have to, as Elaine put it, leap before she looks.

"So how do we do that?" Belinda says. "As much as I'd like to, I can't snap my fingers and have the knitting retreat appear." The Purl is in its default state: spare and lovely with the river on full display. But it was also quiet and seemed empty after the weekend.

Maggie looks around, folds her arms in front of her chest and admits, "I'm not sure yet."

MAGGIE HELPS BELINDA retrieve folding tables from the back office storage closet and set them up in the Purl the way they'd been arranged for the yarn market. Max, catching them in the act during their second trip to the supply closet, offers to help: "Looks like I'm missing a party."

"No party," Belinda says quickly.

She's already advised Maggie that Max is on a need-to-know basis about their plan. "I'm not telling him anything until—if—there's something to tell," she'd said. Maggie understands, and plays along by being vague even as Max asks questions.

If Maggie and Belinda are going to convince Elaine to become a partner in the inn, every detail counts: the way the place sounds, the way it looks, the way it smells. She's tapping out a list on her phone as she paces in front of the fireplace: Food. Drinks . . .

"Do you think you could get that hot cocoa cart in the lobby?"

"It's short notice," Belinda says. "But Max seemed to get her on a whim last weekend, so it's worth a try. I have to say, the bachelors certainly enjoyed it. Genevieve told me she rarely sells out so fast. Speaking of bachelors: You and Aidan Danby seemed to hit it off. Do you think you'll stay in touch?"

Maggie takes a beat before responding.

"I sort of stood him up when I left like that on Sunday night. By the time I remembered our plans, I was back in New York. I texted him an apology but didn't hear back."

Belinda refastens the hair tie at the tail end of her braid and says, "Oh, you know the fragile male ego. They're all-powerful when wielding an axe, but often crumble in the face of emotional nuance. Just let him know you're back in town. I'm sure he's gotten over that mishap by now. Especially if he knows there's the chance to see you this weekend."

Maggie hasn't had time to process the run-in. She doesn't know what to make of the fact that he was clearly on a date. It's none of her business, really. If anything, she's the one who made a big deal out of not looking for a relationship, of making sure he understood that it was just a weekend thing between them.

"Actually, he knows I'm here. I went for a walk after you and I had coffee and ran into him. He seemed to be on a date."

Belinda looks skeptical. "That's a big assumption. You're probably projecting."

"Anyway—I'm not here for Aidan."

"Are you sure about that?"

"Of course!"

"So you're telling me that all of a sudden, you want leave your daughter and New York City—after how many years—and move to New Hope because you have a sudden urge to open a knit shop? As much as I like to believe my retreats are that inspiring, this might push the bounds of credulity."

Maggie nods. "There is more to it. I'm not leaving Piper. I'm giving her some space. I think it'll be good for us. And as for the knit shop—I want to spend my days doing something I care about. Something that brings meaning and joy—to me and to other people. I know you understand that."

Belinda nods. "I do."

Maybe, on some deep level, Maggie factored Aidan into her idea of a future in New Hope. But it's not a concrete thought, or plan. It's formless, barely a shadow in the corner of her mind.

When the room is mostly staged, Maggie's disappointed to see that with only a fraction of the yarn on hand that Belinda displayed at the beginning of last weekend's retreat, Maggie can't get the visual effect she wants. She envisions a symphony of color and textures, the room bursting with abundance; when she walked into the yarn market one week ago, it had felt like a knitter's wonderland. It's imperative that be Elaine's experience tomorrow morning when she arrives.

"This is all the yarn you have on-site?" Maggie says.

Belinda nods. "I've gotten pretty good at knowing how much to order for the retreats without having too much inventory left."

"Yeah. A little too good." She frowns.

Belinda turns on the sound system and plays the Carole King album *Tapestry* while she arranges the worsted-weight yarn on a table next to the hand-dyed cotton.

"I like this music—can you queue this up tomorrow?" Maggie says.

The song "Where You Lead" plays, and Maggie feels a twinge. It's a song Carole King rerecorded with her daughter as the theme for *Gilmore Girls*.

Life is happening too fast. One minute they're huddled on the couch watching Netflix after Piper finishes her homework and the next . . . Piper is married.

Maggie left her a voicemail congratulating her. It was a huge effort to make her tone sound normal—unbothered. Joyful, even.

She hasn't told Belinda about the elopement. When she asked how Piper is doing, Maggie simply said, "Fine." This is a business trip. She needs Belinda to view her as a steady hand, as a potential partner—not as a distracted, emotional mom.

The scarcity of yarn is nagging at her. There's no yarn shop in town—hence, her initial idea to open one. But while the town lacks knit shops, it doesn't lack knitters.

Maggie exchanged numbers with everyone at the retreat, and they already have their own robust group chat going. Two of the people in the chat are local—Kalli and Laurel. Sheila is an hour away, but it's worth a try. So she sends a quick message:

> I know this is totally random and if it's not possible no problem—but can any of you bring your yarn stash to the inn tomorrow morning? Belinda and I need to borrow it for decoration.

She doesn't know about Kalli and Laurel, but Sheila mentioned her mountainous stash during the yarn swap in her room.

The yarn swap.

Maggie stands up. "Belinda. I think I figured out what to do tomorrow."

Chapter Forty-Three
Saturday

MAGGIE STANDS IN FRONT OF the inn with Belinda. Elaine should be arriving any minute.

The morning is bright but damp, the river shrouded under a veil of soft mist. The air carries the fragrance of rich soil. Leaves cover the lawn, and on a morning like this it's easy to remember that under the blanket of foliage, nature is working its alchemy to prepare for winter. Maggie inhales, fortifying herself to work her own sort of magic, to find a way to combine her past and her present to prepare for the future.

The plan is they'll give Elaine a tour of the inn, culminating with the Purl, and then Bucks Tavern to talk over lunch.

Elaine's car pulls up right on time. Elaine steps out of her car dressed in a gray wool pencil skirt and a houndstooth blazer. Her high heels are impractical, and when they sink into the soft earth, she says, "Clearly I've been in the city far too long."

Maggie makes the introductions, and they walk inside, making easy small talk about the area.

"And Maggie told me you grew up here? All through high school?" Belinda says.

"That's right. I went to New Hope-Solebury High."

"It must have been an incredible place to be young."

"Oh, this town in the eighties? Nothing will compare.

When I moved to New York after college, I was the only one unimpressed with the village."

"Well, welcome home. I really appreciate you coming on such short notice."

"My pleasure. I've known Maggie for over twenty years and I've never seen her this excited about anything before. Aside from that gorgeous daughter of hers. But who can blame her?"

"Wonderful young woman," Belinda agrees.

"You two do know I'm still here, right?" Maggie teases. It feels remarkably natural to have the two of them together. By now, they're in the lobby. She wonders if Elaine is experiencing the entrance the way she herself had last weekend—if she's taking in the pumpkin pine floors and the antique moldings and that warm apple butter scent. She looks at the spot where Scott Cavanaugh and his friend tossed around a ball that first morning and feels a weird flash of nostalgia. Can she be nostalgic for something that happened just a week ago?

Belinda sets the pace of their stroll—energetic but leisurely. She asks Elaine more questions, and Maggie can tell she's trying to gauge the extent of her history with the inn.

"My mother used to take me here for Sunday tea," Elaine says. "This predates your ownership, obviously. And when I first revisited a few years ago, I was impressed by how much of the original feeling and sensibility was preserved. You and your husband did a fantastic job."

Belinda thanks her, and the groups makes a turn down the hall toward Bucks Tavern.

Elaine asks if she operates the restaurant as well.

"The restaurant is independently owned—they lease the space. The chef is a Bucks County native, and the menu changes seasonally. The bar serves craft beer, artisanal wine and signature cocktails. There's a table waiting for us as soon as we finish the tour."

Their next stop is one flight up, the second floor, so Elaine can see a few examples of the accommodations. "The common areas and guest rooms are a mix of antique and reproduction furniture . . ."

"And all the guest rooms facing northeast have a water view . . ."

When Elaine asks about the knitting retreats, Belinda looks at Maggie and gives her a nearly imperceptible wink. "Well, any conversation about the knitting retreats should take place in the Purl."

The trio heads back downstairs through the lobby, where a staffer Belinda called in last-minute is busy checking in two guests. Belinda greets them, but keeps things moving. "I created the room we're going to next with the knitting retreats in mind, converting ground-floor guest rooms into a private event space. Its official name is the Pearl S. Buck Room, but we call it 'the Purl' spelled with a *u*."

"I love that," Elaine says.

"Welcome to our little knitters' sanctuary," Maggie says, opening the doors.

The room is full of people everywhere, the couches, the armchairs, the high-back wooden chairs—all filled with knitters. Dozens of people showed up for Belinda's email blast announcing a pop-up "Yarn Swap and Sip & Stitch." The only price of admission was one skein of yarn for donation, and some yarn to swap.

Maggie and Belinda managed to pull off a last-minute rustic morning picnic vibe. Tables are set with burlap runners, bowls of fresh fruit and handcrafted coffee mugs. Shelves and ledges are decorated with mason jars stuffed with zinnias and dahlias, and a hot cider station is surrounded by mini pumpkins. The fireplace is lit, and the misty sliding glass doors open to the backdrop of the river. And everywhere, yarn: soft merino wool in muted earth tones, shimmering silk blends in jewel hues, hand-dyed skeins with unique color gradients. The swap table overflows with bundles tagged with fiber type and yardage, some with notes from the donators with messages like, "Perfect for a summer wrap" or "Leftover from a hat project."

"How delightful," Elaine says, surprised.

The room buzzes with chatter, laughter and the click-clack of working needles. Maggie sees a familiar face: Sheila, dressed in a loose knit tunic, holds court on the sofa nearest to the fireplace. She jumps up when she sees them walk into the room. Then Maggie spots two more familiar faces, one very unexpected: Kalli showed up, and Cole came with her. He's a reminder of the run-in with Aidan yesterday—not that she needs a reminder. She's been thinking about it ever since. She can't help but feel there's unfinished business between them. But that's something that will have to wait.

"Belinda," Sheila says, giving her a quick hug. And then, to Maggie: "I love this spontaneity!"

"So glad you made it," Maggie says.

"Are you kidding? It's not officially a retreat, but I couldn't risk breaking my streak over a technicality." She gives them a saucy wink.

"Elaine, this is Sheila Bevins. Sheila has the unique distinction of attending every one of my retreats over the past twenty-five years."

Maggie wonders what Sheila would say if the inn changed hands and that was the end of the knitting retreats. She hopes she'll never have to find out.

"Quite a feat," Elaine says. "Lovely to meet you. So tell me about these retreats, Belinda."

Belinda launches into the financials, giving them the occupancy rate stats for retreat weekends, the revenue from the standard markups at the yarn market, the percentage of repeat business. But Elaine seems less interested the more Belinda talks.

Of course—Elaine has countless investment opportunities that would be a quicker and more guaranteed return on her money. So why is she here?

Because *Maggie* called her. Because Elaine doesn't go into business for the money; she goes into it for the people.

"I think what Belinda's trying to say," Maggie adds, "is that the retreats remind us that knitting isn't about the yarn. Or the hat. Or the sweater. It's about connection." She glances over for affirmation, but Belinda's distracted. Her eyes are fixed on the other side of the room.

Maggie pivots to see what's got her attention. And it's Max.

"I thought he left," Maggie says.

Belinda turns to her. "I thought so too."

Chapter Forty-Four

THE MORNING AFTER THEIR ALMOST-MARRIAGE, Piper and Ethan take the bus across Central Park to go to the Yorkville farmer's market. It's a very autumn-in-New York thing to do, the stuff of Nora Ephron movies. It's something she and her mother used to do every Saturday, and it's still her go-to place for kale and squash. And today, maybe just a little, she's also hoping to run into Maggie.

Ethan humors her sudden need for farm-fresh vegetables, and patiently waits until they're in the checkout queue before saying, "Why don't you just call her?"

Is it that obvious?

"You make it sound so simple," she says.

"That's because it is."

He doesn't get it. She and her mother have never gone so long without speaking. It feels awful. It also feels too big to resolve over the phone, but scheduling a time and place to meet feels awkward. That's why she was hoping to bump into her. But since that's obviously not happening, she probably should just pick up the phone.

"It went straight to voicemail," she tells him after she tries. The voicemail is almost a relief. She wasn't sure what she'd say if Maggie had picked up. Probably something like, *We need to talk*. Maybe that's too melodramatic. She could go with, *I think we have some things too discuss*. Too formal. The phone just isn't the way go. If she sees her, she'll know what to say. She's sure of it.

Her phone vibrates with an incoming text.

You here, too?

It's from Cole Danby. Odd. She shows Ethan her phone screen.

"Who's that?" he says.

"It's Cole. From the retreat. I don't know what he's talking about."

"So . . . ask him."

'Here' meaning where? she types back.

He doesn't respond, and the exchange leaves her unsettled. She tells Ethan she wants to head back to their neighborhood. They're almost at the crosstown bus stop when Cole's response rolls in:

@New Hope Inn. I'm here w. Kalli.

This does absolutely nothing to illuminate the situation.

Why would I be there?

She tilts her screen to Ethan and he begins reading over her shoulder.

Just saw Maggie. Thought you 2 were a package deal.

Her mother is back in New Hope?

The 79th Street crosstown bus lumbers up the block. Once

they're on board, it should only take about fifteen minutes to get back to the apartment.

She looks up at Ethan. "You probably won't understand why I'm saying this, because I barely understand myself. But I think I should go see her in New Hope."

Ethan seems to consider this. The bus arrives with a screech.

"I do understand," he says. "And I'll tell you what: I'll drive."

BELINDA STANDS BESIDE Maggie and Elaine as Max, having spotted her in the crowd, makes his way over. She knows that she should intercept him, tell him the truth about what's going on before she's forced to make awkward explanations in front of Elaine Berger. But there's no time. All she can do is keep a smile plastered on her face and accept his kiss on the cheek as if this is all perfectly natural. In the background, Elton John sings "Goodbye Yellow Brick Road."

"You're back early," she says by way of greeting.

"Early, but apparently late to the party," he says, looking baffled. Then, to Maggie: "This your celebration?"

"It was my idea, yes," Maggie says, glancing uneasily at Belinda.

Elaine extends her hand. "Elaine Berger," she says.

"How rude of me. I apologize," Belinda jumps in. "Elaine, this is my husband, Max. Max, Elaine is a friend of Maggie's, visiting from New York."

"Fabulous place you have here," Elaine says.

"Well, enjoy yourself. Sorry to interrupt the festivities, but I need to borrow my wife for a moment."

Belinda looks around at the room buzzing with exuberant guests negotiating trades, gushing over textures and swapping stories about projects. The atmosphere is joyous and warm, glowing with the unique, instant intimacy born of knitters on the hunt for inspiration. She wonders if Max truly sees or feels any of it.

She suggests they go outside on the deck to talk. It's chilly, and she turns on the heat lamps. This conversation might take a while.

"Why didn't you tell me you had a knitting event today? I wouldn't have left you alone to manage the inn."

Belinda shakes her head, shivering a little despite the heater. "The yarn swap was last-minute. It's to show Elaine Berger what this place feels like during a knitting retreat."

"Why?" He looks perplexed.

"To see if she'll make an offer on this place. Because I'm not selling my half of the inn." Belinda crosses her arms.

Max cradles his chin with his thumb and forefinger, rubbing his jaw. "I'm not sure what that means. How do you sell half an inn?"

"What it means is this: We own the inn fifty-fifty. You're entitled to sell your half. But I won't sell mine. Elaine is a potential investor. She'd be a silent partner and I could stay here continuing with the inn—and my retreats—as always. If you don't want to live this life anymore, if you want a new chapter, you can take a buyout and move to Philadelphia. But I'm staying."

She waits for his response, her heart beating fast. Max nods, considering what she's said.

"When I was driving back here today, I was thinking how very little I enjoyed looking at houses without you. So I can only imagine how little I'd enjoy *living* in one without you."

"So what does that mean?" she says, knowing but also needing to hear it.

"Bee," he says, "I'm not going anywhere."

Chapter Forty-Five

MAX'S SURPRISE APPEARANCE SHAKES MAGGIE'S confidence in their plan. But if Elaine noticed the tension, she doesn't act like it. Instead, after Belinda steps away, she suggests they help themselves to some hot mulled cider. Maggie eagerly agrees.

"I'm so glad you lured me out here," Elaine says, stirring her drink with a cinnamon stick. They sit on an ottoman near the portrait wall. "It's been far too long since I visited. I love New York—and after all these years I do consider myself a New Yorker. But it's like Dorothy said: There's no place like home. I realize now that when I told you about the retreat, I actually wanted to get back here myself. And now I have a reason to make sure I do it more often."

Maggie feels a surge of hopefulness. "Does that mean you're going to move forward with this idea?"

Elaine nods. "It's certainly worth exploring. Yes. Yes, I think this is something I want to be a part of."

"Oh, I'm so glad you feel that way!" She glances out the windows to the deck, where Belinda and Max are still deep in conversation outside, the breeze picking up Belinda's long braid. Now that Elaine is in, the stakes of that conversation are higher; they need Max on board.

Maggie, too, could use some fresh air. She hesitates to leave

Elaine alone, but she can entertain herself for a few minutes. It will give her the chance to mingle with the knitters. She excuses herself, telling Elaine if she needs anything she'll be on the front porch.

Outside the Purl, she finds the lobby is empty except for the front desk clerk and a guest reading an iPad on the couch. Maggie walks past them both, out the front door to the porch swing. It's the spot where she saw Piper and Ethan in that upsetting moment last Sunday night. She doesn't want to think about it now. Looking back is pointless. She's there, in that moment, to take steps to make things right moving forward. And that's all she can do.

She looks at her phone and sees, to her great surprise, a missed call from Piper. But before she can call her back, she hears someone's approach on the creaky wooden steps. Distracted, she looks up.

Aidan.

He smiles at her, the bright sunlight making his eyes look more auburn than brown. She takes in the dimple in this cheek, the gold stubble along his jaw.

"I didn't expect to find you out here all by yourself. Isn't there a party going on?" he says.

"What are you doing here?" She stands up from the swing and it bounces gently behind her.

"Well, Cole told me he and Kalli stopped by here for something called a yarn swap. And I figured I should come in solidarity. I know how viciously competitive you knitters can get, and I didn't want him to be outnumbered."

She smiles. "Very considerate of you."

They stand looking at one another. She wants to press herself against him, but holds back. She knows, on a rational level, he's not there *just* for Cole. But she still isn't sure where they stand.

"I guess you should go in and find Cole."

"I guess so."

He steps forward and touches her forearm, and she inches closer until they're close enough to kiss. But they don't.

"May I take you to dinner tonight?" he says.

She wants to say yes, but she can't let herself get distracted. This is a business trip, and she needs to be open to wherever the day—or evening—takes her with Belinda and Elaine.

"This party could go awhile, so I'm not sure about dinner," she says, slipping one hand into her back pocket. "But I'm around later." She hands him her brass room key. In her overnight bag, she'd also brought back the one he gave her last Saturday night—she returned it to Belinda. From the look on his face, he remembers what happened last time they exchanged a room key.

"Are you sure?" he says. "Because unlike you, I'm going to actually use this key."

"I'm sure," she says.

He gives her a wink and heads inside just as Elaine walks out. She's wearing her coat. That's not a good sign.

"Are you leaving?"

Elaine walks closer, reaches out to hold both of her arms and says, "Yes. I'm leaving. But I'm so glad I came."

Maggie's confused. They haven't even had lunch yet.

"We have a reservation at the restaurant here. Don't you want to talk things through?" She searches Elaine's expression for any hint that the plan has gone south, but she seems cheerful.

"I already had a little chat with Belinda. It seems there's nothing more to discuss. They've decided not to sell the inn."

Maggie's stunned.

"Well, I'm sorry to have called you out here today." Elaine had closed Denim for this. "I didn't mean to waste your time."

It's the outcome she wanted—Belinda is staying in New Hope—but it didn't happen the way she expected.

The winds pick up and she wants to go back inside. But Elaine makes no move to leave. Instead, she fixes her gaze on her and says, "Why are you out here this weekend, Maggie?"

Elaine knows her too well. Maggie has never taken a day off from work last-minute, leaving her in the lurch. And she owes it to her to be honest about her future at Denim.

There's a reason stitches can be unraveled.

"I want to relocate here and open a knit shop." Admitting this to Elaine makes it feel more real than even yesterday's talks with Belinda.

Elaine seems to consider this. "Do you have a spot in mind?"

Maggie nods, telling her about the yellow building on Mechanic Street.

"I'd love to see it," Elaine says.

"Now?" She glances back at the inn, thinking of the party still inside. But it's Belinda's party now. Her work here is done.

"Sure. Why not?" Elaine gives her a wink. "Maybe I won't go back to New York empty-handed after all."

Chapter Forty-Six

IT'S THREE IN THE AFTERNOON by the time Piper and Ethan pull up to the inn. She's concerned about her mother. There's no question: Maggie ran back to New Hope to escape into knitting instead of dealing with their problems. She kinda gets it; they've never gone nearly a week without talking. If Piper's being completely honest with herself, she'd been trying to escape by running off to elope instead of having a calm, rational conversation. She's grateful Ethan encouraged her to take a step back in the moment. It was that kind of thoughtfulness and care that had made him cautious about proposing, something Piper hadn't appreciated fully until now, with hindsight.

"So, I'll go find a coffee place in town," he says, the car idling in front of the inn. "Just text me when you're ready for me to pick you up."

It was what they'd discussed during the car ride over. But now that they've arrived, it doesn't feel right.

"Come inside with me to say hi. Then I'll ask my mother to sit somewhere private to talk."

"Are you sure?"

She nods. "We're engaged. We're a . . . package deal. This is the right way to handle it."

They pull around to far side of the building, where the parking lot is busy.

"Popular place," Ethan says.

They hold hands, walking past the spot on the front patio where they'd reunited less than a week ago. Her stomach rumbles, reminding her she forgot to stop for lunch.

Inside, she's greeted by the familiar sweet and spicy aroma of the lobby, as if the Sip & Stitch is still going on just as she left it. But the room is quiet except for a staffer she doesn't recognize behind the front desk. When Cole last messaged her, he said there was a knitter's group in the Purl. But when she and Ethan check the room, it's empty except for tables covered with discarded cups and mugs, and few left-behind balls of yarn, and scraps of torn labels and tags littering the ground. No Maggie.

"I'm going to have to call her. Let her know we're here."

Piper hadn't given a ton of thought to showing up unannounced. She's not even sure why she felt so compelled to just *go*. Maybe she was a little afraid Maggie would have told her not to come. No doubt she's hurt by the way Piper handled things.

Her mother had begged forgiveness for the dishonesty and interference in her relationship. Now it's Piper's turn to say she's sorry for shutting her out. They both have to do better.

"Hey," Ethan says, seeing the tension in her face. "It's going to be okay. You said there's a restaurant on-site? Let's go get something to eat while we wait for her. You can call her from there."

"Good idea." She takes one more look around the room, then walks closer to the window, gazing out at the river. "It feels good to be back here. I kinda fell in love with it and didn't get a chance to say a proper goodbye."

He moves to stand next to her, and puts an arm around

her shoulders, sharing the view. "It's beautiful," he says, then, "You know what I think?"

"What?" she asks, wondering if he's thinking what she's thinking.

"It's a perfect place for a wedding."

AFTER THE YARN swap ends, Maggie and Belinda keep the party going with a table for six at the tavern, where Max, Elaine, Cole, Kalli, and Aidan are toasting with the champagne Elaine ordered.

The only thing missing is Piper. But if Maggie's learned anything the past week, it's that she can't let missing Piper spoil the moment. She read somewhere once about "removing yourself from a table that no longer serves you." But she'd never thought about finding herself at a table that feels so much like a new beginning. Sitting in between Belinda and Elaine, across from Aidan, it's like a magical convergence of her past, her present and her future. And she wouldn't have experienced it if she hadn't taken the chance to rethink her life, to look at it from a different angle. Now she knows happiness will come as a result of the deliberate choices she makes in her own life, not vicariously through Piper. And so, in keeping with that spirit, she reminds herself that the moment is complete even without Piper. And it really is.

But a part of her—somewhere deep and subconscious and delusional—must not fully accept that. Because she thinks she hears Aidan say, "Hey, Piper!"

Maggie whips around and finds Piper. Piper and Ethan.

"What are you doing here?" she says, jumping up.

"I wanted to see you. Cole told me you're here."

It's her first time seeing her daughter as a married woman. She swallows a lump in her throat.

"I hope you got my message . . . congratulating you."

"I didn't go through with it, Mom. We're not married yet."

Elaine stands up. "Maggie, you didn't tell me she's getting married."

"Aunt Elaine, what are you doing here?" Piper says.

"Opening a knit shop with your mother. Pretty fabulous, right?"

Piper turns to Maggie. "Um, can we talk outside for a minute?"

That's probably a good idea. They excuse themselves, Maggie offering Ethan her seat at the table.

Outside, the air is chillier than it had been just a few hours earlier. Across the river, the trees of Lambertville are a blur of brown and gold. On the surface of the water, fallen leaves create a patchwork of moving color. They both walk to the wooden balustrade, looking out and not at each other. Piper breaks the silence.

"Wow. Don't I feel like an idiot for not talking to you sooner." She turns to her. "Anything else I missed?"

"Let's see," Maggie says, picking up on the lightness of Piper's tone. "I'm moving to New Hope, going into business with Elaine and opening a knit shop. Hopefully in the spot on that side street where you almost stole the Doc Martens. So yeah, I think that covers it."

Piper crosses her arms with a smile. "I think you're leaving something out. That table in there is pretty full. With some people who have nothing to do with a knit shop."

She understands what she's getting at: Aidan. She's not leaving him out, she's just not sure she wants to talk about him yet. It's all so new and unexpected. But she has a feeling there will be plenty of time to talk to Piper about him.

"You didn't come all the way back here to ask me about Aidan," she says.

"No. You're right. I didn't. I came down here because I owe you an apology. I shouldn't have left here angry without talking to you. And I should have given you a chance when you came to the apartment."

Maggie feels choked up. In all the time she'd imagined this moment over the past stressful week, she never once thought Piper would be apologizing. The most she hoped for was the chance to get her own forgiveness.

She reaches out and hugs Piper, holding her close. After a few seconds, Piper pulls back.

"And I never thanked you for the retreat. For our mother-daughter weekend. It was pretty great."

Maggie agrees. But . . .

"I kinda wish it had ended differently," she says.

Piper smiles. "I'm pretty sure we'll get a do-over soon."

"Really?" Maggie isn't following her, and figures it's just a throwaway comment, something to placate her in the moment. But Piper looks bemused—like it's a real idea. One she's excited about.

And then it clicks. "Wait, do you mean . . ."

"That's right," Piper says. "Bachelorette party weekend, here we come."

The glass door slides open behind them. It's Belinda, concerned about the cold. "Let me turn these heat lamps on for you?"

Maggie puts her arm around Piper. "Don't think we need them. We're all good here, right?"

"Never better," Piper says. And with one last look at the changing light falling across the water, they walk back inside.

★★★★★

Acknowledgments

Thank you to the Ghost Light Inn and Stella of New Hope for a great stay and unforgettable pancakes. Thank you to my extraordinary editor Erika Imranyi, SarahElizabeth Lee, and the entire team at Park Row. Thank you to my ride-or-die agent, Adam Chromy—for all the books. Thank you to my local bookstore, The Doylestown Bookshop, a source of tremendous support and community. Special thanks to Kathy Hammer, who bid at auction to support The Artists Against Antisemitism. The character of Elaine Berger is named after her beloved mother.

Finally, thank you to my readers and the bookstores who make every new novel a celebration. I appreciate you.